Splinte
Tim

The Salvation of Tempestria

Shifting Stars
Gathering Storm
Shadows Fall
Fragmented Control
Splintered Time

Splintered Time

The Salvation of Tempestria
Book 5

Gary Stringer

First paperback edition November 2022

Cover Design by BespokeBookCovers.com

ISBN 978-1-7396096-0-3 (paperback)
ISBN 978-1-7396096-1-0 (eBook)

Published by Gary Stringer

Chapter 1

You are cordially invited to the Wedding of Catriona Redfletching and Dreya the Dark. The place is, of course, the Black Tower. The time is about a year since they returned from the past.

My name is Arshes Megane, and I am your humble commentator. You might consider a commentator a rather odd thing to have at a wedding, gentle reader, but in this case, trust me, it's not.

They called it a private ceremony. None of them could possibly know that was far from true. To the people of my age, thanks to recreational time travel, this wedding has become one of the most witnessed events in history, and there are commentaries galore. We even studied it at college, which, as you can imagine was a strange experience for me. It was presented as 'the first official joint ceremony involving the Original Three since the formation of the Guardianship'. Can you believe that? (Apparently, a betrothal isn't 'official', so it doesn't count.)

My essay on the subject was entitled, 'A Lesson in How to Spectacularly Miss the Point, or How to Make a Lesson Truly Academic.' (And yes, gentle reader, I got marked down for that, too – you're starting to see the pattern, aren't you?)

This wedding was about two people declaring their love and commitment to each other. It was about a friendship for the ages. It was about including their alien friends and helping them feel wanted after the Guardians had inadvertently abandoned them for more than two years. Ossian Miach Kaidool was there, too, standing tall, towering above all. He had missed their betrothal as he had been wandering around Alloria, trying to come to terms with Daelen's death and his own continued existence. The Guardians had no way to find and contact him at such short notice. The wedding, by contrast, was planned, so it was about making him feel relevant. It was about this handful of people coming together not despite their differences, but because of them.

Though they didn't know it, these events were also about their uninvited guest, Princess Zarinda of Ainderbury, who looked on from her favourite spot. These days, she was putting her talents to good use, having set up a healing centre for animals and Faery alike. Humans, too, in principle, but in practice, they were seldom allowed inside the Sylfranian border, so it almost didn't apply. At eighteen, Zarinda would be seen as a young adult by human standards but was still considered a child by the traditional Sylfranian Faery Folk. In less than three years, she would turn twenty-one, which would mark the end of her childhood. Less than three years of relative freedom and it would be her turn to marry, she knew. Only her marriage wouldn't be for love, but for closer political ties with the Quarthonian Faery. Unless her dream came true and Dreya swooped in to save her because she 'needed' her. Given today's events, that dream seemed more absurd than ever.

Watching the loving couple exchange their vows, gentle reader, the Faery princess could have no idea of the role she would play in their future...

...or mine.

Dreya could sense her, of course, but saw no point in banishing her. She had witnessed their betrothal, so in a way, it seemed only fitting that she should see this, too.

The wedding was about all these things, and probably more besides, but it had nothing, absolutely nothing to do with them as Guardians. Honestly, I sometimes think I'm the only person in the world, other than Aunt Mandalee, who can see her, Aunt Dreya and my mother, in any way other than through the lens of the Guardianship.

*****

The weather around the Black Tower that day was bright and sunny – Cat made sure of it. Dreya had chosen a human custom for their betrothal. For their wedding, Catriona wanted something a little more Faery.

"Is it ready?" she prompted Mandalee.

Her friend pulled something out of, of all things, a pocket dimension.

"I've been practising," she said in response to Catriona's quizzical look.

"Well, none of us ended up naked, so you're up on my early attempts," Cat admitted.

Mandalee handed her a garland of flowers – red, white, and black – their stems bound together into a two-foot-long strip. The two Chetsuans didn't know what was going on, but judging by Dreya's reaction, she clearly recognised it.

Standing beside her fiancée, Catriona took Dreya's left hand in her right.

"Dreya," she began, "you have let me get close to you in ways no-one ever has before. You've shown me the woman underneath the robes…"

Shyleen, by Mandalee's side like her feline shadow, as always, making sure only her literal soulmate could hear, quipped, '*If your pocket dimension magic had gone wrong, we might all have seen it.*'

Mandalee had to suppress a smile.

"…but I know there's so much more," Catriona continued, uninterrupted. "Every time I think I know what to expect from you, you do something unexpected. You told me I mean more to you than your magic, and I know what it cost you to say that. In return, I want to say this: I once told you that my Crystal Mage Staff was more important to me than our friendship. My obsession with my staff may have faded in recent times, but I'm sure there is more to learn about it. Still, no matter what mysteries still surround its existence and whatever functions it may yet have, its most vital role is already achieved."

She glanced over at Mandalee.

"It has gained me the best friend I could ever have," she returned her focus to Dreya, "and a love I never imagined I would find." Addressing the Champion of the Gods for a moment, she surmised, "Michael, I assume you've been around long enough to know Faery wedding customs?"

"Although I've never before had the privilege of being invited to one, I do know what they entail, yes," he confirmed.

Cat acknowledged that with a nod. "For the sake of our two Chetsuan friends, then, let me explain that in Faery tradition, when two Faery are wed, the best friend of each party binds their hands together with a garland of flowers. In this case, I believe it's safe to say we share the same best friend?"

Dreya nodded in confirmation.

"Therefore it falls to Mandalee alone. The flowers symbolise the conferring of Nature's blessing, the kiss of Blessed Alycia, on our commitment to each other. The binding, which will keep us connected for the whole day, symbolises our desire to never stray from each other. That this action is taken by a friend, symbolises that the support of those we care about reinforces our love."

To further involve the others, the garland was wrapped around a flexible metal wire mesh from Sara's Lavosian technology. A component of her higher planar energy detector that still stubbornly refused to work.

Jessica had grown the flowers with her druid magic. Like her sister, she had contributed without really understanding, until now.

Mandalee had attached her one remaining sapphire earring from her shopping trip with Daelen and Cat on Earth, so it dangled down between their wrists, further symbolising her joining them together.

Michael imbued the tiny sapphire jewel with a sliver of his own power so that it glowed.

"Dreya, is it your wish that our friend, Mandalee, should bind us in love, helping us to strengthen our bond as we prepare to take the next step in our journey through life together and marry?"

"Yes, Catriona," Dreya answered. "I wish it with all my heart."

Mandalee stepped forward, the garland strip in her hands.

"Although," the sorceress added, "for this to be completely official and legally binding, Mandalee, I suppose you ought to use my full given name."

Naturally, Catriona already knew, but everyone else shared the same puzzled look.

"Dreya isn't your real name?" Mandalee wondered.

"My chosen name is like your body, Mandalee," Dreya offered, cryptically.

"Beautiful, strong and completely awesome?" she suggested with a grin.

Everyone laughed but Dreya shook her head. "No, I mean it's real, and it's me, it's just not the one I was born with."

Mandalee nodded her understanding.

"And if any of you ever use it outside this ceremony, I'll turn you all into toads, or something."

Dreya accepted their word to keep it to themselves. As for Zarinda, as a Sylfranian Faery royal, Dreya would have been astonished if she didn't know already, so she just came out and said it. "Andreyanka."

"Wow!" Sara exclaimed, pulling a face. "That so doesn't suit you at all."

"Not remotely," Mandalee agreed.

'*And I thought* '*Pryshia*' *was precious.*' Shyleen remarked.

"Yeah," Jessica put in, "I can totally see why you pared it back to Dreya. I mean, it's just so fussy and frilly around the edges. It sounds like…" she trailed off, trying to think how to finish the sentence.

Michael finished it for her. "It sounds like a Faery princess."

"Exactly!" Jessica cried, the others nodding and murmuring in agreement. "Good call, Mickey!"

"Don't call me Mickey!" he grumbled.

"Well, a Faery princess was exactly what my parents wanted me to be," Dreya explained. "If they'd had their way, I would have been married long before now to someone I barely knew. All to raise their status and supposedly protect me. Instead, I learned to provide my own protection and status. That choice led me to take this Black Tower, and then one day, this troublesome half-Faery druid girl I'd heard about came looking for a library.

Taking Catriona's hand, she gazed into her eyes and told her, "I still remember that day. The magic you used to 'challenge' me was unlike anything I'd seen before. With your strength, your confidence, your wit…" with a smile, she indicated the three colour roses framing her door, "…and your flowers, you filled my garden, my home and my life with a joy that was infectious. My library, my home, and my heart were yours from that day to this, and I vow in the future, too. A future I wish to share with you and," she added, placing her free hand on her fiancée's belly, "whoever the amazing person growing inside you might be. I give you both all that I am, all that I have, for as close to forever as our fates will allow." To her friend, she concluded, "So yes, please Mandalee, bless our marriage and bind us together."

"Catriona and Andreyanka," Mandalee began, taking care not to trip over the unfamiliar name, "when I first saw you two together, I was…" she hesitated, "…sceptical to say the least."

Both Dreya and Cat flashed a smile at that. "But now, I couldn't feel prouder or more privileged to be the one to help you symbolise the promise you are making here today."

She wrapped the garland strip around Dreya and Cat's clasped hands in an intricate pattern, and sealed it with a little magic from Shyleen, preventing them from letting go of each other until the next day.

(In practice, gentle reader, they would be unbound occasionally, so they could see to certain private bodily functions alone, but immediately afterwards, Mandalee would re-bind them.)

"With this binding, I give you both my blessing and my love, as your chosen friend, so that you may go forward in your relationship, and begin your journey into the marriage you both wish for. Congratulations to you both." She gave each a kiss on the cheek, and then the happy couple shared a deeper kiss with each other, while everyone showered them with a flurry of rose petals.

When her supply was exhausted, Jessica had to sit down and let the tears flow. She just couldn't hold back the flood any longer.

"That's it, I'm done!" she declared. "I can't handle any more emotions for at least a week!"

"Really, guys," Sara sniffled, only slightly more composed. "Thank you so much for letting us be a part of this private ceremony. I've never seen anything more amazing."

"Seconded!" Michael boomed, striding forward and shaking their free hands.

When he stepped aside, the two lovers each held their free arm wide, and Sara hauled her sister to her feet so they could both be enfolded in their embrace.

Finally, Shyleen rubbed bodily against them with a loud purr. The happy couple reached down and stroked the leopard, conveying their appreciation.

The rest of the afternoon was consumed by eating and drinking. Mandalee decided that since Catriona was, somehow, still pregnant, it was her solemn duty to drink her share as well as her own, and consequently got very drunk.

They even portalled over to Zarinda with a selection plate.

After Zarinda had gone home, the evening was filled with music and dancing. Then, when night fell, and all their guests had gone, leaving Cat and Dreya alone…

…Well, what happened after that, gentle reader, is between the two of them and protected by the highest of privacy ratings. Use your imagination.

Chapter 2

Mandalee was going through her training routines in the grounds of the Black Tower, keeping an eye on the place while Dreya and Cat were on honeymoon on Earth. Dreya didn't want to turn her private grounds into a public park, but she had agreed to let Mandalee invite one other person at her discretion. Windell had been curious, and he was available for a few days, so he had joined her, but he was gone now.

After what he'd said, she didn't expect to see him again.

Shyleen was dozing off up a tree, out of the way of Dreya's undead groundskeepers.

On her wedding day, the sorceress had, with the demigod's permission, relocated them to work on Michael's grounds. Their presence would have spoiled the atmosphere, but now they were back and hard at it once more.

Mandalee was doing her best to ignore them.

Her presence wasn't entirely voluntary. It was a condition of the Council of Mages that they would allow the married couple personal leave away from Tempestria only if the one remaining Guardian remained on hand in case of emergency. The Council didn't want a situation like last time when they went missing for over two years.

Dreya had protested that they only intended to be away for two months, not years. The Triumvirate had pointed out that they hadn't expected to be away at all, last time, and look what happened.

Catriona had reluctantly conceded that was a fair point.

Of the three leading mages, only Laethyn didn't particularly object, but since everyone knew Dreya had him in her pocket, that was hardly surprising.

Maia was intent on them not going anywhere at all until the 'current crisis' was resolved.

When they asked, "What crisis?" Maia was incredulous that they didn't know.

"How can you be ignorant about this? Where have you been?"

Cat shrugged. “Lost in Time, for the most part,” she replied with a twinkle in her eye.

Maia was unimpressed. “All the more reason for you to not disappear for such an extended period. The greater good must come first. At least until the current crisis is over.”

“Again, what crisis?” Dreya demanded, reminding them that they had removed her from her position as Secondmage in the order of Dark magic. Therefore she wasn’t as up to date with Council business as she once was.

Justaria explained that the rumours had started less than six months after they disappeared. Rumours of a group who were opposed to Council rule. Some took issue with the new inclusive policy for clerics. Many of those were clerics themselves who objected to the very suggestion that they could sit in conference with clerics of different orders. They also objected to being dictated to by wizards. The Triumvirate had issued statements that all members of the new Council of Mages would have a say in formulating the revised rules. Therefore, the more clerics joined, the better representation they would enjoy. The main problem, however, was one particular group of fanatics that were vowing to put an end to co-operation and order in magic entirely.

Mandalee offered a wry smile. “So basically, there’s a diverse group of magic users who are co-operating to try and end diversity and co-operation in magic, yes?”

Justaria returned the smile. “Believe me, the irony is not lost on me, though I suspect it would be on them.”

“You’re seriously saying you knew nothing of this?” Maia demanded incredulously.

Catriona patiently explained that she’d been busy setting up safeguards against accidental Timeline changes, including, but not limited to, a Timeless spell on Calin’s Tower.

*****

It obviously had to be a version of Timelessness that wouldn’t kill everyone who went there, unlike if they went to Catriona’s Meadow. That proved impossible to achieve with their current knowledge. Yet the need remained for an immutable reference there in the present, in case of future changes to the past.

In theory, she eventually realised, it would be possible to devise a Timeless spell for use on inanimate objects only; specifically, the books. Unfortunately, in practice, there were so many books – and more were being added all the time – that casting a Timeless spell on each one individually was a task that could never be completed.

It was Calin herself who proposed the most workable solution.

"Catriona," she spoke up, one day, when they were taking a much-needed break, "tell me about your meadow."

In an apologetic tone, the Red Guardian told her she couldn't really talk about how their Timeless base worked.

Calin shook her head and clarified, "I don't mean your Timeless one. I mean the original. The one you created on Earth."

"What would you like to know?" Cat asked.

She had already chatted with Calin about many aspects of her adventures with Daelen StormTiger. Including the day she understood the cryptic message left by Rose – the avatar sent by Catriona's Alternative Universe self. Realising that she was meant to combine her magic with Daelen-style brute force to demolish his training centre and find what was buried underneath. Having done so, she transformed the area into a place of natural beauty, a copy of her memory of her childhood home in Quarthonian lands.

"I'd like to know how you did it," Calin replied. "Surely you didn't work your magic on every blade of grass, individually."

Cat laughed. "Hardly! That would be an endless task."

"Exactly," Calin agreed. "So why are you trying to do that here?"

Cat still didn't see what she was getting at, so Calin reiterated her question of how she created her meadow on Earth.

"Well, if I want to grow a field, I don't think about the plants I want to appear; I work my magic on the ground in which I want them to grow."

"Focus on the flower beds, not the flowers," Calin summarised.

"Succinctly put."

"So why can't you do that here?"

Cat wore a look of intense concentration as she processed Calin's suggestion. If the books were analogous to the flowers, then the equivalent of flower beds would be… "The bookshelves!" she exclaimed excitedly, which prompted a lot of shushing from other library users.

All the bookshelves were made of wood from the same trees in the same forest. There was a ready-made connection. Making a spell cast on one bookshelf spread to all the others would be simple. That spell could, in turn, affect all the books placed upon them. The Timeless spell could be done, appropriately enough, in no time. Catriona worked with Dreya to refine the idea and confirm the specifics of the magic itself, and then she executed the plan. That was just a few days before her wedding.

*****

"So," Cat explained to the Triumvirate, "excuse me if we've been too preoccupied with preserving our record of the past to keep up to date with current affairs."

The Council had also issued an order that anyone who encountered anything they thought might be a fragment of Kullos' control device should report it immediately. That left Dreya and Mandalee busy running around Elvaria, investigating those reports. Meanwhile, Michael, Jessica and Sara, who had given up on her tracker ever working again, were doing much the same throughout Alloria.

All proved to be false alarms.

Dreya had tried to decipher her hastily written co-ordinates in Catriona's notebook. One more fragment was definitely sent into Tempestria's past but didn't seem to have caused any Timeline damage. They had been reluctant to indulge in any unnecessary Time Interventions until the books in Calin's Tower had been protected.

In addition to the fragment that had been stolen from Phitonia, they believed there was one more that had remained in Tempestria's present. In her haste, however, she seemed to have made a mistake when she'd written the co-ordinates, so she couldn't be sure. As for the sixth and last fragment, in the cold light of day, she had to admit her notes made no sense whatsoever. She'd been working on instinct at the time, with no time to think, only to try and record the essence of what she sensed. They'd have to worry about the last one when they'd found the other outstanding three.

"Perhaps if we weren't sent on so many wild goose chases," the White Guardian complained, "we might actually get something done."

Dreya agreed. "Now, after wasting our time so much, is it so wrong for my wife and me to take some time for ourselves?"

Frankly, Dreya didn't understand why they were asking permission from a Council that wouldn't even exist if not for them.

"No-one's saying it is," Justaria assured her, smoothing things over. "Are they, Maia?" she added pointedly to her White faction counterpart. Laethyn wisely continued to stay out of it, visibly squirming under Dreya's glare.

In the end, Cat suggested that they would be willing to compromise on the amount of personal time they would take.

"Perhaps the Council might agree to two weeks, rather than two months?"

"That's a factor of four!" Justaria gasped. "If you are willing to make such a compromise, I'd say that's more than generous, wouldn't you agree, Maia?"

Maia relented immediately, clearly believing she had made the Guardians see sense.

"Oh, well, naturally, I'm sure a fortnight is perfectly reasonable for this wonderful couple to celebrate their union. Yes, the White order happily approves the request."

It was further ratified by the Red order on the condition that Mandalee made herself available and contactable for the duration. Hence, she ended up taking up temporary residence in the Black Tower.

When the Council officially approved their two weeks' leave of absence, the Guardians began to walk away from the Council chamber.

Once outside, Mandalee leaned close to her friends.

"Has anybody told them that Time moves four times faster on Earth, so your 'compromise' was actually them giving you exactly what you originally asked for?" she asked quietly. "About two months on Earth?"

Cat made a show of considering the question. "Oh, I'm sure Dreya must have mentioned the Time difference in one of her reports."

"Actually, I don't think it's ever come up," Dreya admitted.

"Really? How remiss of you," Cat teased.

"It just never seemed important."

"Would you like me to explain it to them?" Mandalee asked with a mischievous grin.

"No, Dreya's right," Cat decided quickly. "I don't think there's any need to bother them with such tedious minutiae."

*****

The first two days at the Black Tower, Mandalee had spent with Windell, and initially, it had been nice. She liked him – the first man ever to kiss her, and they'd done more of that. They'd even made use of one of Dreya's spare rooms to do more, exploring her new body further. That had been good, too, but after the initial spark wore off, they found they had little in common. What finally ended things was that Windell didn't understand Mandalee's connection to Shyleen. In fact, on their third day together, he described their silent conversations as 'creepy'. In response, Mandalee immediately portalled him back to his home in Southern Alloria and his regular duty as a ranger, guarding the remote passes into Kelna's Imperial City. That way, he need never put up with her 'creepy' behaviour ever again.

On day four, Jessica and Sara had popped over, having caught a lift with Cat and Dreya to Daelen's Earth base so they could charge their phones and grab a few things. Michael had picked them up according to a pre-arranged schedule.

When the Chetsuans had breezed in with their customary, "Heya, love!" Mandalee was thankful she hadn't still been with Windell. It could have got a bit awkward if they'd interrupted something. As it was, she was happy to see them. Her alien friends had decided they were long overdue what they called 'A Day at the Movies,' so they brought some with them. Sara's cobbled-together technology had helped Mandalee get up to speed with a few of their references. Especially with regards to a remark Sara had made at the wedding, that Dreya's ghoulish guards serving the wedding feast was, "Like Casper meets Beauty and the Beast!"

Sadly, only her sister had known what she was talking about.

Having now watched those movies herself, Mandalee could see it clearly. "Although I wouldn't show that last one to Cat, or she'll figure out how to use her magic to make Dreya's undead guards perform 'Be Our Guest' on demand."

They all cracked up at the idea, with Jessica adding, "Can you imagine Dreya's reaction, coming home to that? She'd probably vaporise the lot of us!"

That had been fun, but now she was starting to feel bored, and it was going to take more than movies to change that.

*****

It was the seventh day, Tempestrian time, and Mandalee was deep into physical training when she heard a noise that she hoped might at last herald excitement. Someone was shouting for help from beyond the gates of the Black Tower's grounds. Calling for the Guardians, plural, obviously unaware that two of them were absent. They were using magic to project their voice, apparently unwilling to approach uninvited. Mandalee opened a portal for herself and Shyleen, mostly just for practice, and went to see what the fuss was about.

When they exited the portal, a Red robe wizard stepped forward, his eyes wide. "Fascinating magic," he remarked. Then, snapping himself out of it, he gasped, "White Guardian! We need your help! We're under attack!"

"Who's 'we'?" Mandalee asked.

The wizard introduced himself as Yanis, a professor at a magic school in Tedstone Warf, on the Southwestern Elvarian peninsula. He went on to explain that a group of renegade wizards and clerics were attacking the school, intent on getting at the young magic students in their care.

"Please come!" he begged. "There isn't much time – I don't know how long we can hold out against their assault!"

"I'm a Guardian," she reminded him calmly. "I have Temporal magic. I can have us there five minutes ago." She'd been practising, so she was much more self-assured about her Guardian powers than before. “So, you have plenty of time to tell me everything,” she insisted.

“What else do you need to know?” Yanis asked.

“Let’s start with how you got here so fast,” she replied.

Yanis explained that he was originally from Gaggleswick before he was invited to teach in Tedstone. “That’s why I was chosen to bring this message – I have a strong memory of the Black Tower, a clear image I could use to teleport here.”

“That explains how,” Mandalee accepted. “What about why? Why not go to the Council for help?”

“Because the group that’s attacking us claimed to be Council representatives until we got suspicious. How could we be sure anyone we spoke to on the Council wasn’t in on it? But we have a lot of respect for the Guardians at our school.”

Mandalee explained that the other two Guardians were away at the moment, so only she and Shyleen were available.

“From what I’ve heard, you’re all we need,” he assured her. “There’s only about a dozen of them.”

Flattery would get him nowhere, even if it was nice to hear.

“Is there anything else we should know about this attack before we risk our necks?”

“Just that there’s something strange about their magic,” Yanis offered.

“Strange in what way?”

Yanis explained that their school had strong historical links with the Council – hence the attack – and many higher-ranking members sent their children to study there. Knowing that made them a target for anti-Council dissidents, the school was equipped with magical shields.

“But these dissidents are cutting through those shields like they’re nothing. My fellow professors are trying to bolster those defences, but the attackers’ magic is laced with a kind of energy we’ve never encountered before. Not just the inter-planar forces all wizards and clerics use for their magic, but something more potent.”

Mandalee and Shyleen shared a glance. Higher planar energy. It had to be. That suggested this group had got their hands on one of the missing fragments. The White Guardian recalled how Dreya had taken her own idea of sharing power with others and found a way to boost the fledgeling Council mages' magic with her own store of higher planar energy. It sounded very much to her as if this group were doing something similar with the power of a fragment of Kullos' dimensional control device. Yanis was right; this was definitely Guardian business.

"Alright, we'll help," she agreed.

She would have helped anyway – she couldn't stand by and let people attack a school, whatever their grievance. She was just trying to take a leaf out of Catriona's book. Getting all the information first, rather than just getting very drunk, armed to the teeth, and going for it, as she had in times past.

Mandalee encouraged Yanis to picture his school as it looked the moment he left and project it to her. Using her enhanced sympathic link, she could see that image in her mind. Factoring in the few minutes he'd been with her, she added a sensible margin for error, ensuring they wouldn't arrive before he left. That could cause some nasty paradoxes. Co-ordinates verified, she opened a portal, and the three of them stepped through it.

Chapter 3

Though she was no expert in architecture, it seemed to Mandalee that the school shared some features with the Council building. All stone archways and high vaulted ceilings.

The building shook with the impact of a powerful magical assault, and Mandalee hurriedly joined the group of magic tutors that were desperately working to shield against the attack.

A sorceress tapped one of her male colleagues on the shoulder and directed his attention. She must have seen their approach out of the corner of her eye,

He greeted his colleague warmly with a beaming smile. "Ah, Yanis! You've brought help, I see."

"Principal," Yanis returned respectfully, but before he could say anything further, Mandalee cut him off.

"Act now, introductions later, yes?" she suggested. "Yanis has explained the situation, so first things first." More magical impacts rebounded off the shields. Through that barrier, Mandalee could sense higher planar energy lacing the magical assault. "How many students, and where are they?"

The principal told her that all six hundred or so were safe in the basement.

"Safe is relative," Mandalee disputed. "If the attackers breach the walls, they'll be trapped down there. We need to get them out."

She could understand why they hadn't. From what she knew of standard teleportation spells, a typical wizard could take one other person with them as long as they were in physical contact. An exceptionally skilled wizard might manage two at a time. Still, even if one of the tutors in this school was that good, that would mean at least three hundred trips, which would take too long to be viable. Besides, the wizard would be too exhausted after a few dozen trips at best. The more wizards that helped with the evacuation, the fewer there would be to shore up the shields, so they would fail sooner. Whichever way one ran the numbers, it didn't end well.

With the aid of a portal, however, there was no theoretical limit to how many could be transported at once. Indeed, there had been no problem portalling the Council-led army at the Battle of Rhynas Desert against Kullos' forces. They had numbered considerably higher than six hundred.

"Where are you thinking of sending them?" asked the principal.

"Well, from what Yanis says, I take it you wouldn't be keen on Walminster?"

"It wouldn't be my first choice, no," he agreed.

Mandalee briefly considered the Black Tower, but if one of the kids did something that Dreya's undead guards misinterpreted as a threat, the results could be disastrous. That left only one sensible option. It was taking liberties, but that couldn't be helped.

"What would you say to a school trip to a reconstructed ancient temple in Northern Alloria, home to the Champion of the Gods and a pair of aliens?"

"Well, technically, we're supposed to get parental authorisation before taking them out of school..." the building shook as a particularly explosive volley struck the ever-weakening shields. The power was enough to penetrate in one place, shattering all the windows in an East-facing classroom. "...but under the circumstances, I think we can make an exception."

"Besides," Yanis put in, "the rule technically says, 'parent or guardian'. Mandalee is a Guardian."

"Good point," the principal agreed. "Very well, I'll allow it. Show our guest the way, Yanis."

Yanis acknowledged that with a sharp nod and led Mandalee through the maze of corridors.

Mandalee had never attended a school like this one. There had only been a few kids in her village, and most of her tutoring had come from her parents and Elric, the village Cleric. Then, once she was joined with Shyleen, she acquired complete understanding of wild things. Beyond that, her education was mainly acquired through experience, according to need. She could see the sense of a school of magic like this one in Tedstone Warf, but she was sure she would have felt closed in by such a place.

When Yanis led her and Shyleen to a stairwell, Mandalee was momentarily confused because the steps only went upwards, but it turned out that the stairs leading down had been hidden by illusion magic. Yanis cancelled the spell, and Mandalee asked

Shyleen to remain at the top on guard. She didn't want to introduce a leopard to a room full of terrified magic users.

Upon reaching the bottom, Mandalee saw the hundreds of frightened kids. Some were crying, others were pale, their eyes darting everywhere, jumping at the sound of every bang and crackle of magic against the shields. A few were trying to act tough and unconcerned, but that was just bravado.

"Hi, everyone!" she called out. "I'm Mandalee, the White Guardian." That was the first time she'd announced her title, she realised. She wasn't sure how she felt about it, yet. She supposed she'd get used to it in time. She hadn't been keen on the White Assassin, at first, but she'd since embraced it. "As a Guardian, it's been agreed that I can send you on a little field trip while I sort things out here. I'm going to open a portal, like a big round blue door in space. It's just a dressed-up teleportation spell, really. It's perfectly safe; the other Guardians and I use them all the time, so it's nothing to be scared of."

"Actually," Yanis put in, "our principal has been working on that same, well, principle, trying to reproduce that kind of magic, and many of our students have seen those attempts. Failed attempts, mind you, so they wouldn't be safe to use, but still…" he trailed off, apparently realising he wasn't helping.

Mandalee supposed she shouldn't be surprised. Like many academic institutions, this was a place for cutting-edge research. Portal-based travel could change the world in many ways, so it made sense that such revolutionary magic would be on the research agenda. She made a mental note to discuss with Dreya and Cat whether they should simply give them the information they needed. On the one hand, the only reason the Guardians had such travel was that they learned it from Daelen – directly or indirectly. So why should they withhold that knowledge? On the other hand, Catriona, in particular, always believed there was value in research for its own sake. She had even refused Daelen's offer of a shortcut to the power of her staff, preferring to do the work herself.

Still, Mandalee thought as the school shook violently once more, that was hardly the most pressing concern right now.

She opened a portal to Michael's home and bade the others wait while she checked who was around. It turned out the Champion of the Gods was out training a group of his followers somewhere in the Corolis Wood, but Sara and Jessica readily agreed to help keep the students safe and entertained for a while. So, anchoring her portal in place, Mandalee returned to the school with Jessica and left her to help the teachers organise the kids' exodus. At their destination, Sara set up her technology for movie time, to keep them occupied for an hour or two.

*****

The assault was penetrating the shields more and more frequently, now. They couldn't avoid a breach much longer. Getting six hundred people through the portal was going to take time, but the way things were going, the school could be reduced to rubble before they were even halfway done. The attack had to stop. Still, Mandalee was entirely confident of taking out a dozen mages pretty quickly, so she could afford to give them one chance to cease of their own accord.

Rejoining Shyleen, she returned with Yanis to where the principal and the rest of his staff were struggling to shield the doors.

Once there, Mandalee, recalling how Yanis had got her attention at the Black Tower, asked if he could project her voice through the barrier to address the attackers. He agreed that was no problem.

"The shield doesn't block sound," he pointed out.

As if to prove his words, the loudest explosion yet rocked the school. Pictures and awards fell off their wall mountings. Chunks of plaster rained down from the ceiling, leaving cracks behind that were spreading with each attack.

Wasting no time, Yanis worked his magic on Mandalee.

"You lot attacking this place," she projected, "listen to me! This is Mandalee, known alternatively as the White Guardian or the White Assassin. I will be coming out to you in a moment, and you get to choose which version of me you meet. If I come out as the White Assassin, our meeting will be brief, and you will die. The White Guardian, on the other hand, is prepared to have a longer conversation with you, in which you can air your grievances and discuss them with me in a civilised way. But if you want to meet that version of me and appease the White Assassin, you'll have to cease your attack on this school. Because while you're deliberately putting innocent children in danger, quite frankly, I don't give a fig about your grievances."

In these situations, she had often seen the person in her place give a countdown, say one minute, to a deadline. The way Mandalee saw it, that would be like allowing them sixty seconds to keep attacking with impunity. In effect, it was granting them permission to attack for sixty whole seconds. They would get no such permission from her. She expected immediate compliance.

It would take her a moment or two to get in position anyway, but there was no sense in removing any element of surprise by telling them exactly when to expect her to strike.

Without waiting for a response, Mandalee asked Yanis if he could teleport her and Shyleen somewhere close by, but where the attackers wouldn't see them.

Since she already had a portal open in the basement, she wasn't sure if she could open a second one. Besides, if she wanted to approach unnoticed, it would be better if there wasn't a big blue light announcing her arrival.

Yanis teleported them to a pub around the corner called the *Wand and Staff*. There, Mandalee and Shyleen split up to approach the school from different directions, just in case the attackers decided that meeting the White Assassin sounded like a good idea.

As she neared her destination, however, all was quiet. Powerful spells assailed the school no longer. It seemed they were interested in talking to the White Guardian, after all, but she wasn't taking anything for granted. They could just as easily be saving their magic for an all-out assault on her. She had to be ready for anything.

From a well-hidden Shyleen, Mandalee got an accurate count of fifteen in the attacking group – slightly more than the dozen she'd been promised. A mixture of wizards and clerics. They had, for the moment, stopped firing at the school as they looked around, most likely searching for her.

'*Fair's fair,*' she told Shyleen. '*Looks like they get to meet the White Guardian.*'

'*A wise choice,*' Shyleen agreed.

The White Guardian decided that projecting an image of authority from a high vantage point would be a prudent next move.

Opposite the school campus, just behind the rebel group, were the stables. It was high but not too high and seemed sturdy enough, so it ought to work quite nicely. To that end, she snuck around the back of the building and climbed up onto the roof, maybe twenty feet off the ground.

'*It really is time I learned levitation,*' she thought.

She could float an arrow or similar object that was designed to fly but levitating herself was a different matter.

Once on the roof, she moved to the front and stood close – but not too close – to the front edge, doing her best to project calm and confidence.

From there, she called out, "Glad to see you heeded my warning!"

'*Though I would not rule out the possibility that the White Assassin may yet be required,*' Shyleen told her, with a note of caution in her telepathic voice.

Mandalee assured her friend she was absolutely on her guard.

"So, why don't you tell me what this is all about, hmm?"

They all began talking at once until Mandalee yelled at them to stop.

"One at a time!" she cried. Picking a White robe wizard at random, she pointed at him and ordered, "You first."

"We're against all these new Council rules," he replied.

That elicited a murmur of agreement from the rest.

"What does that have to do with this school?" Mandalee asked.

"Well, we know we can't attack the Council directly, but all the higher members send their kids here. We just want to make them listen to us."

Mandalee was incredulous. "And you think attacking their children will make them *more* receptive? Did you even *try* talking to the Council first?"

"There wouldn't be any point. They wouldn't listen!"

"I'm here," Mandalee countered. "I'm listening, although I'd now like to listen to someone else." She chose a Black robe cleric and asked, "What's your problem?"

"All this co-operation with wizards and other orders of clerics," she grumbled. "It stifles the cutthroat competition that makes magic stronger."

"And yet here you are co-operating with wizards and other orders of clerics," Mandalee pointed out.

Mandalee listened to grievance after grievance. All petty and jealous and fearful of the changes Dreya had wrought. People often found change confusing and frightening, and she sympathised. There would always be resistance to new ideas, and some of the necessary changes to the Council system would be painful after being ingrained for three centuries.

There were many inconsistencies in the rules that had allowed the inclusion of clerics, such as using weapons. Mandalee herself would have refused to join if she couldn't use whatever weapons she liked, yet she knew wizards were allowed only one.

Still, she wouldn't attack a school over the issue.

A more significant matter was the Triumvirate – all wizards, of course. How could clerics be expected to place themselves under the rule of wizards? Perhaps there could be a ruling commission of six, but would they be the current heads of the three major cleric factions or new representatives? It was unlikely the former would agree to it, and the latter could cause a split within the clerical orders with who knew what consequences?

Moreover, what about druids? They had been part of the Council for most of its existence. An ignored minority. Didn't they deserve representation? But although pockets of druid magic had begun to take root, thanks to Catriona's influence, they tended not to go for unnecessary formal structure as a people.

It was unquestionably a difficult and challenging time, but in general, Mandalee firmly believed the changes could only be a good thing.

"Surely, clerics joining with wizards and druids in some kind of new Council is a natural extension of the Accords," she suggested.

Chapter 4

The Accords, gentle reader, were drawn up in the aftermath of the Demon Apocalypse, about five decades earlier. In fact, Mandalee realised she had missed the golden jubilee during the two years she'd been lost in Time.

The Council of Wizards formed in response to the tyrannical wizard, Ulvarius. He had been the first wizard to tap into the more potent interplanar forces found above the mortal plane rather than the lesser ones below.

Over the following decades, however, other wizards began to learn to do the same. Such progress continued until, a little over two centuries later, more wizards were getting their magic from above than below.

Following the demise of their common enemy, a growing number of clerics had begun to view the growth of wizard magic as a threat. Skirmishes between clerics and wizards gradually escalated into open hostility and eventually warfare.

To try and minimise casualties in this war, both sides came up with the same idea at about the same time. Rather than attack directly, each side focussed on summoning demons to do their dirty work. More and more wizards and clerics summoned ever-increasing numbers of demons. According to the history books, the combined demon armies would have easily put Kullos' efforts to shame. Or perhaps even Kullos simply had more sense. What people didn't realise was that there was a critical mass of demons beyond which all control would be lost.

If you recall my Great Cosmic Sandwich, gentle reader -(and how could you not?)- each plane of reality has less available energy than the plane above. Whether that energy flows from some kind of Creator entity, or whether it's merely the nature and structure of reality, is a matter of sacred versus secular belief. In practical terms, it's a distinction without difference. The point is the demon realms have less energy than the mortal plane. Therefore it requires energy to bring demons here. That's what summoning is. By nature, demons need less energy to survive than mortals, so they have an excess just by being here. That's what makes them so dangerous. The summoner – wizard or cleric – must always retain control over that excess energy to keep the demon in check. The more demons they summon, the harder that is.

During the last and greatest of the wars between clerics and wizards, each side allowed the threat of the other to push them beyond their limits. That meant they were not always in control.

Sometimes, the demons would secretly stockpile energy while letting the mages think they were in control. When enough demons had enough extra energy, they began to summon other demons. Unlike the mortal summoners, the demons did not try to control those they summoned but allowed them free reign. These free demons used their excess energy to summon more demons, which in turn summoned more and more. Ultimately, the free demons outnumbered those who were captive.

During one enormous battle between thousands of wizards and clerics, the free demons attacked, slaying the summoners and freeing more of their kind. As such, the war took a different turn. No longer wizard versus cleric, but all mortal magic users (and many non-magical troops) versus the demons. It quickly became known as the Demon Apocalypse.

It was a watershed moment. For the first time, both sides – cleric and wizard – were forced to put aside their differences and help each other simply to survive. Those hardline elements that refused were soon swept away by the demons.

For almost four years, this new war encompassed most of Northern and Southern Alloria and even, to a lesser degree, Elvaria. The mortals of Tempestria eventually turned the tide, culling the demons. While not all demons were slain or Banished down to the planes of hell, the war was ultimately declared won.

In the aftermath of the Demon Apocalypse, the Accords were signed, outlawing the use of demons in warfare forever. Thus signalling a new era of, if not co-operation between wizards and clerics, then at least tolerance.

*****

"Surely, you're proving the value of co-operation yourselves by joining together like this," Mandalee suggested. "I just wish you'd work together to achieve something good instead of attacking a school."

"We're only working together because we have to," a Red robe cleric insisted.

"Just like you 'have to' attack a school?" Mandalee challenged him.

"It's not just a school," a White robe wizard maintained. "It's a research centre, too,"

"Naturally, it is," Mandalee agreed. However, from what she'd seen inside, there was a college campus for older students not far away. She imagined most of the research went on there and told them so.

"That's just the research they tell us about. We've been told there's secret work going on!" the wizard insisted.

"Well, I'm sure much of their work is confidential," Mandalee allowed. "What's wrong with that?"

"It's wrong because the school's Principal and Head of Research is the new Secondmage of the order of Dark magic, replacing Dreya the Dark."

The Black robe sorceress who had spoken seemed to think that was the crime of the century.

Mandalee snorted. "If you're upset about Dreya losing her position, trust me, she's a big girl and doesn't need you to stick up for her."

The sorceress shook her head. "I'm no Dreya fan!"

"I'm sure she'll be devastated when I tell her."

Ignoring Mandalee's sarcasm, the sorceress continued.

"I just don't think one mage should have free access to the Triumvirate while having the resources to conduct secret experiments."

One Black robe accusing another of having too much power was hardly new. Dark mages often used such notions to justify attacking each other. Even if Laethyn – at Dreya's instance – had done away with the policy of in-fighting, that didn't magically change people's attitudes.

"And what's so bad about these experiments?"

"We've been told he's working on some way to control us with magic. Make us all slaves to his will."

"Who told you this?"

"Our leader."

'*There's a leader!*' Mandalee remarked to Shyleen. '*At last, we're getting somewhere.*'

"And who is that?" she prompted the sorceress.

The whole group shifted uncomfortably at the question. "We don't know," one wizard admitted, finally.

'*So much for that,*' Shyleen remarked in Mandalee's mind.

"He always shrouds himself in his Black robes and uses magic to disguise his voice when we meet. He told us about the secret experiments being done here, experiments that threaten us all. That's all we know."

"Yet he chose not to come himself," the Guardian pointed out.

"He said he has broader plans, and we're just one part of it."

Mandalee was incredulous. "So, some mysterious figure appears to you, sends you on a mission to stop some terrible threat that only they know about, and you just do it?"

'*Why not? You did!*' Shyleen snarked, reminding her friend of the time a mysterious white figure sent her on a mission to stop Daelen StormTiger. In fact, to kill him, or so Mandalee believed at the time.

'*That's different!*' Mandalee insisted, although her soulmate's words got her thinking.

She was in danger of forgetting why she came here in the first place: the fragment. When she reached out with her magical senses, she could feel something emanating from it. It was probing at the edges of her mind, trying to sneak in, but her link with Shyleen – a god, even if she didn't like the term – was proving to be a challenge.

Mandalee suddenly realised that the group had stopped attacking the school because they were concentrating their magic to attack her, instead. The worst thing was, she didn't think they even knew they were doing it.

She didn't bother to listen to whatever nonsense reply was coming her way. She knew it was irrelevant.

All at once, the White Guardian put it together.

"Listen to me, all of you!" she gasped, accessing her clerical powers to raise further shields

"I think you're right. At least partly. I think there *is* some kind of magic trying to enslave you all!" It was trying to capture her mind, too. That's what she was feeling, and the attack was growing in strength. "But it's nothing to do with this school or anyone in it!" Mandalee was sure it was this group's so-called leader, but if she said that, the group would most likely turn on her.

There was something else. A disturbance in nature. Something that didn't belong. She had to focus through the attack and find it. At last, she spotted it, shimmering on the edge of her vision. A small blue spot in the fabric of reality. It was a micro-portal. A tiny Prismatic Sphere. Now that she'd seen it, she could focus on it and sense the magic flowing out. Magic that was being directed at the fragment of Kullos' control device. That device was amplifying the spell.

Shyleen could feel it, too. '*Mandalee, this is shadow warrior power,*' she fretted. '*Way beyond the Pantheon. Even if it's just a fragment, it could be too much for me to hold it back.*'

She knew her friend was going to tell her to escape to Catriona's Meadow, but that wouldn't help Shyleen.

'*Don't even suggest it!*' Mandalee insisted.

First things first, she decided. That portal had to go. There had been plenty of time to transport all the kids to Alloria, so if her portal closed, it should be no problem. Trouble was, she'd never before tried to close a portal that she had not opened. No matter how she focussed and tried to will it shut, the micro-portal resisted her efforts. Whether because of the spell that was sapping her will or just her own poor technique, she didn't know, but either way, it was clear that she would have to try something else.

'*Shyleen,*' she began, '*I have a ridiculous radical plan.*'

Once again, it was something she'd never tried. In fact, Cat had once warned against it, but she could see no other way. She had no idea what would happen if she attempted to portal a portal, but it was the only thing she could think of. Concentrating hard, she opened a portal of her own, forming it in the exact same place as the other one. For the destination of her portal, she chose the Black Tower. She knew Dreya's home had powerful wards against mental attacks – years ago, they had once prevented her from contacting Cat when she needed help. These days, of course, Dreya was her friend, and Catriona was her sister in every way that mattered. Cat still mentioned the incident from time to time.

Mandalee wished she wouldn't. That whole thing was ancient history as far as she was concerned.

Still, those wards were the only thing Mandalee knew that would withstand this assault. Plus, if anybody should be foolish enough to travel through the portal, they would have Dreya's elite guards and, if necessary, all the defences of her grounds to contend with.

The point proved to be moot, however, as the two portals exploded into nothingness.

The concussive blast sent out a massive shockwave that knocked Mandalee off her feet and off the end of the roof. She twisted in midair and reflexively clutched at the edge. One hand slipped, but the other held firm.

'*I definitely need to learn levitation,*' she decided.

She was grateful she'd had time to get used to her new body by now. A few months ago, that would likely have been a nasty fall.

Grabbing hold with the other hand once more, she found the strength to pull herself back up, none the worse for wear. Though the portals were now gone, whatever spell had been channelled into the fragment was still growing. Apparently, it was now self-sustaining, no longer requiring external input.

"Please!" she begged the group below her. "Give me the fragment! You don't know what it's doing to you!"

"You just want to take our power away!" the Black robe sorceress scoffed. "Dreya the Dark uses higher planar energy with her magic; why shouldn't we?"

Once again, for all that they claimed to be against co-operation in magic, the others seemed to be in complete agreement.

"Dreya the Dark knows what she's doing," Mandalee growled, fighting to control her temper despite her growing headache. "And even she knows better than to tamper with these fragments. Don't you understand? Don't you know what they are? How they came to be here?"

She explained that they were once part of Kullos' device. Something the shadow warrior was going to use to activate a terrible weapon that wouldn't have merely destroyed the world but unmade it. The blast would have unravelled history and causality on Tempestria and spread to other worlds, perhaps even other planes. (In fact, he *had* used Heaven's Surrender. Only the Temporal powers of an impossible Six Guardians had saved their reality from its effects. Still, Mandalee thought it best not to stress that detail.) It had taken virtually every scrap of power that Dreya the Dark and Mandalee herself possessed to wrest the device from Kullos and shatter it into fragments. Each of those fragments contained an unstable mix of wizard and cleric magic as well as higher planar energy – the vast energy resources of the plane that sat just two layers below the Creator. Then, to compound it further, each fragment was thrown through a Prismatic Sphere portal in time and space.

"Seriously, what part of that makes you think it's safe to use?" she demanded. "Give it to me, and I can make it safe!" '*I hope,*' she added for Shyleen's benefit.

The assault on their minds was becoming unbearable by now, and it was clear these rebels were not going to listen to her. The White Guardian was done. This was a job for the White Assassin.

Mandalee flicked her dragonclaw knives into her hands. She didn't want to harm these people, who she didn't believe were in control of their actions, but she needed to find which of them had the fragment and take it from them. And she needed to do it quickly. While she was still able.

Even as the thought came to her, she could feel the magic tightening its grip. She tried to use her super-speed, but her speed would not come. She managed to climb down from the roof, but when she made to run around the building, she had only taken a few steps before she could move no longer. It was like she wanted to move and didn't want to at the same time. With a supreme effort, Shyleen managed to run to her friend's side before she, too, was stuck.

Too late, Mandalee realised this whole thing had been a trap – a trap for her and Shyleen. That idea was confirmed when two figures sped into her limited field of vision. A young woman with long, dark brown braided hair and an arrogant attitude. At her side was a golden lioness: Nalani and Pryshia.

Chapter 5

"You've got no friends to help you this time," Nalani sneered, prowling around her captive audience. "You're on your own. Now, you just wait," she added as if she had a choice. "I'm busy. Back in a tick!"

With that, she sped off. A moment later, Mandalee heard the death cries of the group of rebels. Magic flared, fizzed, and sizzled, but Nalani was too quick, and they were all dead in less than a minute.

Rushing back, she remarked. "Had to get rid of the minions. Can't have them telling tales, now, can we?"

"I suppose I'm next," Mandalee surmised.

Nalani shook her head. "Actually, I've got some good news and bad news about that," she said, tossing what looked like part of the hilt of a sword up in the air and catching it repeatedly. It was the fragment, right there within arm's reach, and Mandalee could do nothing about it.

"The bad news is I don't get to avenge my father's murder today. The good news is I'll get to kill you a few days from now, and I'll be hailed a hero. You know why? Because once the boss' magic penetrates your mind, you'll be getting some new instructions. Just like that lot attacked the school because they were told to, only the hold on your mind will be much more powerful. It has to be, you see, because when the other two Guardians come back from honeymoon, they're naturally going to meet up with their best friend. The one person – and one mangy cat – that they trust with their lives. Which makes you the perfect weapons to kill them!" She laughed hysterically at the idea.

"No!" Mandalee cried in horror. "I won't do it. I won't. Never!"

"You won't have a choice!" she snapped. "Even if your friends somehow survived, which they won't, the very act of one Guardian attacking another will break the Guardianship magic." Her rage gave way to a malevolent smile. "Either way, no more Guardians, no more special privilege and no more Time magic. Then, when that's done, I get to kill you. And like I say, best of all,

I'll be hailed a hero for stopping the one who murdered the Guardians, just like you murdered my father. Isn't that brilliant?"

Nalani burst with laughter once more, thoroughly enjoying the prospect of such an outcome.

Mandalee, by contrast, was seething with anger. She would not allow this to happen. She would not turn against her friends. She had to stop the controlling magic before it could get a hold of her.

Acting on another ridiculous radical notion, with a supreme effort of will, she created another portal. This one right next to her, leading to Catriona's Meadow. She had no intention of escaping through it, even if she could move, but in theory, from that Timeless zone, she hoped her magical senses might just be able to reach all across Tempestria in an instant. Maybe then she could sense the whole natural world and all the creatures in it. If so, and if she was lucky, there might just be one with the power to help her shield her mind.

Years ago, when she first befriended Catriona, she wasn't alone. Her companion appeared to be a small green snake, but she was no more an ordinary snake than Shyleen was a regular leopard. She was an Ysirian, from a plane just below that of the shadow warriors. Michael, Champion of the Gods, apparently worshipped her because, as he put it, sometimes even the gods had gods. But to Catriona, she was just a friend. A friend who had taught her how to forge a sympathic link. Catriona had chosen to share that link with Mandalee. Even on the day their friendship ended for a time, she had never severed it.

Cat had not seen Pyrah since the battle against Kullos' forces, but the druidess was convinced she was still alive. Mandalee hoped that wasn't just wishful thinking, because Pyrah was the only being in the world who could block this mental attack.

'*Pyrah!*' Mandalee projected. '*I really hope you're still out there and not dead because that would be brilliant. This is Mandalee, friend to Catriona; please remember me. Serious mental attack. Could force me to harm Cat. You must help!*'

For a moment, there was silence, and then a sympathic message entered her head: '*Open mind. Trust.*'

It was Pyrah. Mandalee recognised the contact that could not be described as a voice, unlike when Shyleen spoke in her mind.

But it was an impression of intelligence, a will, perhaps a soul. She didn't know how best to characterise it, but that didn't matter. What mattered was the message. Pyrah was asking for a leap of faith. She was asking Mandalee and Shyleen to abandon their shields entirely, granting Pyrah full access. The trouble was, that would allow the control magic full access, too. They were going to have to trust that Pyrah could be faster, no matter how far away she might be.

'*It seems we have little choice,*' Shyleen advised her friend. '*I can't hold back the power much longer anyway. Calling the Ysirian was a brilliant idea, Mandalee. It's our only chance.*'

Mandalee agreed and sent out, '*Acceptance. Trust.*'

Without another thought, they dropped their shield of clerical magic. Immediately, she and Shyleen could sense another presence wedge itself between their minds and the mental attack. They both saw the image of a small green snake in their minds, striking at the incoming attack with lightning-fast reflexes. Pyrah's barrier held, the attack was thwarted, and the pair were free once more.

Shyleen sprang at Pryshia, catching her off-guard as Mandalee did the same with Nalani. In a break with tradition, Mandalee fought with only one knife, keeping a hand free to grab her prize. She went for the fragment, and for a brief moment, her fingertips held the cold metal, but Nalani was too quick.

Her dragonclaw dagger swept around to slice Mandalee's wrist, forcing the White Assassin to drop the fragment in favour of flicking her own blade in hand to block it.

"How the hell did you break that magic?" Nalani demanded as they fought. "The boss said there was no way!"

"I have friends," she answered simply. "You wouldn't understand."

Nalani's frenzied assault forced Mandalee back a step, giving the girl an opening to retrieve the dropped fragment. Mandalee aimed a kick at her face, and though Nalani sensed it coming, she still took a glancing blow to the side of the head. Nevertheless, she successfully retrieved the fragment and put it safely in a pouch attached to her belt. It hung at her left side, taunting her while, as if for balance, the Timeless dagger hung on her right.

They were more evenly matched this time, Mandalee thought, given extra time to train and get used to how her new body worked. But the fragment was clearly Nalani's priority. Trying to take it from her was going to be impossible. All of which gave Mandalee an idea.

Mandalee rarely used direct magic, preferring not to waste energy better used for her physical attacks, enhanced speed, agility and shields, but she could do it when she wanted to. She sent out a jet of fire, not at Nalani but at Pryshia. Being so focussed on Shyleen, who was also holding her own somewhat better than in their last encounter, she didn't see it coming. The lioness roared in pain as it singed her fur. Furious, Nalani reciprocated with a fan of flames at Shyleen, but there was no way an assault like that would catch her by surprise. Unlike their enemies, she and Mandalee were always tuned in to each other's senses. Plus, they had an advantage – they had Guardian powers. They were limited without the other two, but it was enough to slow Time a little so that Shyleen could manoeuvre herself to put Pryshia between her and the blast. Thanks to the combined magic, the lioness was severely injured. As before, Nalani felt nothing when her god was hurt and had to be prompted to send out some healing.

The White Assassin focussed her attack on Nalani's left, where the fragment-holding pouch was hanging. Nalani put everything she had into keeping her away from it, as Mandalee knew she would. That was part of the plan. She switched her attack to Nalani's right in a split second, catching her completely off-guard. Mandalee had accepted that she wasn't going to get the fragment and so opted for second prize: the Timeless dagger.

Mandalee's knife sliced Nalani's belt clean away, and the dagger was hers in an instant. Since the girl's combat suit was one-piece like hers, she didn't need the belt to hold anything up.

'*Shame,*' she thought to Shyleen. '*That could have been quite funny, and I could use a laugh.*'

Shyleen disagreed. '*No matter how serious the situation, there is no need to resort to such base comedy. I have standards.*'

Still, it forced Nalani to choose between recovering the dagger or retrieving the fragment that was still attached to her belt on the ground. Except there was no choice at all – the fragment had to come first.

There was no need for Mandalee to explain her plan to Shyleen – the leopard knew immediately why her friend had done what she'd done. The Timeless dagger offered protection from the effects of changing Timelines and, in theory, from the kind of Timelessness that existed in Catriona's Meadow. It was a risk, but there was only one way to find out for sure.

She didn't need to ask if Shyleen was ready.

The leopard put on a burst of speed, sprinting toward the portal. Mandalee flung the dagger and followed its trajectory to dive through with her friend, closing the portal behind them.

The school she had gone to protect in Tedstone Warf was safe; the children had all evacuated. The attacking rebels were slain, and Nalani clearly had no interest in it one way or the other. Retrieving the fragment would have been ideal, but if this worked, there would be time for that later.

'*How are you feeling, Shyleen?*' Mandalee asked. That question was usually unnecessary, given their bond, but in this case, she wanted to be doubly certain.

'*I am perfectly fine,*' Shyleen replied, standing right next to the dagger.

Proximity was required for the shielding effect to work – that was a given – the question was, how close was close enough? Forcing Shyleen to remain in one spot was unacceptable in the long term.

In principle, it would be possible to attach the dagger to a collar, so Shyleen could always have it on her. *On* principle, Mandalee hated the idea of Shyleen wearing a collar. Shyleen wasn't a pet. She was her friend, and she was free. Besides, it would be all too easy for Nalani to do to Shyleen's collar what Mandalee had just done to Nalani's belt.

Still, Mandalee was confident that Catriona would come up with one of her clever solutions. In the meantime, this would at least give Shyleen the same options for escaping to safety as she had. Plus, without the Timeless dagger, Nalani was no longer protected from the full wrath of a trio – or rather a quartet – of very annoyed Guardians.

By all accounts, this Timeless dagger was a product of the future, since Cat hadn't yet invented the spell. She imagined a future Guardian travelling back in Time to try and retrieve it. Much like the present Guardians were trying to find the fragments of Kullos' dimensional control device.

"Well, if some future Guardian has a problem with me using this future magic to help Shyleen," she announced threateningly, "they can damn well come here and try and take it!"

'*There seem to be no takers,*' Shyleen remarked after a moment, '*so why don't we see what the two of us can do, now that we've levelled the playing field a bit?*'

Mandalee nodded and opened a portal to the exact time and place they had left.

From Nalani's perspective, the portal had not so much closed as just flickered for a second. Then they were back.

Flashing a wicked grin, Mandalee flicked her knives into her hands. "Ready for round three?"

Nalani was livid over what had just happened and made to rush at her father's murderer, but Pryshia called out to her in her mind.

'*Leave them!*' she commanded. '*The plan's a bust anyway. We need to get the fragment back to the boss. That's what matters.*'

"No!" Nalani cried. "I can take her! She murdered my father; I have to make her pay!"

'*I told you to leave them. Do as I say. Now!*'

With that, Pryshia sent out her magic, and Nalani screamed in pain.

'*Don't you ever make me tell you twice!*'

"I'm sorry! I'm sorry!" Nalani wailed. "I'll come. Please stop!" Her knees buckled, and she almost fell, but then the pain stopped, allowing her to recover.

Mandalee couldn't hear Pryshia's part of the exchange, but she got the gist, and it was a revelation to her.

Sheathing her knives, she looked upon her enemy with new eyes, filled with compassion and concern.

"Nalani?" she gasped. "Did Pryshia just give you an order and punish you for disobedience?"

With a black look, Nalani replied, "The price of being a Cleric of Nature – you know that!"

Mandalee's eyebrows shot up as she shook her head. "It's really not." To Shyleen, she said, '*Order me to kill her now.*'

'*Order you? I would never—*'

'*—I know, that's the point. Can you transmit it so Nalani can hear you as well?*'

Mandalee knew Nalani would understand. She wasn't sure if the girl knew animal languages as well as she did, but lion and leopard had a common root structure and weren't that different.

Shyleen realised Mandalee's plan and transmitted, '*Mandalee, I order you to kill Nalani. Immediately!*'

'*No,*' Mandalee transmitted back. '*I don't want to kill her; I want to help her see she's being used.*'

'*Mandalee, I gave you an order!*'

'*Sorry, Shyleen, I won't do it.*'

"See?" she challenged an astonished Nalani. "Shyleen wouldn't and couldn't force me to do anything. We're equals. Pryshia's lying to you about what it means to be a Cleric of Nature, and if she's lying about that, what else has she lied about?"

Nalani switched her gaze back and forth between Pryshia and Mandalee, clearly trying to process what she'd just seen and reconcile that with what she'd been told.

Mandalee reached out to Nalani as she pressed home her argument. "Nalani, I did kill your father; I've never denied that, but I swear it wasn't murder, and if you give me a chance, I'll prove it to you."

'*How are you going to do that?*' Shyleen asked privately.

'*I'm a time traveller,*' Mandalee answered vaguely. '*I'll figure something out.*'

Pryshia sent out another jolt of pain. This one did knock Nalani off her feet.

"You'd better go," Mandalee murmured, with a compassionate smile, giving her a hand up and sending some pain relief magic as a further gesture. "I wouldn't want you to suffer more pain on my account."

There were tears in Nalani's eyes as she walked away, feeling the foundation of her whole world crumble around her. She hated Mandalee. Really, truly hated her. Mandalee was her enemy. She murdered her father…but what if she didn't?

Pryshia was supposed to be her friend, but she inflicted pain when she didn't get her own way. If her friend was hurting her and her enemy was healing her, she had to question if she had them the right way around. Much would depend on this ‘proof’ Mandalee claimed she would have. Then she would see.

Chapter 6

When Catriona and Dreya returned home a few days later, Mandalee caught them up with events before they responded to an urgent summons from the Council of Mages. Not just the Triumvirate, but a full session.

"Does anybody else feel like we're in trouble?" asked Cat.

Mandalee nodded. "They probably want to tell me off for not getting that fragment."

Dreya shrugged. "Join the club." She had been unable to get the one from Phitonia, of course, and none of them had had any success tracking down any others.

"As they say on Earth, 'we should get T-shirts printed'," Cat remarked.

Dreya had already discovered that a Black robe wizard had somehow managed to portal to Phitonia while they were lost in Time, and steal the fragment from there. Thanks to Mandalee, at least they knew the reason for this was deliberate obstruction. Now they could add Mandalee's encounter with the rebels who answered to some mysterious Black robe wizard leader and Nalani's casual mention of a boss. A wizard who, as part of his attack on Mandalee, had used a micro-portal. It seemed reasonable to assume they were the same Black robe wizard. Nalani had obviously killed the rebels to prevent them from leading the Guardians back to him. Still, there was one link remaining: Nalani herself.

That was all the more reason to try and save her rather than kill her, Mandalee thought. If they could turn her, she could probably lead them to two of the missing fragments – success at last. Trouble was, they didn't know who they could trust on the Council. They couldn't just suspect all Black robe wizards. The rebellion against Council rules and the changes that were underway seemed to attract wizards and clerics from across the spectrum. Besides, given this wizard's mental powers, anyone might be an unwitting leak of information. The Guardians knew they would have to compartmentalise much of their intelligence. Michael could help. Jessica and Sara, too, given their own mental powers that had even impressed Dreya. As Catriona could attest, Dreya the Dark did not impress easily.

One piece of good news, however, was that Pyrah was alive somewhere.

When Cat tried to mentally reach out to her little green snake, asking if she'd come back to her, Pyrah replied, '*Too soon. Regret.*' It was disappointing, but she was sure her Ysirian friend had her reasons. '*Too soon*' implied that the time would be right at some point, and she would return. As far as Cat was concerned, Pyrah had effectively said, '*See you later.*' That was good enough for her.

"Right then," Catriona declared with a smirk, "let's go and get our wrists slapped, shall we?"

*****

Out of respect for the Council and what it stood for, Mandalee elected not to open her portal directly into the chamber. Rather, she portalled outside the entrance so they could walk inside the conventional way.

Eyeing the shimmering blue Prismatic Sphere suspiciously, Dreya asked, "Are you sure you have these under control now?"

"Hey!" Mandalee protested. "I'm not the one who missed the target by more than two years."

"And I'm not the one who blew up a portal," she countered.

"I would never blow up my best friend's wife…" Mandalee insisted.

Appeased, Dreya stepped through with Catriona. As she did so, she heard Mandalee complete her sentence, "…not unless you really pissed me off."

Shyleen portalled next, and then Mandalee dived through to the other side, where she collided with Dreya, sending them both to the ground with the White Assassin on top.

Standing to one side, Cat burst out laughing.

"How do you keep doing that?" Dreya winced.

"Practice," Mandalee answered.

"One of these days, you're going to do it when I'm in a bad mood, and I'll blast you with magic," Dreya threatened.

"Never!" scoffed the White Assassin. "You'd never lose control like that. Besides," she growled, suddenly brandishing a knife, "I'm not the one who should worry because guess what? I really have been mind-controlled, and now I'm going to kill you!"

The sorceress was equally dismissive. "As if you'd ever announce it first! If you really wanted to kill me, you'd make sure I never saw it coming."

"As would you," Mandalee agreed, standing and offering her friend a hand up.

Dreya smiled and accepted the hand, getting back on her feet. "So, it's a good thing we're on the same side."

Mandalee matched her smile and nodded. "Always."

Shaking her head in wonder, Cat stepped between them and linked arms with them both.

"You two have the strangest friendship," she remarked. "I love it!"

Genuinely, Catriona was incredibly proud of their growing bond, however unconventional it might be. Whatever opposition might be arrayed against them, she knew that the three of them together would ultimately prevail against it. Ready to present their united front, then, the Guardians entered the Council building.

*****

The three women and one leopard stood on the central aisle before the seats of the Triumvirate. All around them were hundreds of mages from all over Tempestria, divided into the Black, White and Red factions. At their approach, a frosty silence had descended on the assembled mages, making Catriona feel uneasy under their intense scrutiny.

"Welcome, Guardians!" Maia called out in greeting, although none of the Guardians felt particularly welcome. "I trust you enjoyed your honeymoon?" she asked, in that polite way of hers that told them she didn't really care.

Catriona decided to call her out on that point, saying, "With respect…" A phrase commonly used before saying something disrespectful. "…I don't believe the Council called us here for tips on how to attain marital bliss." The reaction from those assembled was mainly split between scandalised gasps and amused chuckles.

With an apologetic half-smile, Justaria confirmed, "Sadly not, I'm afraid."

"No," Laethyn agreed. "We're here to discuss the continued failure of the Guardians."

Dreya glared at him, eyes narrowing, warning him he was treading on dangerous ground.

"Failure is a highly pejorative word," Cat objected.

"It's a word that fits," Maia insisted. "Correct me if I'm wrong, but you've retrieved a grand total of one fragment."

"Two, actually," Mandalee corrected her.

"Can you honestly claim credit for the other one?" Justaria asked. "Wasn't that recovered from Lavos by a team comprising Jessica, Sara and Michael?"

"It's not about credit," Cat put in, but Justaria stopped her.

"I'm afraid it is. From a certain perspective, a team of non-Guardians has been, shall we say, equally as successful as the Guardians themselves?"

"And it gets worse," Maia added, addressing the whole Council. "During their most recent failure, according to her own report, the White Guardian literally had her hand on one of the missing fragments and yet did not retrieve it."

"You don't understand," Dreya objected, feeling the need to defend her friend. "Nalani is fast. Even I had trouble pinning her down."

"Maybe you're losing your touch, Dreya," Laethyn suggested.

The Council erupted at that, but Dreya, eyes flashing, raised her voice over the noise to challenge him, "You can test that theory any time you like, Laethyn."

Clearly, with her absences and other distractions, both professional and personal, he had started to forget his place around here. She was going to have to give his leash a good tug, soon, to remind him that he was the leader of the Dark magic only at her sufferance. Indeed, he was alive only at her sufferance. In either case, if she judged it to be a mistake, she could soon correct it.

Justaria magically enhanced her own voice to bring the chamber to order. "I don't think there is anything to be gained by such provocative remarks," she insisted. "Now, can we all please remember that this is the Council of Mages, not a school playground? We will resolve this with discussion and debate, not taunts and threats of violence."

"I apologise to the Council," Laethyn offered, apparently contrite.

"As do I," Dreya agreed formally, though she doubted either of them was fooling anybody.

"Furthermore," Maia ventured, "I am concerned not only by the incompetence of the Guardians but also their selfishness. Particularly that of the White Guardian."

"Excuse me?" Mandalee demanded, arching her eyebrows. "I'd like to hear how you justify that!"

Behind them, the doors to the chamber flew open with a resounding crash. All eyes turned to see a man striding confidently up the aisle. He stood out among just about everyone else bar Mandalee, in that he was dressed not in robes, but in a loose-fitting off-white shirt and trousers that were tucked into tall boots. A black cloak flew like a flag behind him and a sword hung in a scabbard attached to a wide cross-body strap with a large buckle over his chest. That sword slapped his thigh as he walked.

"Yes!" the man boomed as he approached. "I'd rather like to know that, as well!"

Mandalee recognised the man as the principal of the school in Tedstone Warf.

Dreya, too, thought he seemed familiar, or perhaps he simply reminded her of someone. More of the entity in her mind had escaped its prison recently, making it hard to concentrate. She was still struggling to think who this man could be when he offered his hand and introduced himself.

"Don't believe I've had the pleasure," he declared. His powerful voice reverberated around the high-ceilinged chamber without the need for magic as he vigorously shook her hand before moving on to the others. He even briefly dropped to one knee before Shyleen, a hand clamped over his heart in salute before regaining his feet with a flourish.

'*Oh, I like him!*' the leopard approved.

Mandalee hid a smile.

"The name's Dagamir," he rumbled, "Dagamir the Tenth!"

Catriona's eyes widened at the name. "Any relation to the Dagamir from Ulvarius' time?" she wondered, trying to sound casual.

"My direct ancestor," he affirmed proudly.

Ever since they returned from the past, Catriona had been looking for signs that their Intervention might have had unintended consequences. Now it seemed as if one had literally just walked up and shaken their hands. Dagamir the Tenth. A descendant of Dagamir the Third, whom they had met three hundred years ago. He was so much like his ancestor it was almost as if they'd brought him through the portal with them.

Addressing the Council, Dagamir reiterated, "Once again, I challenge you to justify your charge of selfishness! The White Guardian selflessly risked her life to defend my school and save all of our students. Many of them children of those here in this chamber. Send them to safety. Moreover, as I understand it, the Council owes its very existence to the Guardians, who risked everything to travel back in Time and prevent Ulvarius from destroying the foundations my ancestor helped to lay."

According to the history Catriona knew, Dagamir the Third died in the Battle of Compton against Ulvarius. He had been childless. In the new Timeline, Ulvarius struck out at Dreya, not Dagamir, so he lived and built a legacy. A legacy that, it seemed, was on their side. So, they'd effectively travelled back in Time and created themselves an ally. She supposed that could be seen as a little self-serving, but 'selfish' seemed a bit harsh. Besides, it hadn't been intentional, although she was prepared to take full advantage.

"But before we get to that," Dagamir added, quickly, before the Triumvirate could reply, "perhaps you could explain why I seem to be just about the only wizard of rank not invited to this debacle? As Black Secondmage, successor to the esteemed Dreya the Dark," he bowed slightly to her, "I have as much right to be here as anyone and more than most."

Laethyn answered, "I chose not to include you, Dagamir, as I believed you would be too close to recent events to be objective."

"You're damn right I was close! It happened outside my front door – it couldn't have been much closer. As for being objective, I can objectively tell you that those rebels would have broken down our defences had it not been for Mandalee. Our students – our children – were in danger, and she stood in the path of that danger.

"Selfish?" he demanded furiously. "That's about as far from selfish as you can get!"

Maia shifted uncomfortably under the force of his personality, primly smoothing down her White robes.

"That's as maybe," she allowed. "However, instead of doing everything in her power to retrieve that dangerous fragment in the name of the greater good, she chose to take that dagger to help her…" she waved a hand vaguely in Shyleen's direction, "…cat!"

"The word you're looking for," Mandalee growled, "is leopard. If you don't know that, maybe you should spend some time in Dagamir's school."

That drew another thunderous reaction from the other Council mages, forcing Justaria to bring things back to order.

"I believe we are in danger of missing the point here. Perhaps, White Guardian, you could explain to the Council why you chose the dagger over the fragment. You can see how, to some, it might appear as if you put personal gain above your professional duty."

"It was hardly a question of just picking one, from what I saw from my window!" Dagamir objected.

"Excuse me, Dagamir," Laethyn interjected. "The Council needs to hear from the Guardians on this matter. If you can't remember your place, I will be forced to have you ejected from these chambers."

Once again, Dreya thought it was Laethyn who needed to be reminded of his place.

Judging by Dagamir's body language – his magical powers charging up, his hand twitching mere inches from the hilt of his sword – he seemed to hold a similar view.

Mandalee tried to explain about the Timeless spell on the dagger. Then, when she began to flounder, Cat came to her rescue, detailing her own work on such a spell.

She extrapolated how a future version of her magical invention might operate.

"But that's speculation," Maia objected.

"Of course it is!" Dreya replied incredulously. "It's from the future."

"Well, I'm sorry," Laethyn apologised insincerely, "but speculation of future magic is not admissible as evidence under Council rules."

Dreya began to wonder if Laethyn was even worth the effort anymore. From what she'd seen of this generation's Dagamir, he would make an ideal replacement.

Laethyn leaned close to his White robe counterpart, suggesting, "I don't know about you, Maia, but I think we've heard enough."

Maia nodded. "I say we put this matter to a full Council vote." It was not often that she saw eye-to-eye with him, but on this matter, she found herself in complete accord.

"Seconded," Laethyn concurred. "What about you, Justaria?" he added smoothly.

The woman in the Red robes glared at him. "You know full well that two votes are sufficient, no matter what I say."

"Hang on!" Cat objected. "Vote? What vote? What's this actually about?"

"Yes, tell them," Dagamir insisted, his eyes ablaze. "You owe them that much, at least."

Unlike Laethyn, Justaria looked genuinely apologetic as she explained, "They," she emphasised the pronoun, "are proposing to vote on whether the Guardians should be replaced…or just disbanded altogether."

"What!" Dreya and Mandalee demanded at once.

"I don't even know how you'd replace us," Cat considered. "You can't just pick them yourself. I mean, we didn't decide the rules – Magias did a thousand years ago. I accept that the question will arise one day," she allowed diplomatically. "Apart from anything else, I can't imagine any of us will be doing this job a thousand years from now."

She was already going through the world's most prolonged pregnancy, approaching fifteen months. She couldn't be sure how much of that was down to her own Timeless state and how much was related to her baby's unique higher planar physiology. If it was the former, she wondered if she might have to step down as Guardian to give birth this side of the end of the world. If only there were some kind of magic that could at least reassure her that her pregnancy was progressing properly, if slowly. That would surely fall into cleric territory, though, and even Mandalee had never heard of such a thing. Either way, she wasn't prepared to give up the Guardianship just yet. Not without a fight.

"As for disbanding the Guardianship," she continued, "it wouldn't change who and what we are."

As Dreya had once put it, herself quoting Jessica, the genie could not be put back into the bottle. The magic existed now; it was free and could neither be contained nor destroyed.

"Don't bother, Cat," Dreya advised her. "There's obviously no reasoning with these people."

Mandalee and Shyleen were in total agreement, and Cat could only concur. Her own reasoned arguments were clearly getting them nowhere.

"Fine!" she spat, speaking for all of them. "Do what you will. In the meantime, we'll keep doing what we believe is right."

They all turned their backs and walked away. Dagamir let his own vote be known by joining them.

Chapter 7

Once they had left the building, Justaria asked if anyone wanted to voice their opinions. There were a few takers arguing different points of view, but after a few more minutes had ticked by, it was decided that it was time for the vote to be taken.

Before that could happen, however, the Council chamber doors burst open again, and a pair of guards slumped to the floor. Stepping casually over their bodies came a young woman with dark brown hair in a thick braid down her back.

"Hey there!" she called out in greeting. The smirk on her face said she was looking forward to having some fun. "The name's Nalani," she offered. "Just thought I'd drop in. These two weren't keen." The girl shot a glance down at the still forms of the guards. "But as you can see, I didn't let that stop me."

Maia, incensed, stood and demanded, "What is the meaning of this intrusion?"

"Isn't it obvious? My boss has decided that you and your antiquated Council aren't relevant in our modern world, and I've come to put you out of everyone's misery!"

With that, the young woman sprang into action. As the assembled mages looked on, she was little more than a blur. Nalani sprinted to one side of the chamber, where she began ripping into the mages with her daggers, before zooming over to the other side for more of the same. Several on each side fell before they even realised they were under attack. At last, resistance began, and magic began flying everywhere. Spells of fire and ice, air and lightning. But Nalani was too quick to target accurately. Many wizards and clerics were forced to shield against the magic of their peers. Area of effect spells risked damaging the historic building itself, but that wasn't going to stop the mages from using them to try and save their lives.

The chamber shook with every blast, but nothing could even slow their attacker. Any magic that struck Nalani fizzled harmlessly on her magically resistant bodysuit.

A couple of druids on the Council had been studying the technical manual written by Catriona Redfletching. They worked together to try and make some of the decorative plants grow to snare the woman, but she cut them down in an instant.

A few wizards began to experiment with indirect magic, making chairs and other heavy objects fly around the room in hopes of scoring a hit. None were successful.

The massacre had been going on for no more than five minutes, but already around half the Council representatives had fallen. At last, the Triumvirate yelled for everyone to get down as they worked their magic to create walls of compressed air, closing in from three sides. At last, something had an effect, as Nalani could not break through.

The assassin managed to take out many more defenceless mages before being cut off from her prey and forced into the centre of the chamber where the Triumvirate sat.

She cancelled her super-speed and began stroking her braid with one hand while juggling her dagger in the other. “Nice trick. Although all I have to do now is kill the three of you, and your walls of air will blow away on the breeze.”

“Somebody teleport and fetch the Guardians!” Maia commanded, and one White robe wizard obeyed.

Nalani pulled a face. “Aww! Now, why would you want them to come and spoil the party?”

“Because now you’re scared!” Maia shot back. “Let’s see how fast you are when they Freeze Time!”

“I’ve got a better idea,” Nalani countered. “Let’s see how many more of you I can kill before they get here!”

In short order, Maia saw Laethyn and Justaria collapse beside her. As Nalani predicted, Maia could not sustain the magical barriers alone with her fellows down. She expected to be the next to die, but instead, the assassin resumed her culling of the assembled masses. Maia was powerless to stop it.

At last, a blue portal shimmered into the middle of the Council chamber. Nalani was instantly aware of the danger and sprinted for the exit, but despite her speed, she had only just reached the doors when the Three Guardians stepped out of the portal with Shyleen and worked their Temporal magic.

In the second or two that it took the magic to take effect, the assassin had managed to get halfway out, but then, from Maia’s perspective, Nalani was stuck.

“Still think we should be disbanded?” asked the White Guardian pointedly, raising her eyebrows.

Maia frantically shook her head.

That was when Nalani unfroze. Maia called out a warning as the girl ran to the Guardians’ side, but to her surprise, the assassin did not attack.

Instead, she seemed to object to the White Guardian’s words.

“Excuse me? What do you mean ‘we’?”

“I mean ‘you’.” She offered a sheepish grin. “Sorry.”

“Better. Don’t bury yourself in the part.”

“What’s going on here?” demanded a bewildered Maia.

Her shock was compounded when Justaria rose from the dead. “What’s going on is you’ve been had, Maia,” she replied, “and it was a highly effective demonstration, I’m sure you’ll agree.” Beside her, Catriona worked her druid magic on Laethyn, and he, too, came back to life.

Maia still didn’t understand until the White Guardian shapeshifted before her eyes. In her place stood the swashbuckling figure of Dagamir the Tenth. Then Nalani’s body shimmered with magic, to be replaced by Mandalee.

“You!” Maia gasped in horror, pointing accusingly at the White Guardian. “You killed all those people!”

“Oh, get with it, Maia!” Justaria retorted, fixing her with a withering stare. “They’re no more dead than we are.”

As if on cue, the two guards that had been ‘slain’ first recovered, followed gradually by the rest of the fallen Council members, and it became clear that it had all been part of an elaborate plan.

*****

“How can they do this?” Mandalee had demanded, rhetorically, when they got outside the Council building.

Dagamir tried to explain.

“Maia’s prejudiced against you as a cleric – she’s not a fan of Dreya’s reforms. Plus, well, she’s not exactly an animal lover, and she doesn’t get your unique relationship with Shyleen. Laethyn sees a chance for power, and he’s grabbing it as you’d expect. You can tell Justaria wants no part of it, but—”

"—but it's two against one," Mandalee finished.

Dagamir nodded. "The thing is, though, it's not up to the three of them – it's a full Council vote."

"How does that help us?" Catriona asked.

"You need to convince them that taking the Timeless dagger instead of the dangerous, unstable fragment was the right decision."

Mandalee opened her mouth to object, but he held up a hand to ward off anything she might say, clarifying, "I'm not saying it was a choice. I know better. I'm saying that's how they see it, or rather, it's how it's being presented to them."

The White Guardian conceded that Dagamir made a valid point, and he went up in her estimation.

"You've seen that trying to tell them otherwise is futile," he continued, "so maybe there's a way you can show them, instead."

Dreya was warming to this man more and more. If she had her way – and she usually did – he would have a bright future ahead of him.

"Actions speak louder than words," she remarked. "Earth expression," she clarified.

"Jessica?" Cat asked.

The sorceress shook her head. "No, it's actually something Daelen said to me once."

It was Shyleen who came up with the idea. Mandalee liked it immensely and told the others.

"Looks like your ridiculous radical plans are contagious, Cat, because Shyleen's starting to get them, too."

To pull off her plan, they were going to need help. Excusing themselves from Dagamir's side for a moment, they opened a portal to Catriona's Meadow and discussed how much they felt they could trust him. In the end, they decided to share everything with him – including things they'd only just worked out themselves.

When Mandalee had portalled to Dagamir's school to put a stop to the attack by anti-Council rebels, she had naturally seen the name. At the time, she'd been too busy to give it any thought, but meeting Dagamir just now had brought the memory back.

It was called Melrose Academy.

They told Dagamir the full story of how they went back in Time to take the fragment from Ulvarius at the height of his reign of terror and the formation of the Council. Much of that was well known, but there were some parts they had so far kept to themselves. He, in turn, shared some details of the history of his school.

'Mel' and 'Rose' were the names Mandalee and Catriona had adopted in that time. Names they had shared with a group of school children from Tedstone. Children they had saved from Ulvarius' hideous magical experiments. Dreya, using the name 'Darla', had taken them to the Wizards' Forum, now the Council building. At Catriona's suggestion, she had even played with them for a while, trying to prove she could be good with kids, ready for whenever Cat's child might be born.

Clearly, the Three Guardians had made an impression. As those children had grown up, some had remained in Tedstone and become teachers themselves. In time, the school was renamed Melrose in honour of their mysterious saviours who had never been seen again. The children had, in turn, made an impression on the mages of the fledgeling Council, who began the practice of sending their own magically gifted offspring to Melrose Academy. Over time, a second site was established as the world's first college of magic for the education and training of older students, as well as a research centre.

Shyleen remembered seeing something pinned to a noticeboard in the school – something about Professor Dagamir's Illusion Workshop. Dagamir confirmed he ran that class since he was something of an expert in that field, having won the prestigious 'Darla Award for Excellence' three times.

"In that case," Mandalee decided, "you are the perfect person to help us make our point to the Council."

"If you're willing," Cat added.

"If you are," Dreya put in, "we might also discuss how we might promote you from your Secondmage post to a seat on the Triumvirate, replacing Laethyn."

Dagamir smiled regretfully. "I appreciate the thought, Mistress Dreya," he returned formally, "but like you before me, I would prefer to remain where I am and avoid the paperwork. I have quite enough of that already, running Melrose."

"Understandable," Dreya acknowledged. She knew exactly where he was coming from.

"But you have my total support, and I'd be perfectly happy to keep an eye on Laethyn for you while you're busy with all things Guardian."

Dagamir believed Laethyn was a relic of a bygone era, while he was very much in tune with Dreya's desire to reform and update the Council system for a new age. Now Dagamir had learned that he owed not only his career at Melrose Academy but also his very existence to the Guardians, so he was even more motivated to help in any way he could.

Before executing the plan, the Guardians needed a few supplies, but thanks to their Temporal magic, from Dagamir's perspective, that took almost no time at all.

Then, making sure they were unobserved, Catriona transformed Dagamir's appearance to match Mandalee's with the aid of her now little-used shapeshifting magic.

"Curious sensation," he remarked when his body finished changing. "Painful but curious. I've never been female before."

Mandalee-as-Nalani quipped, "Cat could fix that for you if you like."

Cat shook her head. "Not enough power in Michael's technology," she reminded her friend. "That was a one-time only deal."

Next, Dagamir worked his illusion magic to make Mandalee's appearance match how Nalani looked when he saw her attack the White Guardian outside his school.

Catriona didn't use her shapeshifting magic on Mandalee to avoid the risk of tampering with the body she had worked so hard to give her friend. Therefore, illusion magic would suffice.

For Dagamir, however, their plan was going to involve the disguised Dagamir travelling through a portal, and he couldn't be sure how his illusion magic would stand up to that. He'd never had the chance to test it because his portals were not stable enough to travel through. Therefore, it had to be shapeshifting.

One last bit of illusion magic, and all was ready. Time for 'Nalani' to attack.

She took out the guards first and then made a grand entrance before tearing into the Council of Mages. However, contrary to all appearances, she wasn't using her dragonclaw blades. Instead, her weapons of choice were two tubes of lipstick disguised with perception filters and magically imbued with an enhanced herbal tranquilliser. They would deliver a brief moment of pain as if one had been cut and then a few minutes of unconsciousness.

*****

Even as the Guardians explained this to the Triumvirate, more Council members began to recover, none the worse for wear.

"And what was the point of this charade?" Maia demanded.

"It's simple, Maia," Mandalee replied. "Nalani is incredibly dangerous–"

"–All the more reason you should have taken the fragment from her!" Laethyn interrupted.

Mandalee shrugged. "I didn't use a fragment or any higher planar energy when I attacked just now," she pointed out. "I attacked you with lipstick. Nalani will use knives, and she'll have Pryshia with her, using tooth and claw." Mandalee had taken out nearly half the Council in under five minutes. Given the dual attack and the fact that Nalani was even faster, she fully believed the pair could probably slaughter them all in that time.

"It doesn't matter what weapon is used to kill you, Laethyn," Dreya pointed out, allowing genuine threat to creep into her tone. "Dead is dead."

"Except maybe not," Mandalee put in, "because we're Guardians of Time and Magic. If an incident like this were to happen for real, we could reverse it." In her mind, there was a 'probably' after that sentence, but she chose to leave it unspoken.

Dagamir raised his voice to address the whole Council, who were now mostly recovered if a little groggy.

"The Guardians have put a lot of work into ensuring this Council's past," he announced, "and they can secure its future, too!"

"But not if Nalani still had her Timeless dagger," Catriona pointed out.

Mandalee nodded. That was the one weapon they knew could nullify their powers. "If I had not taken it from her, then any attack would be permanently fixed in Time."

That drew a general murmur from the crowd as the idea began to sink in. None of the mages had appreciated how vulnerable they were, surrounded by powerful magic within the supposedly secure Council chambers.

"So," Dagamir concluded, "do you still offer a charge of selfishness and incompetence? Do you still wish to disband the Guardianship? Or would you like to reconsider?"

Looking flustered, Maia hastily retracted the charges. "W-well, in light of what you have shown us, well, I-I must admit that does put a…different complexion on things."

Coming to her rescue, Justaria suggested that it would be only fitting if the vote were to go ahead as planned. Then the entire Council could respond to the Guardians' evidence.

"Just one problem with that," Laethyn objected. "Given the Guardians' affinity for Temporal magic, how can we be sure they will abide by any decision that is made? How do we know they won't change it, somehow?"

"We've thought of that," Cat spoke up.

Sharing a nod, Mandalee opened a portal to Catriona's Meadow and retrieved the jagged Timeless dagger. Closing the portal, she handed the weapon to Maia, reminding the assembled Council that the Guardians' Temporal powers could affect nothing within the field generated by that weapon's magic. "So, anything that happens here is fixed."

The Guardians' actions and that gesture of trust persuaded the Council to vote overwhelmingly in favour of allowing the Guardianship to continue in their safe and capable hands. At the end of the proceedings, Maia returned the dagger, and the Three Guardians left with their new ally, Dagamir, feeling flush with their victory.

Chapter 8

Keen to press on with their jobs, since they still had them, the Guardians began to speculate on how Nalani's boss – whoever that might be – could have known about the fragment the rebels were using.

"Better still," Dagamir put in, "how did that Black robe wizard know it would appear when it did? Assuming it's the same wizard, I suppose."

"What wizard?" Mandalee asked.

"Didn't Yanis mention it?"

The White Guardian shook her head.

So, Dagamir explained how a few days ago, he was working in his office when a flash of blue light caught his eye. Looking out of the window, he saw that it was a blue Prismatic Sphere portal. The kind used by the Guardians. The kind he had been trying to recreate in the Melrose laboratories. Out of that portal flew what looked like a metal shard of some sort. It was giving off some extraordinary magical readings, and he quickly realised it was higher planar energy he could sense, mixed in with cleric and wizard magic. As far as Dagamir knew, there was only one thing it could be. One of the fragments of Kullos' dimensional control device, which the Guardians were trying to retrieve because they were deemed too dangerous. He could see why. It certainly didn't feel like a particularly safe or stable mixture. Before he could do anything about it, however, as one portal closed, another opened. A Black robe wizard stepped out, claimed the fragment and portalled away again.

"Why didn't you report this?" Dreya asked.

"I did," Dagamir assured her. As Secondmage in the Black order, he had felt obliged to use the official Council reporting system. Contacting the Guardians directly was strongly discouraged so as not to overload them with false sightings.

"But we get those anyway!" cried an exasperated Catriona, throwing her hands up in the air.

"That's *all* we get," Mandalee agreed.

They were a part of everyday life, and while the Guardians may be Timeless, they didn't enjoy wasting their time on those false reports.

When Dreya asked if Dagamir would mind sharing his memory of events a little more directly, he replied, "For the chance to touch minds with Dreya the Dark? Absolutely."

"Flattery will get you nowhere."

"Sorry," he blushed, "but I've long been an admirer of yours…" he trailed off, and his brow furrowed as realisation struck. "…but in your old Timeline, I didn't exist, did I? That's weird."

"Don't worry," Dreya replied breezily, "I probably wouldn't have known you existed anyway."

"Dreya!" Cat gasped while Mandalee snorted with laughter.

"That sounded better in my head," Dreya admitted with a half-smile.

Then she used her little-used mental magic to tune into Dagamir's memory. The last time she had done this, of course, was with Scarlett on Phitonia. She pushed that memory aside – she couldn't afford to get distracted. The mental image he projected was more detailed than anything the other Guardians could see with their magic. Sadly, it didn't reveal much more, but it did feel strangely familiar, as if she'd seen it before. At first, she wasn't sure why – she'd never been to Tedstone Warf. But when she expressed her sympathic impression as co-ordinates, she recognised them immediately.

Having broken contact, while Dagamir nursed a headache, she asked Catriona for her notebook. On a blank page, she wrote the symbols that gave them the sympathic impression of Temporal co-ordinates. "Now, compare those to the ones I wrote when we beat Kullos," she coached.

Catriona flicked back a few pages and gasped when she saw those same symbols. Symbols that would guide their portals. At last, they all realised why they hadn't made sense before: they had been in the future.

"And I'm betting that's why the last set seems equally nonsensical," Dreya concluded.

Their sympathic co-ordinates were supposed to generate an image of where and when the Guardians needed to go, but an image from the future must necessarily be imaginary. Therefore, future co-ordinates generated a blurry image. The further in the future that image was, the more blurred it would be.

Mandalee couldn't understand how Kullos could have created stable portals into the future, but Cat had an explanation. What she called the Day of the Angel was also the Day of the Monster. Kullos had been working with that same Monster while he was building his army. Kullos had been alone when they attacked, and there had been no further sign of that Monster. Daelen's visitor had indicated that it was from the future. If so, it easily could have provided Kullos with future co-ordinates for his portals. But linear Time being what it was, those future co-ordinates were now in the past. So that was where they needed to go.

As for the last fragment, an inanimate object could survive such a trip into the future – although it wouldn't have made the power of the fragment any more stable. The Guardians couldn't risk such travel themselves, though. They would have to wait for their present Timeframe to naturally come around to whenever that fragment was. Still, at least they could do something about the one Dagamir had seen from his window.

*****

For this mission, the Guardians would have to retain their connection to Catriona's Meadow to remain invisible to people in that native Timeframe. If they didn't, Dagamir would have seen them from his window. So, they portalled well out of sight of Melrose. Behind the same building Mandalee had used for cover to spy on the attacking rebels. After all, there was little point in being invisible if they lit up the area with a blue Prismatic Sphere.

As soon as they ran around the building, they saw the scene that Dagamir had described. It was frustrating being so close to one of the much sought-after fragments and yet unable to grab it.

It was tempting, but they knew the anomalies in their own Timelines would be too important to ignore. Without that fragment, there would be no attack on Melrose Academy, no confrontation with Nalani, and Mandalee would not have the Timeless dagger. Such anomalies in the Guardians' own Timelines could weaken the fabric of reality, even allowing *IT* to gain a foothold to rain true destruction upon Creation.

Still, if they could identify the Black robe thief, they could use that information in their present.

True to Dagamir's word, a second portal opened moments after the first and out stepped the Black robe wizard in question. The Guardians' plan had been to freeze the Timeframe at that point, allowing them to have a good look at him. Unfortunately, it seemed the thief had thought of that because there, dangling from his belt, was a weapon with a distinctive jagged, lightning-bolt-shaped blade. The Timeless dagger. The proximity of that weapon meant that the Guardians were locked into the natural flow of Time, unable to slow or stop it.

The wizard was so buried in his robes that it was impossible to discern anything about him. They could no more take the dagger from him than they could take the fragment. If they took the weapon now, how could Mandalee take it from Nalani later? The Guardians were left with no choice but to watch helplessly as he collected the fragment and portalled away.

Still, it wasn't a total loss. The presence of that dagger confirmed a direct link between Nalani and this Black robe. Clearly, he must be the 'boss' she referred to, so she most probably knew who he was. Moreover, unless there was more than one Black robe wizard who could open portals and track down fragments, he must also be the wizard that stole the one from Phitonia. Of course, they had guessed much of this already, but now they had evidence. If Mandalee could find a way to get through to Nalani, that could be just the breakthrough they needed to get their hands on two of the missing fragments. Then they could shove the Council's charge of incompetence down their collective throats.

There didn't seem to be anything more they could achieve in the past, so they returned to their present. Once there, Mandalee and Shyleen went off by themselves to train for their next encounter with Nalani and Pryshia, leaving Cat and Dreya to make their way home to the Black Tower.

*****

At home, as the couple shared a meal together, Cat had an idea.

"Dreya," she spoke up, "have you thought about travelling to the past on Phitonia?"

Dreya nearly choked. She still hadn't told her about its destruction at the hands of the Angel called Purity.

"What ever for?" she wondered, schooling her voice and facial expression to give nothing away.

"To try and identify the Black robe wizard, of course."

Dreya told her that she'd already seen – in Scarlett's memory – that he had the Timeless dagger on him. The sorceress hadn't known what it was at the time, but when she'd replayed the vision, she was convinced it was the same weapon.

"I know it's a shot in the dark," Cat accepted, "but all it takes is for a gust of wind to blow his hood off, and you'd see him. Can't do any harm, surely?"

Dreya's mind raced. She needed to get her wife off this trail.

"It could do more harm than you realise," she countered. "Every time we open a portal to another world, there's a risk of attracting attention."

Catriona frowned. "Attention from whom?"

Dreya shrugged. "Who knows? It's a big cosmos. Anything could be out there."

"All the more reason to explore, surely."

Cat knew that Justaria had actively sought ways to take up the Lavosian invitation to establish formal contact. So far, she hadn't found any way to achieve that, but she was certainly amenable to the idea.

Dreya shook her head emphatically. "It's not worth the risk. Even if she did find a way, I'd recommend to the Council that off-world travel be banned."

"That could be seen as a bit self-serving," Cat pointed out with raised eyebrows. "We've just persuaded them to drop that charge; maybe we shouldn't give them an excuse to revisit the issue. After all, we did just spend our honeymoon off-world."

"That was a mistake," Dreya muttered darkly.

Cat couldn't believe what she was hearing. "You think our honeymoon was a mistake?" she demanded with real anger. "What about our wedding? Was that a mistake, too?"

Dreya realised how her words sounded and knew she needed to do damage control quickly.

"Of course not!" she protested. "That's not what I meant at all!"

"Oh? Well, in case you've forgotten, there were two off-worlders at our wedding. Was that a mistake? Should we tell them to go home? But of course, they can't go home, can they?"

Dreya winced. She knew Cat was just referring to the fact that Sara and Jessica were Chetsuan plague carriers who could never see another of their kind again without passing on a fatal disease. What they and Cat didn't know was that if Purity had since moved on from Phitonia by now – and the entity in Dreya's mind was convinced she would have – then, ironically, they actually could return to Phitonia…because there was no-one left to infect.

Dreya took a deep breath, trying to regain control. Imploring her to understand despite being unwilling to fully share her reasons. "Cat, you know I love you, and I don't regret a single thing that we've done," she promised. "And I certainly don't begrudge Sara and Jessica their lives here, but maybe we shouldn't be treating the cosmos as our playground. Not until we've solved our problems here."

"Maybe going out there is how we solve our problems here," Cat suggested.

Trying to subtly change tack, the sorceress leaned over and clasped her wife's hands in her own.

"Look," she sighed, "I just think we need to be careful, OK? We've seen the consequences of playing around with Time on Tempestria. I don't believe there's anything to be gained by doing it on Phitonia, too. We could screw something up and, not having any reference points, not even know about it. We don't have the right to start interfering unnecessarily."

Catriona had to concede she did make a rational point. It just seemed strange that Dreya the Dark would make it.

"OK, if that's how you feel about it, I trust your judgement, and I'm sorry about the misunderstanding. Of course you don't think our marriage is a mistake; I shouldn't have said that. But there's something different about you lately, Dreya. You don't seem quite yourself. I'm worried."

Dreya pulled her wife to her feet and embraced her, relieved that she hadn't damaged their relationship.

"I'm just changing, Cat," she assured her. "I have been since we met. It's entirely down to your influence, of course. I can't take any credit. So, if I'm a little more cautious and even protective these days," she pulled away and looked her in the eyes as she finished, "it's only because I have more to protect."

Cat appreciated the sentiments, but there was more to it; she was sure of that. Dreya the Dark would often go to great lengths to simultaneously avoid both lying and telling the truth. She remembered the day that Dreya had tried her hand at working on her grounds with her own magic rather than getting her undead minions to do it. Her magic wasn't well-suited to the task, and a wave rose up in the lake, soaking her.

When Cat came home and asked why she was wet, Dreya, embarrassed to admit her own failure, simply replied, "It's raining."

It was a true statement: it was raining, and that was definitely part of the reason she was wet. It just wasn't the primary reason. She was doing the same thing now, and Cat knew it. Everything she had said was true, but she was avoiding the primary reason for whatever was going on with her.

Moreover, Dreya knew that Catriona understood her well enough to recognise that and realise she was asking her not to dig any deeper.

Catriona wasn't going to invade her wife's privacy, even with the best intentions, so she let the matter drop.

"Alright, Dreya," she acceded, "but if there's ever anything you want to talk about, you know I'm here for you, don't you?"

"I know."

Chapter 9

Over the following few days, Cat and Dreya took the opportunity to look through the pile of messages they had missed while they were on honeymoon. Aside from the junk, most were reports of possible fragment sightings passed on by the Council.

In other words, more junk.

Of the six fragments, they had two, this mysterious Black robe wizard had two, and one was in the future and therefore inaccessible at present. That left one more that had been sent into the past. Catriona supposed they ought to make that excursion their next priority. Before she could voice that thought, however, Dreya found a message that got Cat intrigued.

The message was from Renjaf, the old White wizard recluse who Cat had met when she was still in college. It was from him that she had obtained the scarce book, *Shifting Stars*, which contained information relating to the Angel who had appeared to her on the day that strange and powerful Monster killed her parents. The latest in a series of such appearances by that shining figure throughout history.

To say Renjaf had been 'reluctant to part with the book' would be to describe a mountain as 'reluctant to move'. He had obstructed her at every opportunity, delighting in denying her dreams. In the end, he had pushed her too far, and she had taken matters into her own hands. Demolishing his tower and grabbing the book out of the rubble. He had been unable to stop her, even with her fledgeling druid magic. Despite him attacking her with some impressive mental magic, her sympathic connection with Pyrah had protected her.

That was about seven years ago, and Catriona's life had changed radically from those days. Cat supposed Renjaf must be into his seventies by now, while she had not aged perceptibly. The Guardians had existed for more than half that time, during which Cat only aged while in sync with the Timeline in the past. In the present, she was Timeless and so did not change, apart from her pregnancy.

For some reason, that had developed noticeably since returning to Tempestria, post-honeymoon, and she'd had to buy new robes. On a regular pregnancy timescale, the druidess would say she was perhaps four months along. Except, even discounting her two and a half years lost in Time, it had been at least double the length of any typical pregnancy. But her pregnancy was unique because the father was a higher planar being, and the mother was a Timeless Guardian. She could only guess how many more months it might be before she gave birth. If that was even possible while Timeless.

Seeing this message from Renjaf, now, asking to meet with a Guardian for undisclosed reasons, just brought it home how much had changed. Why he should want to meet a Guardian, she couldn't imagine. Neither did his message specify which one he wanted to see. Since he was aligned with the White, she supposed it would make sense to send Mandalee, but Catriona couldn't help but be intrigued. So, despite the cautionary expression about her namesake animal, Cat decided to indulge her curiosity.

*****

Stepping from a portal outside the grounds of Renjaf's tower, a few miles outside Compton, she was pleasantly surprised by what she saw. His garden looked reasonably well-maintained – a far cry from the overgrown jungle it had been the first time she had come here. How many hours had she spent working on them, tending to them? It had been time well spent, as it had helped her begin to hone her druid magic.

She remembered flying out here, literally free as a bird. She missed shapeshifting into animals. She could picture her red-banded falcon in her mind so clearly. The first form she ever mastered. She'd had to give up shapeshifting while she was pregnant, but one day she'd be able to get back to it. After all, she couldn't be pregnant forever…could she?

As she walked up his garden path, she saw his pond off to the left and, with a smile, remembered the time Renjaf had thrown her into it with his magic. The day she was here with Jacob, the delivery boy whose form she had taken to try and trick her way into Renjaf's home. She had failed, and despite the terrible way she had used Jacob's friendship, he had taken pity on a half-drowned Cat and taken her home in his cart, wrapped in a blanket that was meant for his horse, Bonnie.

The 'Cat who Smelled of Horse' she'd called it. It was one of her favourite stories from her younger days.

Being in Renjaf's grounds was bringing back so many good memories. Would it be too much of a self-indulgent use of her Guardian powers, she wondered, to travel back and watch it all play out again? She could remain invisible and incorporeal, so it wouldn't do any harm. Still, she supposed she ought to stay focused on the present.

Finally reaching his door, she knocked and waited, preparing herself for what was sure to be a frosty welcome at best. After a moment, Renjaf opened the door, squinting at the unexpected caller.

"Good morning, Mr Renjaf," Catriona greeted him breezily. "I'm Catriona – the Red Guardian. I received your message—"

"—My message, of course!" the wizard exclaimed. To Cat's astonishment, his face lit up in a broad smile. He took her hand in both of his and shook it vigorously, then he stepped aside. "Please, come in," he offered in verbal confirmation of the gesture.

She thanked him politely, if a little warily, and stepped inside, where the old man directed her to a sitting room just off to the left of the hallway.

Inviting her to sit on the sofa, he immediately offered her some refreshments. "Tea, perhaps?" he suggested. "And biscuits, of course…" A slightly puzzled look passed across his face as he added, "…I'm sure I have some somewhere."

"Well, I don't want to put you to any trouble," Cat ventured.

He dismissed the idea with a wave of his hand. "Nonsense!" he insisted. "It's no trouble at all. It's an honour to have a Guardian in my home. It's just that, well, I don't often get visitors. No family, you see, and to be honest, well, I have a few friends, but I can't say I'm exactly overburdened with them. Never was a social butterfly, and at my age, many of those I once had…" He looked sad for a moment but quickly snapped himself out of it. "Anyway, I may not be used to entertaining, but you really are quite welcome here."

"In that case, tea and biscuits would be lovely, thank you."

Renjaf excused himself and walked into the kitchen to prepare everything, leaving Cat alone, trying to come to terms with the situation. Maybe he'd changed, too, after seven years? It wasn't unreasonable, she supposed, and perhaps her fame as a Guardian helped matters, but could that account for this? He was like a completely different person.

She rose from her seat, deciding to examine the room in which she found herself. She'd never got this far inside Renjaf's home when she was younger.

The room was part lounge, part study, with a desk by the window, and bookshelves containing, for the most part, books on magic. She didn't suppose his eyesight had been up to the task of reading for many years, but it looked as if the books had been well used in their day.

Her attention was drawn to a section that seemed separate from the others, in a shady corner, containing perhaps two dozen books that appeared to be brand new, or at least untouched. There was no evidence that they had ever been read but had nevertheless been kept free of dust and dirt and out of direct sunlight. They were clearly prized possessions, and a quick glance at the spines revealed why: they were all written by Renjaf himself.

She didn't feel it was right to touch them, but judging by the titles, they all seemed to be academic texts on mental magic. Apparently, it was his speciality. That, at least, struck a concordant note with when he'd tried to assault her mind all those years ago.

One of the titles caught her eye: *Altered Perception.* She turned that over in her mind for a moment. Though she was wary of judging a book by its cover, it seemed to imply he might have been working on a magical equivalent to perception filters. Another read, *Perceptual Environmental Substitution.* Substitution: swapping one thing for another. Had he developed a way to make a place appear to be somewhere else, like illusion magic of the mind? She found that fascinating.

Turning her attention to the walls, she noticed an Honourable Service Award from Calin's Tower. Apparently, he had been one of her Custodians, protecting Calin and the knowledge she collected in the world's paramount library. Cat hadn't realised that Renjaf had enjoyed such an illustrious post.

Cat knew the present White Custodian, Kadessa, had been in the post for longer than anyone else. Something about which she had a chip on her shoulder, so Cat delighted in being a thorn in her side as often as possible. She supposed Renjaf must have been her predecessor.

The way these things were displayed told her that Renjaf was a man who was justifiably proud of his past achievements. Moreover, all those she'd seen so far had been in his past, even the last time they met. All of which continued to feel at odds with the resentful man who had once told her that he was disinclined to do anything for anyone else because others in his life had been less than forthcoming with offers of assistance for him. Except he hadn't phrased it quite that politely.

Academic awards caught her eye. Three that were apparently won in consecutive years made her go cold – the Darla Award for Excellence in the field of mental magic from Melrose Academy. The institution that only existed because of their Time Intervention three hundred years in the past. The Guardians, it seemed, had inadvertently rewritten Renjaf's life story.

It was becoming clear that many things had changed, not just for him but for many other people, and for the most part, that was probably a good thing. If someone studied at Melrose in the new Timeline, from what she had learned, that would surely be a positive experience. And if they didn't, well, in the old Timeline, Melrose didn't exist, so surely that meant nothing had changed. But Renjaf's past directly intersected with Catriona's. If that were changed too much, it could create a paradox in the Guardians' Timelines. Such a paradox, if sufficiently important, could weaken the walls of reality and potentially allow a breach by the entity known as *IT*, the embodiment of chaos that could, if unleashed, unmake everything.

Still, the odds of such an extreme paradox were remote, Cat reminded herself. She was probably worrying over nothing.

When Renjaf returned with a tray of the promised tea and biscuits, placing it on the low table in front of the sofa, she returned to her seat.

"I see you went to Melrose college when you were younger," she remarked, trying to break the ice.

He nodded. "Yes, I had the privilege of a full scholarship there. It meant moving a long way from home, but as a young man of sixteen, I was keen to see the world, and Tedstone Warf seemed a good place to start. It's going on sixty years since I started there. It's amazing where the time goes."

Fifty-seven years to be exact, Cat calculated from the date on his certificate. "That was before the Demon Apocalypse, wasn't it?"

"Good to see someone of your age knows their history," Renjaf approved by way of answer, momentarily facing away from her as he poured the drinks. "Times have changed so much since then. It's hard to keep track of it all."

"You have no idea," Cat muttered under her breath so he wouldn't hear her. When Renjaf was finished, she replied aloud, "It's not easy, but I try. Where were you from originally?" she asked, continuing the small talk between biscuits.

"Kelna," he replied. "The city itself," he clarified, to distinguish it from the rest of the Empire that spanned the lower half of Southern Alloria.

"From Imperial Kelna to Tedstone Warf!" she gasped. "That really was a long way from home."

Way across the ocean. The only time she'd even been to Southern Alloria was when she and Dreya had come to Mandalee's rescue when she first ran into Nalani, a little way North of the Imperial border.

Thinking of her friend reminded her to say, "I hope you don't mind that I came to you rather than my friend the White Guardian."

"Not at all!" he assured her. "Why would I mind?"

"Well, you are aligned with the Light, and so is she…"

"Oh, I don't think that matters so much these days, especially for you Guardians."

"…and then, of course, there's what happened the last time I was here…"

Renjaf frowned in puzzlement. "Last time? I'm sorry, have we met before?"

It was Catriona's turn to be confused. While the passage of years had undoubtedly had a more significant impact on him than on her, she didn't think it was too conceited to assume he'd remember her.

"I'm Catriona Redfletching – the same Catriona who came to you years ago, trying to get her hands on *Shifting Stars*."

Renjaf looked blank. "What's that?"

"The book," she told him. "Surely you remember it?"

"I'm sorry, my dear," he apologised, "but I really have no idea what you're talking about."

Cat realised it wasn't uncommon for people of his age to develop a few gaps in their memory, and she didn't want to distress him by highlighting them.

"Oh, it's not important; it was years ago. Don't worry about it," she laughed, dismissing it with a wave and quickly moving the conversation along. "Anyway, much as I'm enjoying your hospitality, Mr Renjaf, perhaps you ought to tell me why you asked to see a Guardian. How can we help you?"

"Actually," he replied, rising from his seat, "it's more a question of how I can help you."

"Oh?"

"I have something for you. If you'll excuse me a moment, I'll go and get it." With that, he left the room.

A few moments later, he returned, and Cat was instantly on alert. She couldn't see the object he was carrying, but she could sense the power emanating from it – it fairly crackled with an unstable blend of magic, bound up with higher planar energy. It could only be one of the missing fragments of Kullos' control device.

"I know we're supposed to report these to the Council, not directly to you," Renjaf accepted, "but what with these Anti-Council rebels stirring up trouble, I'm sorry to say I'm not at all certain whom to trust these days. So, when I came across it in my attic the other day, I couldn't help thinking it would be better all-around if I gave it directly to those who ought to have it."

He reached out to hand it to her, but she jumped up, almost knocking the tea over in the process, and hastily backed away. She wasn't sure why she was reacting like this, but she was sure it was the right thing to do.

"Your attic?" she demanded, her pulse racing, blood pounding in her ears. "What was it doing there? How do you even have it?"

Uncertain what to do, Renjaf placed it on the table by the teapot.

"I was just having a long-overdue clearout. I've had it for decades, but I'm afraid I'd forgotten all about it."

"Perhaps you'd better explain from the beginning," Cat suggested, still staying as far away from the fragment as the dimensions of the room would allow. Every Guardian-related instinct was telling her this was wrong. She must not accept this fragment. Not here, not now. She didn't know why, but somehow, this was a critical moment in the Timeline. One wrong move now could spell disaster. The fragment was right there, and it was so tempting to grab it, take it before the Council and say, "See? We can do our jobs! We can collect these fragments if we're not inundated with false reports and unfounded accusations of selfishness and incompetence!"

But that action *would* be selfish and completely irresponsible. Cat needed to know the history of this fragment so that she and her fellow Guardians could work out how to deal with it safely.

Still, since it seemed Renjaf had the good sense not to thrust it at her, she decided it would do no harm to at least sit down on the chair at his desk, keeping her cool while keeping her distance as she listened to his story.

Chapter 10

After graduating from Melrose, Renjaf was offered a research position there, but then the post of White Custodian opened up at Calin's Tower. The opportunity to work there in that capacity was a rare honour, and he readily accepted the Council's invitation.

He had been there for about a year when the news broke about what became known as the Demon Apocalypse. It started in Northern Alloria, somewhere between two major cities: Houisbury and Qiapolis, further to the North, which was more-or-less where Kullos built his fortress a few decades later and where the alien city of Rhynapolis stood in their time. Death and destruction swept across Alloria, such that neither city existed any longer. Depending on which version of events one believed, they had either been wiped off the map in the conventional sense, or dragged, intact, down to the hell dimensions. It was a matter of some debate whether the latter was even possible.

"If not for the Melrose scholarship," Renjaf continued, "I would almost certainly have studied in Qiapolis. Had I still been living there, assuming I wasn't in the city when it was destroyed, no doubt I would have been involved in the fighting."

"But you weren't?" Cat prompted, her eyes growing wider by the moment.

He shook his head. "As I'm sure you know from your history, a great many Elvarian people – wizards, clerics and warriors – travelled across the ocean to fight."

*****

She did indeed know that. It was one of the biggest wars in modern history, and its effects were still being felt. Alloria was devastated, which was, at least in part, why the dual continents were still sparsely populated. Imperial Kelna to the far south was just about the only major area that withstood the terrible events, thanks as much to its geography as its defences. There were demon outbreaks in parts of Elvaria, too, but they were minor skirmishes compared to events across the water. Elvarian troops massing to fight in Alloria wasn't purely altruistic – better to fight the demons over there than in their own backyards in Elvaria.

Given the tensions between wizards and clerics on Alloria, it was highly unlikely that an Allorian studying at an Allorian college at that time would have become Custodian. It would have risked dragging Calin and her Tower into the conflict. But studying in Elvaria would have made him eligible.

However, Calin's Tower was universally recognised as a vitally important site. Therefore the Custodians were not merely exempt from war duty but actively forbidden unless it should be necessary to defend the Tower itself.

*****

Offering a grim smile, Renjaf admitted, "I can't say I was sorry about that. If push came to shove, I like to think I would have done my bit, but to face death on that scale…as I say, I'm glad I wasn't there."

"About the fragment?" Catriona prompted, lest Renjaf forget what he was supposed to be talking about.

She sympathised with what he was saying, but she still couldn't shake the nagging feeling that this was all wrong, and she needed the whole story so she could work out what to do about it.

"Oh, yes," he remembered. "Well, it just appeared outside Calin's Tower one day – the very day the Demon Apocalypse started. It flew out of a big blue spherical doorway and landed practically at my feet."

He had no idea what it was, but he was worried about the strange magic that was emanating from it. He picked it up and immediately took it to Calin. After all, if there was anyone who could identify a strange magical object, it was undoubtedly the keeper of the world's paramount library.

Cat asked if he would mind sharing his memory of that moment a little more directly.

She couldn't do mental magic as well as Dreya, but given Renjaf's expertise, she didn't think that would matter. "I need to check the co-ordinates sympathically," she explained. "A simple date, time and place aren't enough. I need an image to lock onto with my Temporal magic."

As an expert in mental magic, he understood very well and consented to the meeting of minds while he continued his tale.

Although Calin could not possibly identify it as a fragment of Kullos' control device from the future, sent back in Time, she was apprehensive about it. So much so that she refused to allow it to remain in her Tower, deeming it too dangerous to risk knowledge of its existence spreading. She charged young Renjaf with keeping it safe and hidden, even from the Council, although that broke the law. Calin's Tower was supposed to share knowledge, not suppress it, but Calin believed this to be a necessary exception. They never so much as spoke of it again.

Cat had the co-ordinates clear in her mind, now, and after breaking the connection, she thanked him and opened her pocket dimension, out of which she pulled her old notebook. Flicking through the pages, she found where Dreya had written symbolic representations of the co-ordinates for the portals through which Kullos had sent the fragments. One was a match.

As the years passed and he lived his life, Renjaf had simply forgotten all about the fragment until, a few days ago, he found it quite by accident and realised what it was. Recalling his promise to Calin that he would never tell the Council, he again broke the law by contacting the Guardians directly, sending a message to the Black Tower.

"I assumed you would want it," Renjaf concluded. "Why don't you?"

"Because something's wrong with Time," Cat replied. "I can feel it. Are you sure you don't remember meeting me before?" she asked once more.

He spread his hands helplessly. "I'm sorry, I don't."

"What about the Conclave?"

"Conclave?"

"You filed a grievance against me."

He shook his head emphatically. "Never," he denied vehemently. "You must have me confused with someone else. I've never filed a grievance against anyone in my life. Don't believe in it."

"And you've never heard of *Shifting Stars*?"

Again, he shook his head.

Growing increasingly worried, Cat excused herself for a moment and, sympathically calling for Dreya, opened a portal to Catriona's Meadow. Her wife took a moment to respond, but when she did, she immediately asked what was wrong.

"I need you to find *Shifting Stars* for me," Cat replied.

"Wow, I haven't seen that in a long time!" she remarked. "What do you need that for?"

"Renjaf doesn't remember it."

"Maybe he just forgot?" Dreya suggested.

"That's what I'm hoping," Cat agreed, "but I have a bad feeling it's more complicated than that."

Questioning no further, Dreya used the locator spell that Cat herself had taught her not long after they first met. The idea, at that time, of any mage being able to teach her magic that she didn't know was a novelty. In fact, before Cat 'proposed' to her on Midsummer's Day that year, she would have dismissed the idea as preposterous. Little did she know how many new concepts that pesky druid girl would open for her. Neither had she imagined, at the time, that that same girl would become the woman she loved even more than magic itself.

The Black robe sorceress smiled at the thought, but her smile faded as her locator spell drew a blank. Had she cast it wrong? She was apt to be a little distracted, these days, with everything she had going on in her head, but surely, she hadn't made a mistake with such a rudimentary spell! She tried again with complete focus. Same result. There was no such book in the Black Tower.

Returning to Catriona's Meadow, she suggested that Cat might have put it in her pocket dimension at some point and forgotten.

Cat shook her head. She'd tried that when she took out her notebook. The way her pocket dimension worked, all she had to do was open it and think about the thing she wanted. If it was there, it would instantly come to her hand. If it didn't come out, it wasn't there; it was as simple as that.

Thinking for a moment, Dreya experimented with adding a Temporal element to Cat's locator magic. If she couldn't find the book in the here and now, perhaps she could locate it in the past. The sorceress could remember, clear as day, when Catriona first moved in with her. Dreya had set aside space in her library for Cat's many research materials, including *Shifting Stars*.

She had to be careful. She couldn't let her past self see a big blue Prismatic Sphere open in her library – that could seriously screw up her own Timeline – but she remembered that evening very well. Remembered taking Cat out to a meal in Gaggleswick to celebrate what, at the time, had simply been friendship. Love developed later. That might be a safe time to open a portal, but her elite guards could have wandered into the library at some point during those hours, and if they had seen a portal, they would have reported it. Still, a micro-portal would be sufficient for her needs and her tower's defences at the time would have been unable to detect such a minor disturbance.

Yes, she decided. That was what she would do.

She opened the Temporal micro-portal with the utmost concentration and sent her locator spell to the other side.

Nothing.

Shifting Stars was not there on a day she was absolutely sure it had been.

Dreya tried a few more occasions when she was convinced she'd seen the unattended book, but it wasn't there. Recalling some of the other books Cat had studied that referenced *Shifting Stars*, generally to point and laugh, Dreya checked those. Those books existed but no longer contained any such reference.

There was only one conclusion: in this Timeline, *Shifting Stars* did not exist. But without that book, Cat would never have known how the stars moved whenever her Angel used the Crystal Mage Staff. Without that connection, she may not have felt so compelled to come to the Black Tower to find an untouched library. If the druidess never went to the Black Tower, she would never meet Dreya. That would be a disaster on a personal level, but beyond that, she, Cat and Mandalee had to come together to form the Guardianship. So much hinged on that. This was precisely the kind of personal paradox that, if left unchecked, could unmake everything.

As if she didn't have enough to worry about with Purity on the rampage in the mortal plane, now there was this.

From within Catriona's Meadow, Dreya called Mandalee, who quickly appeared with Shyleen. Thanks to the Timeless dagger, of course, the leopard could now exist there. Dreya hastily briefed them on the problem, and Mandalee grasped the implications immediately. This was precisely the kind of situation where the Guardians needed to act.

What the White Guardian didn't understand – and Dreya was with her on this – was, "How could this happen?"

It was Catriona who put it all together. All those years ago, when she was researching her staff, she had tried everything to find another copy of *Shifting Stars*. Renjaf had the only one. Why? She'd never given it much thought at the time, but now, having seen that Renjaf had been a published academic writer in this Timeline, she couldn't help but think it was because he had written it.

She recalled the book's account of the author's encounter with her Angel when he witnessed the stars move. As with many other such appearances, it had been at a particularly disastrous moment in the history of magic. In this case, the dawn of the Demon Apocalypse. For some reason, the author believed her Angel had somehow caused it, despite the actual cause being well-known. If *Shifting Stars* did not exist, that implied the would-be author never witnessed those events. Presumably, because he wasn't there…because he was doing something that made him exempt from fighting…because something in his past had caused him to be on another continent at the time.

In the old Timeline, when Melrose Academy did not exist, Renjaf had lived somewhere near Qiapolis on the day of the Demon Apocalypse. He was there. He saw her Angel with the staff, witnessed the stars move and subsequently wrote *Shifting Stars*. She could imagine the reaction. Basically, blaming the Demon Apocalypse on a mystical glowing figure that only he could see, somehow moving stars around with a staff with a blue crystal on top. It sounded ludicrous. He would have been ridiculed throughout the academic world. More than that, many would have found it offensive and a threat to the Accords that came out of the ashes of that terrible time. If Renjaf published such a work in his name, that could have put a swift end to any kind of notable career. It would also explain how he came to be so angry and resentful at the world that had mistreated him.

"But the author of *Shifting Stars* was anonymous," Mandalee pointed out. "I distinctly remember that."

Cat had finally acquired the book on the day they met. Mandalee recalled her friend reading it aloud for the first time when they were together in the appallingly named *FaerWay Tavern*.

"I know," Cat replied, "but I have some ideas about that. Hold on while I check something."

With that, she returned to Renjaf, although from his perspective, she'd never been away.

Indicating his books, she invited him to tell her about his research.

"What would you like to know?" he wondered.

"Well, let me give you a hypothetical scenario. Imagine someone has written and published something they'd give anything to take back, or at least disassociate themselves from. From your research, would there be a way to change the author's name to 'Anonymous' and make the world forget it was ever any different?"

Renjaf blinked in surprise at the oddly specific question but turned it over in his mind for a few moments and eventually gave his answer.

"Well, ultimately, I'd use substitution magic to find and replace the author's name."

"But people would notice that," Cat pointed out.

Renjaf nodded. "That's why I'd have to use perception-altering magic first. I'd start with a locator spell to find every copy of the book."

Cat nodded. That was an extension of her own magic.

"Then I'd use perception-altering magic to make the author's name emit a low-level mental disruption," he explained. "If it was mild enough, it shouldn't even trigger any magical defences."

"And what would that do, exactly?" Cat wondered.

"It would make the name memory proof, so over time, everyone would forget, and from then on, no-one could retain it."

"That would take a lot of effort to sustain, wouldn't it?" Cat asked.

"Absolutely," Renjaf confirmed, "and it couldn't be sustained indefinitely. That's why, when everyone had sufficiently forgotten, I would then make the substitution. After that, I could let the perception-altering magic fade."

Cat nodded, understanding. "So, everyone would assume they couldn't remember the author's name because it was unknown in the first place."

"You've got it," Renjaf agreed. "Mind you, that could have some nasty side-effects, like making even friends and family forget the author's very existence."

'*Then, one day,*' Catriona thought, '*some young upstart druid girl comes knocking on his door asking to borrow the book that ruined his life. No wonder he lashed out.*'

There was just one more thing she needed to know.

"Do you know if there are copies of your books in Calin's Tower?"

"Oh yes, definitely," Renjaf replied. "Given my past association, I made a point of sending Mistress Calin a copy of each one. Why do you ask?"

"Because thanks to my own work there, they are protected by a Timeless field, so they won't be affected by changes to the Timeline."

"And that's important, is it?"

Cat nodded. "It's vital. Believe me, I wish it weren't, but there's no other choice, I'm afraid. I have to do it."

In times past, whenever she'd had one of her ridiculous radical plans, she'd felt a certain thrill at the prospect of executing it. There may have been trepidation when she first thought of confronting Dreya the Dark, and regret when she'd been forced to flood that ancient repository of knowledge. But in the latter case, she had taken solace in the fact that she was saving people from a rampaging horde of True Undead.

This time, she felt only a profound misery at what she was forced to do. She was a Guardian of Time and Magic, and she had a responsibility to prevent major paradoxes that could endanger their world and more besides. Only a few days ago, she stood before the Council and convinced them that she and her fellow Guardians were not selfish in their actions, but surely this was.

Yet she had no choice.

"What about the fragment?" Renjaf asked.

Cat smiled weakly. This version of Renjaf was so lovely, so helpful. He had protected this fragment since long before she was born, never once tempted to try and use it or tap into its power. He'd built a good life and had many wonderful memories. But this Timeline was a contradiction. He couldn't be at Calin's Tower, collecting this fragment, and in Qiapolis witnessing the start of the Demon Apocalypse and her Angel's activities simultaneously.

He had to write *Shifting Stars*. It was no exaggeration to say the fate of the world depended on it. No *Shifting Stars*, no Guardians and no way to prevent the world from being unmade at the hands of Kullos.

But what of the consequences? What of the cost?

Rising from her chair, Cat replied, "You've kept it safe all these years. Thank you for that. Now I'm going to have to ask you to hold onto it for..." she hesitated before lying, "...a while longer."

In fact, he wouldn't be holding onto it at all. By the time Cat was finished, he would never have had it in the first place.

"If you think that's best," Renjaf accepted. He didn't understand why the Red Guardian wouldn't take it, but he wasn't going to question it.

It broke Catriona's heart. It was all she could do to hold back the tears. "I'm so sorry," she lamented as she opened a portal. "I really am. If there were any other way...I'm so very sorry."

"For what?" asked Renjaf with a deep frown.

Catriona did not answer until she had stepped through the portal to the other side and closed it so he could not hear her. Instead, she told only Dreya and Mandalee.

"I have to restore the old Timeline, as best I can, and to do that..." she broke down as she concluded, "...I have to ruin that lovely man's life."

Chapter 11

Catriona was all for going into the past alone, seeing it as her responsibility and hers alone. The others refused to allow it.

"I was the one who pushed you into interfering in the first place," Mandalee reminded her.

At first, Cat had been reluctant to risk meddling in the past any more than necessary to retrieve the fragment Ulvarius was using. Mandalee convinced her that stopping the influx of prisoners to the Black Tower was the right thing to do, regardless of the circumstances.

"And I pushed you into doing it in a more overt way," Dreya added.

Mandalee and Cat had kept their true abilities under wraps, trying to appear as if they were no different from the other small pockets of resistance in that age. But then Dreya came up with her plan to goad Ulvarius into attacking the fledgeling Council in Compton, in line with the history they knew. That required them to attract the tyrant's attention. It had been on the last of these occasions that they saved a group of children from his clutches. In doing so, they had inadvertently made an impression, the consequences of which were still being felt three centuries later.

"But I still say saving those kids was the right thing to do," Mandalee insisted.

Dreya agreed.

Though she couldn't say so, she had done something similar on Phitonia, saving a young Chetsuan girl from being murdered by a trio of fanatical Cultists. Sadly, the effect of her efforts had not lasted anywhere near as long because, barely an hour after she left, the Angel, Purity, had wiped out all sapient life. One day, Dreya was determined, when she had amassed the right kind of power, the right weapons, Purity would pay, but that wouldn't bring Amber back. Still, regardless of what happened later, saving Amber had been the right thing to do. In the same way, saving Vashti, Fumika, and the other children of Tedstone had been right, regardless of the consequences.

"Besides," Mandalee added, "remember the other thing that happened when we last went back in Time? We got lost for two and a half years."

"I've apologised for that!" Dreya objected.

Mandalee smiled reassuringly. "Don't worry, I'm not blaming you anymore. It was a mistake. They happen. My point is, what if Cat goes back in Time without us and gets lost in Time like last time, but this time she's all alone?

Despite her feelings, Cat spared a half-smile. "Four 'times' in one sentence. Not bad. But you're right, it is too risky, although at some point we're going to need to use solo time travel to set up the time loops that helped us save the world from Kullos."

For the other two Guardians, that meant appearing to their younger selves and giving them a nudge that would make them want to kill Daelen StormTiger. That would help keep Time on the right track. For Catriona, it meant moving a tiny spider slightly to brush her ear to make her fall, naked, into Mandalee's demon trap and leaving messages for herself under Calin's Tower and Daelen's base on Earth. The latter was supposed to involve writing adventure novels, which she'd never attempted in her life and, somewhat more awkwardly, having a relationship with Daelen. Given that she was now happily married to Dreya, she was going to have to find a way around her other self's ridiculous radical plan.

Still, for now, this being only their second major Intervention significantly in the past, she accepted that it was best to stick together.

Before that could happen, they needed Renjaf's textbooks from Calin's Tower to study his magic. Dreya volunteered to do it because it was wizard magic. Trying to adapt the techniques for druid or cleric magic could have unforeseen consequences. They all agreed there were enough of those already.

As soon as Dreya had the necessary volumes, she returned to study them in Catriona's Meadow. That way, there could be no interruptions. For a sorceress of Dreya's ability, acquiring a working knowledge of this new magic took only a single readthrough. Then they were ready to go.

Meanwhile, Cat had been getting the details of the plan clear in her head and decided that their first port of call should be Melrose Academy, the year Renjaf's name first appeared in front of Melrose college staff. To get co-ordinates to lock onto with their Temporal magic, Mandalee paid a visit to Dagamir there in the present. At her request, he guided her to college records from decades past. That information would allow her to pinpoint precisely when the college board began to discuss the intake of students that would include the sixteen-year-old Renjaf. She then found materials that described what the college was like in those days. There was no photography back then, but paintings and sketches were enough to generate a clear general impression of where and when they were going.

At last, they were ready.

*****

The Melrose Academy college campus in Tedstone Warf was a few miles East of the school. It enjoyed the same Protected status as the school and the Council building, whose features were once again echoed here. Its exterior had remained unchanged in at least six decades and most likely a long time before.

Remaining in their Timeless state, invisible and incorporeal to the natives of that time, the three women and one leopard strolled through the college with impunity. Although, it was a little disconcerting when staff and students walked right through them.

Mandalee was happy to have Shyleen with her this time. Typically, Catriona had quickly found a way to magically link the leopard to the Timeless spell on the dagger without needing to have it physically on her. It was the same thing she'd realised during her time with Daelen on Earth. When she'd been cut off from Tempestria, she had been unable to access her magic. Worse, it transpired that, just as many Faery – her father included – could not stray far from their forest homes without becoming ill, Catriona's Faery half needed a connection to Tempestria to survive. Her solution had been to always maintain an active micro-portal home when off-world. Likewise, Shyleen needed a connection to Catriona's Meadow to sustain her magical link with the spell on the Timeless dagger so she could be Timeless in the past. Severing that connection would cause her to enter the native Timestream, just like the other Guardians.

When the Guardians had travelled back three hundred and twelve years to face Ulvarius, they had arrived about a fortnight later than planned due to Temporal Lensing. Since then, they'd had the opportunity to study the *Chronicles of Magias* and learn from their mistake. Without adjustment, given the shorter journey, they would have been out by perhaps two days, but as it was, they arrived at the correct time, give or take an hour.

A student intake meeting was going on, precisely as documented, so, remaining unseen, they slipped into the room where it was taking place. Dreya didn't need to be this close to cast the spells, but she did if she wanted to see the results.

First came the locator spell, which confirmed references to Renjaf in the documentation in the college building. Thankfully, his name wasn't exactly common, so there was no chance of a mistake. Dreya had made a slight adjustment to the spell such that it would highlight the name within a Timeless field. Through this, the Guardians could keep track of those pieces of paper that bore his name. That done, Dreya worked her perception-altering magic to make the name memory-proof.

Watching the college staff trawl through the piles of applications had to be the most boring job the Guardians had ever had to do. In the end, though, they were confident that every reference to Renjaf had been forgotten. Since his application was so forgettable, it had naturally ended up on the reject pile. They would probably even forget to send a rejection letter. If Renjaf were to chase up his application, he wouldn't get anywhere. They would be unable to find any record of it.

Of course, in the original Timeline, Melrose Academy did not exist for him to apply to. Instead, he ended up studying at Qiapolis University in Northern Alloria. That was their next port of call, to ensure that part of Renjaf's Timeline was back on track.

Since that University no longer existed in the future, having been destroyed or dragged down to hell with the rest of the city in the Demon Apocalypse, no records survived. But Renjaf's story – and simple logic – suggested that he had applied to many colleges at the same time. Sure enough, his application had arrived safely in Qiapolis, along with glowing references and recommendations that ensured the institution grabbed the chance to mould the young man's potential.

Post-graduation, Renjaf was offered a research position at the University, which he gladly accepted. However, much as he enjoyed working in the big city, he preferred a home that offered a quiet life. Therefore, he bought some land about halfway between Qiapolis and Houisbury. There, he commissioned the building of a wizard's tower to be his home. He had no way of knowing that the following year, that was going to be a dangerous place to be.

*****

Before travelling to Alloria in the past, Cat had paid a flying visit to Alloria in her present. Specifically to the no-longer-ruined temple on the edge of the Rhynas Desert where Michael shared his home with the Chetsuan sisters, Sara and Jessica. Once again, Cat needed their help, or Sara's in particular.

To participate in the fighting and protect Renjaf during the Demon Apocalypse, they would have to sever their Timeless connection and become visible. Cat thought it best if their involvement were not widely known for the sake of their own personal histories. The last time they had travelled to the past, they had used false names. This time, she wanted to go one step further. After all, there were many people in the world in their time that had been alive during the Demon Apocalypse. That hadn't been a problem on a timescale of three centuries. Not even the Faery lived quite that long.

Back when their Chetsuan friends lived on Earth, they had used perception filters – tiny pieces of Shadowkin technology that attached to the neck and made them appear human. On Tempestria, after fighting Kullos' army on the back of a pair of dragons, trying to hide who they were would be very much a case of closing the door after the horse had bolted. (An expression that seemed to be universal.) However, they had used them once, since, and Michael had made one, too – for their mission to the world of Lavos. When they retrieved the fragment and saved a continent full of innocent people and dragons, they used their perception filters to appear to be Lavosian citizens.

For this Time Intervention, Cat borrowed that technology to allow the Three Guardians to hide in plain sight.

*****

Dreya felt as though the cosmos were conspiring against her. A nonsense idea, of course, and not one she took seriously. All the same, history was repeating itself.

In her quest to stop Kullos, Catriona spent most of her time with Mandalee while Dreya was alone. When they travelled back in Time to deal with Ulvarius, again, Cat was mostly with Mandalee while Dreya was alone. Now, on their latest adventure together, yet again, Cat and Mandalee were together while Dreya was alone. It wasn't that she resented Mandalee or begrudged Cat being with her best friend. Besides, she and Cat had just spent two months together on honeymoon. Even so, Dreya thought it would be nice if these adventures could stop forcing her and Catriona apart.

It was a sound strategy. Dreya would collect the fragment when it emerged from a portal outside Calin's Tower. Meanwhile, Cat and Mandalee stayed close to Renjaf to protect him and ensure he saw Catriona's Angel like he was supposed to. Cat obviously had a personal interest in that, and as for Mandalee, well, if demons were on the rampage, what you needed was a demon hunter.

If the Guardians used their Temporal powers, they could very well be in two places at the same time. They'd done it before. But Dreya knew it would be a bad idea to introduce the unstable power of a fragment into the middle of the Demon Apocalypse.

Still, the fact that it made sense didn't make Dreya feel any better.

When the fragment arrived on schedule, she stabilised it sufficiently for Temporal transport, but she knew it could not be characterised as 'safe' until it was with the other two in Daelen's Tomb.

After that, there was nothing more to do but wait. It shouldn't be too long. Cat and Mandalee were not planning to guard Renjaf for the rest of his life. All they could do was make sure he saw the Angel and survived the initial demon uprising. After that, they would have to trust history to take care of itself.

In the meantime, Dreya supposed she could visit Calin's Tower since it was right there, but frankly, she doubted there was anything useful there in this Timeframe that she didn't already know. Then she remembered that she still had Renjaf's textbooks with her. They could be worth further study. She supposed those books would never be published now, which was a shame because from what she'd seen so far, some of his ideas had been quite intriguing. Especially his expertise in mental and perception-altering magic. Those could be valuable weapons, with the proper application, under the right circumstances. With that thought, then, she sat down to study.

*****

Today was the day the Demon Apocalypse began. Or so the history books attested.

In reality, pinpointing that day was not unlike identifying the day the Eastcliff Waterfall started flowing. There was no such day. Mandalee had seen that cascade of water on her way to be reunited with Shyleen after two years lost in Time, and it was an impressive sight, but the waterfall did not suddenly start. That's not how nature worked. In reality, it probably began as a trickle, perhaps hundreds of thousands of years before Year Zero. The kind of timescales that made even their trip back to the time of Ulvarius seem like no more than the blink of an eye. That trickle would have increased imperceptibly day by day, year by year, even century by century. But increase it did.

Then perhaps that increase began to grow exponentially as the water eroded the rockface until a whole section fell away. That helped the water to flow even faster, with increasing force, eroding the rock more quickly, releasing more water, which eroded more rock…until the Eastcliff Waterfall became what it was in her time: the largest waterfall in the world.

Most likely, the process wasn't even as linear as that. During those thousands of centuries, there were probably periods of drought when the waterfall retreated to a trickle or even ceased altogether. Ice ages when the water froze. But then the ice melted, flooding the area, and the waterfall returned, growing and growing until it became the spectacle Mandalee had seen.

In the same way, wizards and clerics had been summoning demons from the day they had the power to do so. Even before that, demons would have found a way to invade the mortal plane, some of which would have soon found a way to summon others of their kind without mortal assistance. That was the trickle. As more and more people summoned more and more demons, that trickle grew exponentially.

When did the Eastcliff Waterfall become the Eastcliff Waterfall? One could argue it was the day people named it. The day people recognised it.

When did the Demon Apocalypse become the Demon Apocalypse? The day people named it. The day people recognised it. That day was today, for this was the day the rockface broke away under the strain. The day the walls between the mortal plane and demon realms shattered.

Chapter 12

Qiapolis, to the North, was a wizard's city. Houisbury, to the South, was a cleric stronghold where something remarkable had happened. Clerics from different Orders had begun working together. It wasn't exactly a mirror of the Council of Wizards. It was more a case of recognising a common enemy. The clerics of Northern Alloria were especially devout, and they viewed wizard magic as blasphemy against all the gods of the Pantheon. Wizards, on the other hand, often belittled and scorned the clerics for their 'backward thinking' and 'blind faith', showing no consideration or respect for their beliefs. Such attitudes did much to fan the flames.

There had been skirmishes aplenty across the continent for decades, but today was different. How or why this day was chosen for the conflict to escalate into total war is unknown to history. Clerics blamed the wizards, wizards blamed the clerics, both sides blamed the demons, and nobody cared what the demons thought.

Renjaf was in his tower when it started. His was the only home for miles around. He lived alone and had chosen that site specifically for peace and quiet. He had never been one to involve himself in conflict. He just wanted to be left alone and was happy to leave everyone else alone in return. But today was the day the demons attacked. A pair of them. Which side those demons were supposed to be on mattered little to the demons and even less to Renjaf when he was forced to defend himself. Renjaf managed to use his mental magic to turn them on each other, giving him time to escape.

In the fading light of dusk, he saw a line of magical torches to the South. There were so many that even from two or three miles away, he could detect clerical magic signatures. It was an army, obviously heading for Qiapolis. Renjaf himself had nothing against clerics, personally, but it seemed unlikely they would let him reason with them. He had no choice. He would have to head North. Having made that decision, he noticed another line of torches in that direction. It was an army of wizards. It looked like thousands on each side, so there was no going around them.

It at was times like this that he wished he had learned to teleport.

*****

Mandalee and Catriona were going to have to split up. That's all there was to it.

Despite what Dreya thought, they were not going to get to stay together. More than that, they were going to have to be on opposite sides. They didn't like it, but it was the best way to ensure history happened the way it was supposed to. They would stand out enough as it was since neither of them could summon demons, which was standard practice on Alloria in this era. They didn't need anyone making a connection between the Red robe druid and the White fighter-cleric. They didn't want any mistakes this time. They needed to remain unnoticed, or at least unmemorable.

The armies each numbered more than five thousand, with demon numbers four to five times that, so it should be easy enough for them to get lost in the crowd. The last time they took a trip to the past, Mandalee had, at first, swapped her combat suit for more traditional white leather, hoping to avoid drawing unwanted attention. This time, Mandalee decided to take a leaf out of Nalani's book and wear both. These days, she routinely kept a few changes of clothes in her pocket dimension. She just needed Cat to use a bit of shapeshifting magic on the leather to take it up a size so she could wear it over her combat suit without it being too tight.

While Mandalee put it on, Cat retrieved her bow and arrows out of her own dimensional storage. If she was going to limit revealing her druid magic too much since it was no longer safe for her to shapeshift herself, it seemed a wise precaution.

To further limit the chances of their involvement here becoming part of written history, Shyleen was going with Cat, not Mandalee. The practice of wizards keeping familiars was considered old-fashioned even in this era, but a few mages still clung to the idea. For a cleric to have one would raise questions that were best avoided.

Frankly, as much as Mandalee's reasoning made sense, Cat suspected she simply didn't like the idea of leaving her best friend alone and unguarded. So, if Mandalee couldn't be by her side, she would let Shyleen be her proxy.

They had portalled in using the co-ordinates for Renjaf's home as a landmark. If history was on track, the White wizard would be too busy to either notice or care about a flash of blue light in the distance. From there, Cat headed North to Qiapolis with Shyleen, while Mandalee went South alone to meet up with the clerics coming up from Houisbury.

According to the history books, the battle began in earnest at sunset. Apparently, both sides believed they would catch the other by surprise by attacking at night. That wasn't going to work out for either of them. Nobody knew it at the time, but the demons had sown the seeds of this idea, trying to force events to come to a head, creating a critical mass of demons in one place, along with two enormous armies full of sweet mortal life. To demons, that represented a feast of energy.

As the sun's dying tendrils faded from the sky, Cat and Mandalee met up with their respective forces. Catriona hadn't used her wizard magic for years but still remembered enough for a basic light spell, conjuring a fiery light bob that floated in midair. If the wizards identified her as a druid, she would be confined to healing duty since they believed that was pretty much all such magic was capable of. Unless somebody wanted a gardener, and that was hardly a priority now.

She had seen a few druids together at the rear of the advancing army, dismissed and forgotten, and her every instinct was to tell them that their magic was capable of so much more. Convince them to let their imagination loose of the ties in which the wizards' attitudes bound them. But although she was a druid, Catriona was first and foremost the Red Guardian, and she couldn't risk screwing up history, not even for a worthy cause. To do her job, the Red Guardian needed to ignore her fellow druids and get closer to the action because that was where she would find Renjaf.

*****

Being surrounded by thousands of demons was terrifying. The only thing that scared Mandalee more was that those around her *weren't* afraid. She could scarcely believe the people of this time could be arrogant and complacent enough to imagine they could control these denizens of the hellish planes. Mandalee's every instinct was to warn these misguided clerics. Convince them to cut the demons down; send them tumbling back down where they belonged before it was too late. But although she was a demon hunter, Mandalee was first and foremost the White Guardian, and she couldn't risk screwing up history, not even for a worthy cause. To do her job, she needed to ignore the fact that many people would be slaughtered tonight. She couldn't save them. She'd learned her lesson about changing history unnecessarily. From now on, she would not tamper with events that ought not to be tampered with any more than they already had been.

Thanks to her years of experience as a demon hunter, Mandalee had learned how to tell when demons were really under control and when they were faking it. The clerics here didn't have a clue. Every now and then, a few demons would try and escape the clerics' control and attack them. In truth, they were doing little more than growling menacingly. They had no intention of breaking their bonds just yet. It was all for show. It reinforced the mages' belief that they were masters of their demon pets. It also drew their focus, so they wouldn't look too closely at the demons that were perfectly obedient and docile. The clerics had no reason to question who had summoned them. They all just assumed it was somebody else, not realising the real answer was that nobody had summoned those demons.

They were free.

*****

It took Catriona the best part of an hour to find Renjaf among the army of wizards. It was strange to see him so young. The only reason she recognised him at all was that through his mental magic, she had seen an image of him as he was at this time. Back when he was happy. Before everything went wrong. For now, her job was to protect him so he could see her Angel and write *Shifting Stars* in response. Or, to put it another way, she had to keep him alive long enough to use him and help ruin his life for the sake of the Timeline.

Sometimes she hated being a Guardian.

Having spotted him, it was a question of how to gain his confidence. Catriona could see that he had sustained a few scrapes in his retreat from his home. Combining that with the observation that he seemed uncomfortable being there, she thought that might be a way in.

Making her way through the crowd in a way that appeared to be random, she got close to him. Then, at the last moment, she accidentally-on-purpose tripped over someone's leg and sprawled straight into Renjaf, who caught her.

"Oh, thanks!" she breathed with a well-timed blush. Making a show of regaining her feet, she rolled her eyes self-deprecatingly. "The fight hasn't even started yet, and here I nearly impale myself on my own arrows!"

"Are you alright?" Renjaf checked.

"Right as rain," she replied, then seeing his puzzled look, she clarified. "Sorry. Something a friend of mine likes to say. It means I'm fine. What about you?" she asked. "How did you get yourself injured already?"

"I live out here," he explained. "Demons attacked me, forced me out of my home. It's nothing major. For now."

"Well, one good turn deserves another, so…" she used some straightforward healing magic to fix him up.

"You're a druid," he observed.

"Part druid, part sorceress, part archer," Cat shrugged. "Bit of all kinds of things, really. I'm Rose, by the way." She offered her hand, and he shook it.

"Renjaf," he returned. "Shouldn't you be behind the lines with the other druids?"

Cat shook her head. "I never was any good at staying out of things. I get involved; I can't help myself. Besides, you've probably noticed I'm part Faery, too, and there's a Faery community down in the heart of the Corolis Wood, but I can't get there at the moment because there's a big army in the way," she pointed out, trying to stick to only implying a lie.

It was true that the Corolian Faery lived there, and she couldn't get there if she wanted to. Of course, the reality was she didn't want to, but then she'd never actually said she did. She couldn't help thinking it was precisely the sort of half-truth that Dreya would use.

"So, you're cut off from your home, like me," he surmised. Keeping his voice low, he added, "Then I guess you don't want to be here any more than I do."

Cat shook her head. "Believe me, if there was any way to avoid what's to come, I'd take it." That much was true.

Just then, Shyleen turned up.

"Oh, there you are!" Cat exclaimed, as if delaying her introduction hadn't been part of the plan. "This is my familiar…" She hesitated, realising that if the Guardians were using false names, then she needed one for Shyleen, too. She went with the first one that popped into her head and braced herself for her feline friend's reaction.

"Pryshia."

'*Pryshia!*' Shyleen objected in her head, in the language of leopards that Mandalee had taught her. *'Of all the names, you pick that one?'*

'*Sorry,*' Cat sent back. '*I don't know any other Pantheon names. I should have thought to ask you sooner.*'

'*I have a good mind never to speak to you again!*' Shyleen sulked.

'*Look, I can't change it now, but I promise you can choose a name next time.*'

'*Well, I suppose, under the circumstances, for the sake of friendship, I can rise above the unintended insult,*' she decided magnanimously.

Aloud, to Renjaf, Cat explained, "I know familiars are a bit old-fashioned, but you know how we Faery are – affinity with nature and all that."

The White wizard waved that aside. "No need to explain. If I could have a magnificent golden leopard looking out for me right now, I wouldn't worry about how fashionable it is!"

'*Magnificent?*' Shyleen echoed in Catriona's mind. '*Are you sure we have to change his Timeline? I like him the way he is.*'

'*So do I,*' Cat agreed, '*but I can't base my Guardian decisions on how much I like someone. I have to fix Time, whether I like it or not.*'

"Well then, Renjaf, perhaps the three of us can protect each other."

"Three?" Renjaf returned. "Or four?" His gesture indicated Catriona's pregnancy. "How far along are you?" he asked. "If you don't mind me asking."

"About four months," she answered.

'*That's not true,*' Shyleen objected.

'*It is in terms of how far my pregnancy has progressed,*' Cat returned. '*What do you want me to say? That I've really been pregnant for a year and a half?*'

It was actually getting close to four Tempestrian years since she first got pregnant, but she had been lost in Time for more than half of that. She wasn't sure whether that should count or not.

'*I see your point,*' Shyleen conceded.

"Is this the part where you tell me a pregnant woman shouldn't be fighting?" Cat asked Renjaf.

The wizard shook his head. "Only in the sense that, in an ideal world, none of us would be fighting."

"In another sense, I suppose none of us is doing the actual fighting," Cat pointed out, staying in character for someone of that era. "Isn't that what the demons are for?"

That was undoubtedly the original reason for the practice of wizards using demons in warfare: so that the wizards could avoid having to fight themselves. The aim was to prevent wizard casualties because clerics had an advantage: healing. If they sustained injuries, their fellow clerics could help them. Who was going to help an injured wizard? Well, druids to an extent, but they weren't necessarily on the side of the wizards by choice. Unfortunately, as Renjaf had found out, being neutral wasn't an option when one was unexpectedly caught in the middle of a war. The fact was, wizards needed druids, whereas clerics had no use for them whatsoever. Therefore, many druids sought the protection of wizards in exchange for healing. That was the main reason for the albeit limited involvement of druids in the Council of Wizards in the first place. It was also why some druids were against the inclusion of clerics in the newly reformed Council of Mages. They worried they would lose their niche position with the wizards and sorceresses.

There in the past, though, the Allorian wizards had thought that it would be even better if they could avoid the need for healing by not getting injured in the first place. So they turned to demon control. They would let the demons fight for them, bleed for them, even die for them. In turn, clerics had sought to nullify the wizards' advantage by asking their gods to give them the power to summon demons of their own. Their prayers were answered, and that was how battles had been fought for decades. A practice that was about to come to a head.

"That's the theory," Renjaf agreed. "Never gone in for summoning demons, myself."

Cat nodded. "Me, neither."

"Which brings us back to protecting each other," Renjaf concluded.

Cat smiled. "Much better all around, I think."

Renjaf returned the sentiment. "I agree."

Chapter 13

Renjaf's words were almost drowned out by the rising noise. The two armies were within striking distance now. The wizards halted, and as per the pre-arranged signal, the demons rushed forward.

Just as the two sets of demons clashed, both sides glanced up as one. A figure whooshed to a halt overhead. Someone who looked like a three-dimensional negative image of Daelen StormTiger. The dark clone who would one day call himself Aden-El.

None of the Guardians had thought of that. In their own time, Daelen had combined with his dark clone and died a handful of years ago. But this was the past. In this period, both versions of him were still alive, as was Kullos, of course. Catriona was thankful that in the middle of these two armies, each five thousand strong, there was no reason for the dark clone to pick Mandalee or herself out in the crowd. That could cause some nasty Timeline anomalies.

"What's this?" the dark clone remarked to no-one in particular. "Are you mortals having a demon scrap? Is it a new sport?" He laughed. "Well, I'd love to stay and watch, but I'm planning on some sport of my own – basically exterminating all the mortals in a village or two. I could do that here, I suppose, but where's the fun in that if you're just going to kill each other anyway? I'll see if I have time to stop by and check on your corpses later. Bye, y'all!" With that, he flew away.

Cat hoped Daelen and Michael could catch up with him before he did any real damage. This continent was about to have enough problems without him adding to them.

*****

The demons had used the distraction well, as the assembled clerics and wizards lost concentration and let their control magic slip, just for a moment. Taking full advantage, some of the captured demons quietly Descended, giving up the energy they jettisoned to the free ones. They, in turn, used that same energy to summon them back again. When the dark clone had gone, the clerics and wizards saw the same demons as before, not realising anything had changed. In fact, everything had changed. Now almost all of them were free.

That was a detail previously unknown to Mandalee, but having witnessed it, she thought if ever there was a moment one could point to and say, "This was when the Demon Apocalypse began," this was it.

Then, three things happened almost simultaneously.

First, some of the demons turned on the mortal mages, tearing apart those few who still controlled some of their fellows, thus freeing them. This pulled everyone's focus back to the battlefield, the sky no longer relevant.

Second, a glowing figure shimmered into reality in the sky directly above. The entity held a wooden staff, about three feet tall, with a large blue crystal on top. It was Catriona's Angel with her Crystal Mage Staff. The staff emitted a light that seemed to paint symbols in the sky as if projected onto an invisible ceiling. Then, as the Guardians discretely watched, a section of stars moved out of alignment. Cat risked a glance at Renjaf. He could see the Angel, she was sure of it, and he'd noticed the stars.

Finally, as if in response, demons and hellspawn appeared to pull themselves out of the ground, although they were actually entering the mortal plane from the layer of reality immediately below. They swarmed onto the plain to attack wizards and clerics alike. Some of the mages tried to regain control, but it was futile. Dozens on both sides died before the mages desperately turned to conventional magic.

"Where the hell did this lot come from?" someone cried out, even as they lashed out with magic.

"Isn't it obvious?" Renjaf shot back, invoking his magic in a desperate attempt to keep the horde at bay. "That Angel did it!" He pointed. "Something they did with that staff made all these demons appear!"

When Catriona had read *Shifting Stars*, she had never understood why the author would connect her Angel's actions to this catastrophe. Just because two things happened at the same time, that didn't necessarily mean one caused the other. Now, as she and Shyleen prepared to defend themselves, she could see it as plain as day. If she were in his place, she might very well jump to the same conclusion.

Others looked where he was pointing, but they could see nothing.

"What are you on about?" a wizard demanded.

"There! Can't you see? They made the stars shift, and that brought the demons!"

"He's lost it!" scoffed a sorceress dismissively.

Other similar comments spread through the ranks, and Renjaf turned to his companion, desperate for a lifeline.

"Rose?" he prompted.

Hating herself, Cat pretended to be too busy shooting arrows to look him in the eye.

"Sorry, Renjaf, I've no idea what you're talking about," she lied.

*****

In the middle of the cleric army, Mandalee had been keeping mostly to herself as they marched. The other clerics, especially the pure mages in robes, weren't at all sure what to make of her in her white leather, with her array of weapons.

It had been a while since the White Assassin had used traditional weapons, generally favouring her dragonclaw daggers, these days. As with her combat suit, however, they were anachronistic and best left hidden except in an emergency. As long as they were sheathed, with their perception filters active, no-one would even see them. At times like this, she really missed her Pureblade. Seeing it shatter along with Kullos' control device had been heartbreaking.

When the fighting started, she naturally didn't harm any wizards, focussing instead on the enemy demons. At first, she'd had to pick her targets carefully, fighting defensively against any demons that broke through the line.

Then the noise level grew as they got within striking distance of the wizards. The clerics ceased their advance and unleashed their demons to fight those of their enemies. Some direct magic was cast from both sides, but the main focus was demon control. At least, that was the plan.

Now, however, everything had changed. Now, all the demons were the enemy, as it should be, and she could unleash herself. Even so, she had to be careful not to be swept away and surrounded. The combined demon army numbered over fifty thousand, and that number was growing. Every time a demon killed a mortal, they absorbed their life force, their energy, adding it to their own.

She vaguely wondered if this was how Dreya had learned to drain magic and even higher planar energy from others – by studying demonic energy absorption. After all, from a demonic point of view, mortals were higher planar beings.

Dismissing such thoughts, she admonished herself to focus.

*****

Having absorbed that energy, those demons had withdrawn their attack and returned to a central position on the battlefield, protected by the horde while they summoned other demons. Some groups began delving deeper into the planes of reality, bringing forth Greater Demons. They, in turn, could summon perhaps a dozen Lesser ones.

In this way, even as the mortal mages fought for their lives, no matter that they were slaughtering demons by the dozen, the demon army was still growing.

Seeing this, both mortal armies sent magical messages to the other side, requesting parley. They agreed on a neutral meeting site and chose a handful of representatives who could teleport. For the first time in half a century, there was an open dialogue between wizards and clerics. Suddenly, their differences seemed insignificant in the face of the simple reality of the situation: Tempestria was invaded.

That the two sides could no longer afford to fight each other was a given. Demons did not discriminate; they would slaughter every adult and child in their path. The more they killed, the stronger and more numerous they would become. The demon army had to be crushed before it could spread. Everything else was secondary.

One other thing was agreed by both sides: summoning demons to fight their wars had to stop immediately. Anyone caught doing so in future had to be considered a renegade and traitor. In the years to come, this would become formally enshrined in Tempestrian law as the Accords. For the moment, however, their job was clear: to spread the word across both Northern and Southern Alloria. They even sent a desperate plea across the ocean for help from Elvaria.

Accounts of this period said that the battle here would be officially over in a matter of hours, but not before hundreds of demons had spread in all directions. Also, very few members of the two original armies would survive. The Guardians just had to make sure Renjaf was one of them.

The Demon Apocalypse would continue for the next four years before it was officially declared won. The devastation would last for decades beyond that, but they were content to leave that to history.

*****

The White Assassin sliced the hellish creatures apart with a sword in one hand while sending out her returning blade with the other. She killed them by the dozen, the score, but she knew it wasn't really making any difference. She was already covered in demon blood and ichor, and the hilts of her weapons were getting slippery, but she couldn't stop to wipe them. She would just have to grasp them tighter, literally hold on for dear life, for those weapons were the only things that would keep her alive out here.

Amid all this, however, Mandalee's primary mission was the same as it always was: protect Catriona. As Guardians, of course, they could both easily pull themselves out of the flow of Time, becoming invisible and incorporeal. But if they wanted to preserve history, they couldn't very well do that in front of thousands of witnesses on the battlefield.

There was no way to be sure if their Guardian tricks would even work against the demons. Nor did they want to give them any ideas that they were somehow special and might have more magical energy than the average mortal mage. There were dozens of different demon species there already, some of which had perception beyond that of mortals.

Through her dual connections, she knew Cat and Shyleen were both fine, if busy. She would just have to keep fighting until she could get to them. At the moment, given the swarm of demons in the way, meeting was impossible. There was no way they could open up a portal without everybody noticing. The people here were scared enough already without seeing magic they couldn't explain. Perhaps that was why Catriona's Angel kept themselves shrouded. The one person who had seen her – Renjaf – had not reacted well, believing them to be a threat, so it made sense.

The Angel was still there, doing whatever they were trying to achieve, but Mandalee had noticed a change. The entity had begun to glance at their wrist as if checking a portable timepiece. Did the process with the staff require a particular length of time, Mandalee wondered, or did Angels have schedules to keep to, just like mortals?

Before she could think of it any further, Mandalee spotted something else. Something that made her blood run cold. A group of fifty enormous Greater Demons from about five planes down had banded together. Standing in a ring, they were ignoring the battle entirely in favour of doing something more important: summoning magic. But the way the space between them was shimmering suggested only a single individual was to be made manifest. There was only one thing they could be doing. They were bringing forth something from a plane even lower down.

The White Assassin was already terrified beyond words. This was far worse than her fight against Kullos' army because, as bad as that was, she had friends and allies around her. Here she was alone. In the face of that fear, though, Mandalee would react the way she always did when her back was against the wall: fight harder. There were already more Greater Demons here than she had encountered in her life. As far as she knew, there had only ever been one instance of anything being brought forth from below, and that wasn't here. That was happening a few miles further South at the ancient temple ruins that would be the future home of Ossian Miach Kaidool.

What the people around her did not know was that the free demons had not put all of their eggs in one basket. About a hundred of them had banded together at a second site, miles away from civilisation. According to history, the only reason that spearhead had failed was that the demons were in the wrong place at the wrong time.

*****

Only moments ago, the dark clone of Daelen StormTiger had flown by. However, an unfathomable distance away on another world, the other Daelen had received an alert and acted immediately.

He portalled directly outside Michael's Tomb and entered. Even he could not penetrate the building when the security systems were active. If he could bypass the security, then his enemies would be able to do likewise.

Waking from his rest, the Champion of the Gods quickly charged up and followed his friend through a portal to a small town a little way outside the Corolis Wood, where the dark clone awaited them.

Like Daelen, the dark clone spent most of his time off-world, returning to Tempestria to fight. Ever since he'd been split from the original Daelen StormTiger, his one goal had always been to recombine. Unfortunately, he was worried that even if his light half agreed, it would be that half that would end up in control. The dark clone could never allow that. However, in his exploration of other worlds, he sometimes found a tool or a weapon that he believed might give him an edge in their battles. Then he could wear his light clone down and forcibly recombine, keeping that half of his nature subsumed. This was his latest such attempt.

To draw out his other half, all he had to do was terrorise some mortals. He didn't need to do anything to them – that would be a waste of power – the threat was enough. The fact was, he could very easily wipe out a whole mortal town if he wanted to, so Daelen would never call his bluff. Just in case he wasn't bluffing.

Looking up at the sky, the dark clone sensed the portal before he saw it. Clouds gathered, unleashing a storm, and the lightning shaped itself into the form of a tiger. Daelen had arrived with Ossian Miach Kaidool by his side.

The clone greeted them breezily with, "Hello, you! I don't suppose you fancy a chat before we fight?"

“Hardly!” Daelen replied. He and Michael tried to fly down to grab him, but the dark clone shot out a beam cannon blast, forcing Daelen to shield Michael against its terrible power. Unfortunately, as was always the case, the explosion slammed into the town and levelled a few buildings.

The mortals in the town fled the scene – at least, those who could still move after that initial onslaught. Daelen and Michael did their best to limit the damage their powers did as they fought, but they couldn’t afford to hold back – the dark clone certainly wouldn’t. After a few minutes, the combined power of Daelen and Michael was enough for them to force the dark clone away from the town, driving him North towards the ancient temple ruins. As a rule, they would find very few people around these parts, but today was different. There was a large force of mortals, both human and Faery, heading North, having quickly rallied to fight a demon invasion. None of that concerned the shadow warriors, however. They were consumed by their own struggle.

Chapter 14

No matter how the shadow warriors' battles began, gentle reader, they almost invariably ended the same way. Although Michael was not Fated to die as he was against Kullos, at some point, the dark clone would get bored of the fight and focus his powers on Michael, almost always slaying him before flying away. This time looked to be no different, as the dark clone's latest scheme failed to live up to its promise. However, just as he was about to kill Michael, a slimy black tentacle shot out from below and grabbed the demigod's ankle, yanking him down at the last second, causing the dark clone to miss. The three looked down to see what had happened. The tentacle was one of a dozen that belonged to a hydra-like creature about the size of a whale with oozing black skin, guarded by a large group of Greater Demons. It took only a moment for Michael to chop off the tentacle that held him, but another quickly grew in its place.

Understandably, that proved to be enough of a distraction for Daelen's dark clone to get away. Daelen, not being one to get involved with mortal affairs, wasn't going to stick around, either.

However, since this was one of those rare times that Michael was still alive, the demigod decided to stay and help with the situation unfolding below. Ossian Miach Kaidool, Michael, had been created by the gods, and this hellish creature was known to the Pantheon. They called it an Ostium. Even as Michael watched, demons began to spawn from its massive bulk, but despite appearances, it wasn't birthing them. The Ostium could exist across multiple planes simultaneously, and some types of demons used the creatures to traverse between the levels of hell. It was uncertain whether it was a natural creature or whether demons grew Ostia artificially. Michael considered it a distinction without difference.

Never before had one been summoned to the mortal plane, but now that it was here, if it wasn't destroyed or Banished back down to the lower planes, it could provide easy access to Tempestria for untold numbers of demons. On any other day, the demons would have chosen their site well. The temple ruins were deserted. As you will appreciate, gentle reader, given the escalating hostilities between clerics and wizards, and now the demon invasion, it was hardly an ideal time for tourists. The Ostium could have quietly done its work for days without being found. The demon army it could have spawned in that time could have been unstoppable. As it was, Michael wasn't going to give it that chance.

Ossian Miach Kaidool rallied a force of mortal mages and fighters around him, and together they managed to eradicate the threat. The battle became woven into history and legend, but only a few days later, Michael was forced to leave them. Kullos had returned, which had to take priority. Even after the Demon Apocalypse ended, large sections of his fighters stayed together, having forged a bond through Michael, who, as always, was slain by Kullos in that never-ending cycle. Those fighters passed on their stories of Michael, or 'Mickey' as they had taken to calling him, to their children and grandchildren. That gave rise to an Allorian myth that one day, Michael would once again have need of a force of brave warriors, wizards and clerics to fight by his side, and they would be honour-bound to answer his call to arms.

*****

Most of these details were unknown to Mandalee at the time, but she knew Michael had won that battle, and nothing they had done to Time could possibly alter that fact. Therefore, she could leave that second lot of demons to the demigod and history. But the monsters arrayed before her could not be allowed to complete their spell.

Taking a deep breath, she sent a sympathic message to Catriona, asking her to forgive the interference. She'd promised not to do it this time, but as a demon hunter, she just couldn't stand by and let this happen.

As she charged forward, Mandalee saw her friend's answer even before Shyleen spoke in her mind. The grass and other plants around the Greater Demons quickly grew to bind them in place, and the faintest hint of a rainbow road flickered before her, forming a bridge over the battlefield. The coloured light was gone in an instant so as not to draw too much attention, but Mandalee didn't need to see it.

Shyleen's voice entered her mind, '*You are never alone, Mandalee. You can trust that.*'

Mandalee smiled. Of course she could. It had been foolish of her to ever think otherwise. Trusting in her friend to keep the air solid beneath her feet, she sprinted over the heads of the fighting masses towards her targets.

She'd never fought so many Greater Demons at once before, but the key was not to allow it to be fifty against one, but one-on-one fifty times over. Her speed and skill made that possible, and as she felt the windy path beneath her begin to curve back down to the ground, she realised her friend could help her gain even more momentum. It was what Cat herself had done against Nalani. Embracing the trust exercise, then, Mandalee threw herself onto her backside on the invisible path, sliding all the way down. At the last moment, she jumped off and used her momentum to plunge her sword into a Greater Demon's neck. It died before it knew what hit it.

Leaping down to the ground, she ducked under the mighty blows of its two neighbours. She hamstrung and killed them. They collapsed before the others could even mount a defence, swiftly followed by another pair and then two more. Using the cover of a sudden deep fog, which she could counter with her Cat's Eyes spell, she darted around to the other side of the ring of demons. Her weapons sliced their way through vital arteries and severed tendons in a further half dozen Greater Demons.

Typically, Greater Demons could lash out with powerful magic. If they did, her magically resistant bodysuit should protect her, but she didn't know if it had been tested against demon magic. Hopefully, she thought, if they had designs on summoning whatever horror they had in mind, they wouldn't have the magic to waste, especially with their numbers cut down by a quarter.

She was wrong.

The remaining demons injured themselves, pulling free of Catriona's snare, but they didn't seem to care. Ignoring their bleeding wounds, they lashed out with magic, causing walls of air to slam into Mandalee from all sides. She was left with nowhere to go, which effectively nullified her super-speed. The invisible walls began to squeeze tighter, threatening to crush her, but before they could, the plants proliferated once more, towering above and reaching down to pull her free. She mentally thanked her friend. Three Greater Demons advanced on her menacingly, throwing magical bolts at her, but thanks to her super-speed, she was able to dodge them.

Catriona was doing her best to use crowd control druid magic to prevent any other demons from attacking her friend, but she couldn't hope to stop them all with plants alone. Her friend was sure to have a water bottle on her, she realised. With a bit of communication, she could get her to spill some. Freezing that into an ice wall as a more substantial barrier would be a simple matter. She was just about to suggest it when she had a better plan, plagiarising the demons' ideas and using air instead. Conjuring walls of air was no different to how she created her windy steps. They just required more interactive magic, demanding her constant attention to maintain, whereas her ice walls needed a source of water but, once formed, required no further thought.

Just before she worked that magic, however, she shot a few arrows, using the wind to guide them to their targets and, at the last moment, igniting them with her little-used wizard magic. Then, even as her windy walls protected her friend, she used more druid magic to turn her flaming arrows into a great conflagration. The flames grew into a ring, burning with fierce intensity. A further incentive for other demons to keep away.

Beside her, Renjaf gasped, "Did you do all that?"

Cat shrugged. "I told you: part sorceress, part druid, part archer. No reason I can't use all three at the same time!"

She wasn't too worried about revealing some of her powers to him. If history was back on track, he was going to end up a recluse who barely left his tower except to spite her. Who was he going to tell? Even if he did, who would believe him? He'd claimed a glowing Angel, which no-one else could see, was responsible for starting the demon invasion, so his credibility wasn't exactly high.

What did worry her was where these Greater Demons were going to get the energy required to complete their summoning. There was no way to do an exact calculation, but even a rough estimate of the available power was well short of the minimum they would need. Her fears were confirmed when, at the height of the spell, they simultaneously sliced open their throats, their blood flooding out and adding to their conjuring. Blood magic. She knew from Dreya how much more potent that could be, and that would definitely make up a significant percentage of the shortfall, but it must still be well short of what was needed.

But those demons wouldn't have sacrificed themselves for nothing. They must have been convinced they could do it.

Sure enough, as the last of the magic-infused demon blood spilt from their bodies, a ferocious-looking demonic monstrosity pulled itself up through the planes. The Angel chose this moment to vanish, Cat observed, although she suspected it was motivated by time rather than fear.

At more than thirty feet from head to tail, it towered above all others on the battlefield. Mandalee thought it looked something like a bipedal, wingless dragon, except it was covered in sharp spikes instead of scales. It opened its massive jaws and roared loud enough to wake the dead. Given the reddish glow of its eyes, the shiny metallic texture of its exoskeleton and the smell, the demon hunter began to wonder if it had somehow swallowed a blacksmith's forge. The other demons were clearly in awe of this hellish horror. Any that were not actively fighting for their lives took a moment to bow before it as if, to them, it was a king among demons.

Warriors had begun to arrive by now. Some on horseback, others on foot and still more teleported by mages. The magic users, grateful for the protection, did their best to let them make their way to the front lines. A small strike force had the misfortune to teleport close to this deep-level demon, attracting its attention. It strode forward to meet them, every step shaking the ground. The spears the warriors threw bounced off its metallic hide. Swords were equally useless. Catriona's barrier didn't even slow it down. Even fire worried it not at all.

The creature didn't rush to slay the mortals. It seemed to enjoy seeing their dawning realisation that there was nothing they could do against this monster. With another blood-curdling roar, it grabbed one of the warriors and physically pulled him apart, throwing the two bloody halves at the others, knocking them over like skittles. It stepped on the prone forms of two more, dissecting them with the claws on its toes. The demon king smashed the life out of a few more with a lash of its tail, then finally, it projectile-vomited molten metal like a volcanic eruption, killing the rest of the group.

Wizards and clerics alike began to assail the beast with magic with little success. Cat wanted to help, but she had her hands full, trying to keep all the other demons from getting too close to Renjaf or herself and maintaining a close watch on Shyleen. She was considering a mental call to Dreya, but Mandalee had other ideas. She was a demon hunter. She didn't care what foul realm this one was from – she was taking it down. Sheathing her sword, she raced towards the demon.

Mandalee had noticed the creature had a habit of flicking its tail up at regular intervals, so with precision timing, she leapt lightly onto it, using its powerful thrust to propel her upwards to land halfway up its back. The protruding spikes made for natural hand and footholds as she swiftly climbed higher, up to its neck. Using her thigh muscles to keep herself from falling, she flicked her dragonclaw daggers into her hands and plunged them into the base of its neck.

The monster roared in anger, fury and pain. It tried to dislodge her, but she held firm and struck again. Her daggers were small, but they were ultra-sharp. Ideal for slicing and cutting through its flesh. Its armoured exoskeleton was tough, but it was no match for dragon claws. The blood that began to pour from its wound was like molten lava, forcing Mandalee to use some cleric magic to keep herself from being scalded. A combination of a violent shake and the slick blood finally managed to dislodge her, but even as she slid down its back, her daggers formed a pair of clean slices. A colossal, clawed hand clamped around her and started to squeeze, but she refused to panic. Her own hands were free, and their motion was a blur as she repeatedly sliced at its thumb joint. It was forced to let go before she could cut it clean off, but it threw her to the ground with such force that she was momentarily stunned.

Seeing her vulnerable state, Cat had an idea.

"Renjaf," she prompted, "I think that demon hunter could use your help."

"What can I do?" he wondered.

"Mental magic?" she suggested. He'd told her that was how he escaped from the demons that attacked his home, and she'd seen him use it a few times since, against the demonic horde before them. Not to mention the way he'd tried to use such magic against her many years ago in the future when she demolished his tower to get her hands on a book that he would write as a result of what he'd seen today.

"Might not last too long," he warned, but he tried anyway. Catriona knew full well how fast Mandalee could be: she didn't need long.

This king of demons felt the magic assail its mind, trying to control it, and used its own mental strength to fight back. Renjaf was repelled from its mind after only a few seconds, but for Mandalee, Cleric of Nature, White Assassin and White Guardian, a few seconds were almost an eternity. While it had been distracted, she had momentarily sheathed her daggers, worked her cleric magic, and conjured a flame hammer. Spinning around and around to gain momentum, just as it returned its focus to her, she slammed it into the back of its left knee. It staggered and fell…straight into the demon trap she had set. It had been a hasty job – she'd obviously never tried to trap one of these creatures before. All she could do was conjure a larger version of the kind she'd used to capture Greater Demons. It might not contain it for long, but it would just have to be long enough.

Chapter 15

Mandalee's demon traps had come a long way since a young Catriona blundered into her early ones. Now they could contain a demon and drain its energy over time. For Lesser Demons, it could force them to Descend. Greater Demons could sometimes resist the process; she was sure this monster could, too. That was why the magic of her traps allowed her access, so she could go in and force the issue. In this case, she had no intention of letting this demon king escape back down to hell. She wanted the demon horde to witness its total destruction, to deter them from trying anything like it again.

Darting through the barrier, she reverted to her dragonclaw daggers, using them to slice through its hamstrings. Now, should it have the power to escape her demon trap, such power would do it no good when it couldn't even stand. Demons moved to rush to the scene, but that meant turning their backs on the growing numbers of mortal troops, leaving them vulnerable. At the same time, the sky overhead darkened, and hail began to fall. Where it landed, the individual hailstones quickly stuck together and grew into an ice wall, forming a semi-transparent barrier around the demon trap.

The demon king howled in pain as Mandalee resumed her work on the base of its neck. When the wound was sufficiently deep, she used a pair of swords to hold it wide open, allowing her to neatly separate the vertebrae before pulling its massive head from its shoulders. That done, she used simple levitation to make the head fly up and over the barrier to land amid the demon army.

At the same time, Catriona found what she was looking for. Even while she was fighting, snaring the enemy, and keeping tabs on Mandalee, Shyleen and Renjaf, she had been scanning the battlefield with her magic because what she'd just witnessed didn't make sense. Even with blood magic, there was no way Greater Demons alone had the power to summon that creature from the deep planes. Therefore, they had to be getting more power from somewhere. Now she'd found it. At first, it was a bit like catching a faint scent on the breeze, only for the wind to shift before she could identify it. It had taken her a while, but now she knew what it was: unstable higher planar energy infused with mortal magic.

Exactly what she would expect from one of the missing fragments. But how? The only fragment in this time was with Dreya at Calin's Tower.

Then something caught her eye – a tiny speck of blue light shimmering in the sky. She'd only seen it because of the way it reflected off her ice wall. It was a micro-portal, and now that she knew where it was, she could focus her senses and detect the stream of energy flowing through it. That's what the demons had used. That's where they'd got the extra power.

She still couldn't work out what the source of that power could be, but thanks to technical discussions with Dreya, she could determine where and when the portal originated by interpreting the sympathic readings.

Filing that thought away to deal with later, she took a leaf out of Mandalee's playbook and forced the portal to explode by forming one of her own in the same spot. No sooner had she done so, however, than a new, much larger portal opened not far from her position. For a moment, Cat feared what fresh trouble this might bring, but instead, it turned out to be salvation in the form of Ossian Miach Kaidool leading an army of more than ten thousand onto the battlefield. The demons suddenly found themselves in a real battle, their advantage having evaporated.

This wasn't their plan. The demonic realms wanted a permanent foothold in the mortal plane, and this world had opened the door for the demons through their practice of summoning. They had hoped to wipe out the mortals here, draining their energy, and they had gained much already, but it would do them no good if their invasion were halted here. The demon king was slain, and their source of higher planar energy was cut off, so they needed to spread out to survive.

The demons seemed to make the decision together without any observable communication passing between them. They began to fight even more ferociously than before, hacking, slashing, biting and magicking their way through the mortal army, but as soon as they got a sniff of freedom, they took it.

Catriona's ice wall shattered, and a triumphant Cleric of Nature burst free. That naturally drew Michael's attention. Catriona was thankful that they'd thought to wear perception filters. It could definitely create some issues with their Timelines if he met them now, a few decades early.

Seeing the headless corpse of the demon king, Michael's eyes widened.

"She slew that monstrosity by herself?" he remarked.

His question was largely rhetorical, just thinking aloud, but still, Cat couldn't resist replying.

"Well, she did have a bit of help," she countered, introducing Renjaf, and herself as Rose.

The demigod regarded her strangely and took in Renjaf with a glance. Cat realised he must have been probing for magic because he marvelled, "A cleric, a wizard and a druid working together? There's hope for your world yet!"

"That might not mean much to her if someone doesn't do something," Renjaf spoke up. He pointed to a group of about forty demons that, perhaps realising they were too close to the centre of the battle to escape, decided to take revenge on the assassin who was looking rather spent. "We have to help!"

Once again, Cat felt a stab in her heart. This version of Renjaf was so warm-hearted, but she knew it wouldn't last. The more he talked about the Angel that he believed started the Demon Apocalypse, the more people would ridicule him. When he refused to let it go and published a book that claimed the Angel was also appearing throughout history and using the Crystal Mage Staff to move the stars, things would only get worse.

Through splintering the Timeline during the Battle of Compton, Catriona had saved him from what was to come. Inadvertently, but she'd done it. She could have left it at that, but instead, she had actively manipulated the Timeline again to put him here in this time and place. All so he could see the Angel, write *Shifting Stars* and end up a bitter and twisted old recluse. He was going to all but erase himself from the world because that was better than continuing to suffer the humiliation of his peers.

The two people she loved most in the world thought she was being too hard on herself. After all, she wasn't forcing him to make those life choices, and she wasn't responsible for how other people would treat him. Plus, she hadn't really changed anything, just put things back.

Was that a valid excuse?

According to the *Chronicles*, aberrations in the Guardians' Timelines had to be avoided for fear of unleashing total destruction. But did that mean they were justified in using any means necessary to protect themselves? That seemed a bit convenient.

All that aside, Cat couldn't help thinking that Renjaf's fate could easily have been her own. They had both seen the Angel, both seen them do what they did with the staff. Cat had told other people, just like Renjaf, most of whom didn't believe her, but despite that, Cat couldn't let go any more than Renjaf could. No matter how many people had told her that she should. The only difference was that Catriona had found a few people who believed in her. Jacob was the first. He had helped her so much in the early days, and looking back, she felt guilty that she hadn't done more to tell him so. After Jacob came Mandalee with her ever-present leopard friend, Shyleen, and then Dreya. Add to that list Michael, Daelen, Sara and Jessica. Somehow, despite their remarkably similar experiences, Renjaf had ended up shunned and alone, whereas Catriona had become a celebrated Guardian of Time and Magic, surrounded by the love of friends.

The worst thing was that Cat knew Renjaf was right. Not his conclusion that the Angel was evil, but about everything else. His life and work should be celebrated, not forgotten. Yet history had to play out. That was her responsibility. When they faced Ulvarius, Cat had referred to it as her job. Mandalee had preferred the word calling. She was right. It was much more than a job, she realised, as she followed Michael's charge to the centre where Mandalee still fought valiantly. It was a privilege, a sacred duty, and sometimes…duty sucked.

With the aid of Michael and a group of fighters, Cat, Shyleen and Renjaf swiftly cleared a path to Mandalee, and not long after that, the battlefield was devoid of demons. People said the demon attack was over and declared victory, but the Guardians knew this was far from an end.

There would be four years of hell to endure in both Northern and Southern Alloria, and the two continents would never be the same again. Still, out of that would come the Accords, ending open hostility between clerics and wizards. Distrust and disagreement would remain, but this would be the last serious conflict between the different types of mage. It also saw an end to clerics summoning demons. Whether that was entirely down to individual restraint or an act of the gods refusing to grant that power any longer depended on one's religious beliefs.

To Mandalee, it was a distinction without difference.

Unfortunately, as she knew all too well, summoning did not entirely cease among wizards. Perhaps she could push for such a reform now that she was the White Guardian. Something to discuss with Dreya, she decided, rather than promote it herself. Probably better if it came from a wizard rather than a cleric.

The stench of death was all around, overpowering their senses. More than ten thousand were dead. Ten thousand people who wouldn't be going home to their loved ones tonight, or any other night.

It took all of Catriona's self-control not to throw her arms around Mandalee and tell her how glad she was that she was OK after fighting the demon king and the rest of the horde. She knew Shyleen was also craving some attention and reassurance from the friend with whom she shared a soul. Shyleen didn't like that Mandalee kept fighting these major battles without her by her side. But they knew they had to resist acting on such feelings for now. They could not afford to arouse suspicion that they knew each other, especially not with Michael around.

The demigod spoke to Mandalee with respect in his voice.

"You did well to slay this beast," he rumbled appreciatively. "Actually," he amended, "you did well just to survive. You all did."

"That's all I wanted to do," Renjaf grumbled. "Just survive. Live. I didn't ask to be dragged out of my home and shoved in the middle of a warzone. All because some Angel decides to Descend and unleash a plague of demons!"

'*Or because the Red Guardian of Time and Magic drags him here by manipulating the Timeline,*' Cat remarked to Shyleen.

"Angel?" Michael wondered.

Cat opened her mouth but was saved from having to say anything by a wizard – one of the few survivors from the onset of battle.

"Renjaf here seems to think it's all some Angel's fault," he smirked. "He says the Angel turned up, brought the demons and made the stars move."

Others laughed at the ridiculous notion. Cat and Mandalee didn't join in, but neither did they speak out in Renjaf's defence.

Michael didn't laugh, either, but he was clearly sceptical. "Did anybody else see this?" he wondered.

"Don't you know?" the wizard grinned, slapping Renjaf on the back in mock camaraderie, "The Chosen One here's the only one who could see this visitor from the heavens!"

"Perhaps," Michael ventured, "the fault really lies not with the Angels, nor with the stars, but with yourselves. If you play around with demons, don't be surprised when your world goes to hell."

"Look, I'm not saying we're blameless in all this," Renjaf insisted, "but that Angel appeared in the middle of the battlefield just before the demons started pouring out." The laughter caught on, but Renjaf was undeterred. "You can't tell me that's a coincidence. I'm telling you, the Angel brought them here!" The laughter began to spread throughout the battlefield. At that moment, many of them were too far away to hear what was being said and were just laughing as a release of nervous tension and relief at simply being alive, but that was about to change.

"You hear that, everybody?" the wizard shouted, using his magic to project his voice. "Beware, all of you! Renjaf says there are Angels among us! Angels among us!"

Hearing this, one of a group of Corolian Faery that had joined the fight spoke up. "There's an old Faery lullaby that translates as Angels Among Us."

"Sing it!" called out another voice in the crowd. "Maybe if we sing him a sweet lullaby, he won't be so scared of imaginary Angels coming to get us!"

"I'm not sure if I can translate all the words into the human language," the Faery faltered when the laughter died down, but the other Faery encouraged her, promising to help her fill in any blanks.

Accepting that, then she began, haltingly, "'*Angels among us, stars in the…night; Guard your rest*' – no, not Guard…" As she floundered, the Faery beside her suggested, '*Watch,*' but another advised it was more like, '*Watch over.*' "That's it!" she agreed. "'*Watch over your…sleep,*' not rest…"

At that point, Catriona excused herself and walked away, Shyleen by her side, maintaining her cover as her familiar. That lullaby was special to her, and she couldn't bear to listen to it being defiled in this way, used as a weapon to mock Renjaf. Especially when it was her fault that this was happening to him. She couldn't even bear to look at him as she walked away, betraying him with every step.

A short distance from the battlefield, Shyleen told Cat, '*It's not your fault. The fault lies with Kullos. He scattered those fragments in time and space. You, Mandalee and Dreya are just trying to clear up his mess.*'

'*But are we clearing it up, or just making more of a mess?*'

Not long ago, she had stood before the Council and argued that the Guardians were neither selfish nor incompetent. Now she wasn't so sure.

'*I think you are doing your best to deal with an almost impossible situation, and I defy anyone to do it even half as well.*'

Cat thanked her feline friend, but since they didn't need to keep up the pretence any longer, she suggested she should join up with Mandalee, who was approaching by a completely different route.

'*When she joins you, you should meet up with Dreya at Calin's Tower,*' she told Shyleen in her very best leopard speak. '*I have a quick errand to run first.*'

Shyleen was curious, as cats are known to be, but didn't question her, offering instead, '*That's the best I've ever heard you speak my language. Well done. It was almost as good as Mandalee.*'

Cat smiled at the high praise but remained silent as Shyleen slunk away.

Chapter 16

Opening her pocket dimension, Cat took out her notebook and wrote the co-ordinates that represented where the micro-portal had come from. She verified that they gave her the right sympathic impression before flicking back a few pages to find Dreya's handwriting. She found it – the six sets of co-ordinates where Kullos sent the fragments of his dimensional control device. There was one set in particular that she was interested in right now. She found it and compared it with her own symbols. They weren't a match, but they did share a key element. One that had massive implications.

For now, though, she filed that away for later discussion with the others. Before that, as she had told Shyleen, she had an important errand to run. It meant travelling further back into the past, further than she'd ever been before – more than nine centuries. About as close to Year Zero as it was possible to get. It needed to be done sooner or later, so there was no time like the present. She had reliable co-ordinates, so there was no danger. She just wanted to be alone with her thoughts for a while, and this errand didn't need the others, so it was ideal.

She found the co-ordinates written on a piece of parchment that she kept attached to her notebook, the co-ordinates for Ellinsford, long before Calin was even born, let alone had a tower built there. Written on the parchment was a letter that she had dug out of a pocket dimension under Calin's Tower. It had been left for her by a kind of self-aware copy of her Alternate Universe self as a clue to help her realise that she needed to unlock the *Nameless Book*, using the same keys as for her staff. The book turned out to be the *Chronicles of Magias*, which had given rise to the Guardians of Time and Magic. That other, original Tempestria had been unmade so that this one could survive, maintaining cosmic balance. That meant she and her fellow Guardians had to replicate the clues for their past selves. This would establish what the Chronicles called a 'Reinforcing Paradox.' Reading between the lines, the book hinted that this was a tool the Guardians would often employ to ensure critical points in history could not be altered.

According to the letter, this was her Second Intervention, whereas everything she did on Earth was her First. This time it would be the other way around, but she couldn't see why that would matter. As long as her letter *said* it was her Second, that was enough to preserve the Timeline. Besides, the voice from her staff had indicated that this was the Red faction's first attempt.

Since Dreya was waiting for her at Calin's Tower in this Time zone, Catriona also had exact co-ordinates for her return trip. As Time Interventions went, this one was about as straightforward as it got. It was time she started creating Temporal portals herself, rather than relying on Dreya all the time, and this was an easy opener. She just needed to compensate for Temporal Lensing.

She peered at the letter once more. After her signature, there was a cheeky postscript:

p.s. Tell our boyfriend, he was adorable when he was younger.

Years ago, in Calin's Tower, while Mandalee had first read the letter, another line had appeared on the back. A p.p.s., warning them of the imminent threat of Daelen's dark clone. At the time, Cat had joked that next time she was going to give herself more time. Only later had she realised it was another clue: where there was one time-delayed message, might not there be another?

Sure enough, not long ago, her staff had warned her that something significant had happened, and after a bit of searching, she looked at the letter and saw there was now a p.p.p.s., giving her a set of temporal-spatial co-ordinates. The spatial element was familiar to her as the site of Calin's Tower in Ellinsford. The sympathic impression of the temporal component matched the age of the parchment itself, just a few years since Kullos' strange weapon split Daelen StormTiger in two.

Acting on that information now, checking there was no-one around to see her do it, she opened a Prismatic Sphere and focussed on the co-ordinates. They wouldn't take her to the exact spot where she had to leave the letter. Instead, if she was interpreting them correctly, she would step out into Red Street, from where she would have a short walk to her destination. She didn't know why, but her other self must have chosen those co-ordinates for a reason, and she wasn't going to argue.

*****

Catriona stepped out of her portal without looking and immediately fell with a splash into the River Ellin, but the current wasn't fast, so it was simple to swim to the bank. Sitting there, her clothes water-logged and her hair a complete mess, she burst out laughing.

"Of course!" she cried. "I'm an idiot! Red Street doesn't exist yet!"

In her time, the river was long gone, replaced by the narrow passageway known as Red Street, leading to Calin's Tower. Cat knew that history very well, but she just hadn't thought. Her other self must have known that too, which meant she had done this deliberately as a kind of practical joke. It was also why she had chosen to seal the letter inside an airtight silver box, to protect it from the water.

"Oh, well done!" she called out to her other self as if, in some cosmic way, she might hear her even though she now technically never existed.

She had to admit the shock of the cold water had really helped her. After witnessing the terrible atrocities committed by Ulvarius, plus the horrific bloodbath that began the Demon Apocalypse, and her manipulation of young Renjaf to satisfy the demands of Time, this was a welcome moment of fun. It was a good reminder that history wasn't all death and disaster, and while her calling as Guardian came with burdens and responsibilities, they were offset by many extraordinary privileges. To swim in the water of the River Ellin, a few decades short of a thousand years before she was born, was mind-boggling.

At this stage in history, the population of Esca Isle consisted of only a few nomadic tribes. The conflict that this place would see wouldn't happen for centuries, yet. For now, as far as the eye could see, there was nothing but a green expanse of gently rolling hills, trees and flowers, birds, insects and wild animals. It was the beauty and majesty of nature arrayed before her, like a feast for her druid senses. A few minutes ago, she wouldn't have been in the right frame of mind to appreciate it properly, but a dip in the river had fixed that.

As she walked toward the spot where she needed to hide the letter, Cat began to use her magic to evaporate the water and dry herself slowly. It was a pleasant summer's day, so she was in no particular rush. When at last she reached the right spot, she used her magic to dig a deep hole in the granite bedrock. Then, when she was sure it was the correct depth, she opened a large pocket dimension at the bottom of that hole. She had copied the original letter, complete with its time-delayed clues, and she was ready to leave it for her younger self to find. Taking the small silver box out of her robes, Cat decided to open it one last time. As she did so, a few droplets of water dripped off her hair and landed on the page.

"So that's where those marks came from," she remarked to herself.

When she'd first seen them all those years ago in the future, she'd wondered if her magical copy had been crying at the time, having just walked away from her relationship with Daelen. But no, it was only a few droplets of water after she had been dunked in the river. At least, it was this time around.

She paused in her thoughts as realisation dawned: this time around, it wasn't some magical copy doing this; it was Catriona herself. In effect, she had just played a practical joke *on herself*. By her actions here, she would set in motion a series of events that would lead her to fall into the river and cheer herself up.

She had dunked herself!

But that was only possible because her younger self had made all the right choices to take her to Calin's Tower with Mandalee and Daelen in the first place. It was reassuring to know that free will still played its part.

Catriona closed the silver box, making sure the seal wasn't compromised in any way. Then she dropped it into the pocket dimension, manipulating the air to guide its trajectory, making its fall slow and gentle. When the box disappeared from view, the druidess reshaped the stone, smoothed it out and carved the three symbols that, in her personal shorthand, read: DIG HOLE HERE. That done, she cast a Timeless field over it so it would remain unaffected by the passage of time for the best part of a millennium.

Though her work was now done, she remained standing in silence, remembering the day Daelen and Mandalee lowered her younger self into that pocket dimension so she could solve the

Mystery of Calin's Tower. She bathed in the warm glow of nostalgia for a moment. She remembered being that young free spirit, off on a wild adventure. Not to save the world or correct anomalies in Time, but for the simple joy of discovery, of learning. She just had to know. As a Guardian, she had to be careful to avoid significant changes to her own Timeline, but even if she could change something about her past, she wouldn't want to.

Of course, she wished Daelen hadn't died at the Fall of Kullos. Wished she'd found a way to save him, but as the druidess placed a hand on her swollen belly, she realised that a part of him was still with her, growing inside her.

At that moment, as if in response to her thoughts, Catriona felt her baby kick for the very first time.

"Telling your Mum to stop standing around and get on with her life?" she asked her baby. Another kick. "Alright then," Cat chuckled. "That's me told! Let's go and see Dreya and Auntie Mandalee."

*****

Dreya watched as a portal opened in front of her. Out of the blue Prismatic Sphere leapt Mandalee and Shyleen. For once, her friend chose not to land on top of her, for which Dreya was grateful, given the state she was in,

"Sorry, Dreya. Just us," Mandalee said with a smile. "Shyleen says Cat's gone off on some errand or something."

The White Guardian was obviously in a good mood and rushed forward to hug her, but Dreya quickly stood and teleported out of the way.

"You are not coming near me covered in demon blood!" the sorceress insisted.

"But it's not the blood of just any demon," Mandalee objected. "It's the blood of a demon king from way down in the cosmic planes."

"I don't care if it's the blood of the Keeper of the Underworld; you're still not getting it on me."

"But Dreya, I killed it!" she bragged. "OK, I had a bit of help, but it was mostly me."

Dreya had to admit that was impressive, but while she was keen to hear all about it, she still maintained that Mandalee could keep the physical evidence to herself.

Mandalee held up her hands in surrender and sat down. "Alright, no hugs," she promised, but as soon as Dreya got close, she grinned and declared, "Sorry, I lied!" The White Guardian leapt at Dreya, forcing her to teleport again.

For the next five minutes, a giggling Mandalee kept trying to hug Dreya so she could cover her in the slimy stuff. She invoked her super-speed, but the Black Guardian's teleportation was quicker. Just. As much as Dreya was doing her best to avoid contact, she was soon laughing at the game as much as Mandalee.

The fun continued until a teenage girl approached them. She could be no more than seventeen, though she was trying to seem older as she wagged her finger, putting on her very best scowl.

"You two pack it in!" she scolded them.

The girl's White robes and official Sash of the Office of Calin's Tower identified her as the White Custodian. One of Calin's personal assistants and guards.

"This is a place of serious academic research and study," the Custodian fumed, "not a playground!" Then, taking in the sight of Mandalee, covered in demon blood, she warned her, "And don't even think about trying to enter Calin's Tower looking like that, young lady!"

'*Young lady?*' Shyleen wondered incredulously. '*When she's barely out of childhood herself? Someone has an over-inflated sense of their own importance!*'

Mandalee hid a smile as the girl continued, "There are outdoor facilities around the back that you can use…although," she wrinkled up her nose, "they can't work miracles."

"That's OK," the White Guardian replied, "I'm not planning on going inside anyway."

The girl breathed a visible sigh of relief. "Thank heavens for small mercies," she prayed, but the raised finger returned as she delivered a final warning. "Now, please, both of you, conduct yourselves with greater decorum, or I shall have you escorted off Esca Island entirely!"

The truth was, she didn't have that kind of authority. Custodians could eject someone from Calin's Tower, but not the whole island. Even so, Mandalee and Dreya acted suitably apologetic…at least until she disappeared back inside, at which point their suppressed laughter burst forth as they sat back down together.

"Wow!" Dreya remarked. "I can't remember the last time anybody told me off like that!"

"Me, neither!" Mandalee agreed, wiping away a tear.

*****

Having calmed down from her exhilaration, Mandalee told Dreya all that had happened, including a blow-by-blow account of her battle with the demon king.

"Aside from Kullos, that has to be the most powerful creature I've ever fought. Seriously, no-one else in that place could have done it," she bragged. "Well, apart from Michael, of course," she amended, "but he wouldn't have got there in time. He was busy destroying an Ostium."

Dreya's ears pricked up at that. "Michael destroyed an Ostium?" she wondered, trying to sound casually interested. "Where? When?"As a demon hunter, Mandalee knew far more about the Demon Apocalypse than Dreya.

"Strangely enough, it was at the ancient temple ruins, where his home is now. Maybe that's why he chose it," she speculated.

She supposed it made sense. That was the first time Michael had been free to act on his own, not just as Daelen's support. Now that he had his freedom, perhaps he saw that as a symbolic place to build a life.

"As for when, well, it was about the same time as it all kicked off where we were."

"Kicked off?" Dreya echoed. "Jessica expression?"

Mandalee nodded. "Catchy, aren't they?"

"Very," Dreya agreed. "So, how do you know about this Ostium business? Research?"

Mandalee snorted. "Research like that's more Cat's thing. No, while you were on honeymoon, I got chatting to Michael about my demon hunting days. That's when he told me all about the Ostium. I could see it so clearly as he told me. It sounded terrifying."

“Says the woman who slew a demon king!” Dreya said pointedly.

Dreya’s mind was racing. Since Mandalee had gained such a clear image from Michael, it was a simple matter for her to see it, too. Thanks to Renjaf’s fascinating research on mental magic, she didn’t even need to enter her friend’s mind, as such. While she was talking about it, it was as if she were projecting the image like one of those Earth movies. Adding that image to what Dreya already knew about where the other two Guardians had just been and the location of Michael’s home, the sorceress could generate precise temporal-spatial co-ordinates. Now the Black Guardian just needed to get her companions out of her hair for a few moments.

“Well, while we wait for Cat to turn up,” she said, “I suggest you make use of those facilities that the Custodian told you about. With all that demon blood on you, I have to say, you’re really starting to stink.”

‘*I wasn’t going to mention it,*’ Shyleen put in, in Mandalee’s mind, ‘*but she’s not wrong.*’

“Shyleen agrees with you,” Mandalee told her friend, standing and stretching out her aching limbs. ‘*Coming, Shyleen?*’ she asked the leopard.

‘*Oh, I’m not letting you out of my sight,*’ she assured her. ‘*We’ve been apart for too long on this trip as it is. It’s a miracle you haven’t got lost yet.*’

Mandalee laughed, and with a, “See you later,” to Dreya, they headed off.

“Well, Cat,” Dreya whispered to herself when they were gone, “if you can have a little solo side trip, then so can I.”

Chapter 17

Dreya stepped out of her portal just outside the temple ruins and closed it again while maintaining her Timeless connection. It was imperative that she not be seen. Not by any passers-by, not by the Greater Demons that were approaching, and most definitely not by Michael or the shadow warriors.

The demons chose a suitable spot for their magic and began their work. Dreya, confident in her Guardian abilities, stood close and studied the process intently. As she watched, a pool of darkness formed on the ground like a black whirlpool. Gradually, the pool began to thicken as if it were turning into an oil slick. Out of that ooze, a creature rose up with a flexing, bulbous head and flailing tentacles. It looked like an octopus in a tar pit, but Dreya could sense the magical power crackling through its body as it channelled energy from the mortal plane back down into the deeper realms. Out of those depths, demons began to appear. It was like a cross between exiting a portal and being born.

Ordinarily, there was no way any mortal could watch this happen up close without being in the fight of their lives. Even Dreya conceded she couldn't battle the demons with her magic and study this process in detail at the same time. But thanks to her powers as Black Guardian, she was so close, she could practically reach out and touch the Ostium, though she didn't.

After a few moments, three figures whooshed to a halt overhead: Daelen and Michael fighting the dark clone. Dreya couldn't be entirely certain about the extent of the shadow warriors' powers, so as a precaution, she took care to shroud her own. She watched as one of the Ostium's tentacles shot out and grabbed Michael, sensing the demigod's energy and seeking to use it, absorb it, but it had bitten off more than it could chew. Michael chopped off the offending appendage, which promptly grew back. The dark clone made good his escape, and Daelen, too, quickly portalled away, leaving Michael alone.

Dreya decided that it was time for her to leave, too. She didn't care about watching the battle. She had witnessed the formation of an Ostium, and through that, she'd got what she came for: a detailed analysis of how it worked to bring demons from the lower planes to this one. It would take time to study and think about what she had learned, but if her theory was correct, she should be able to adapt it for her own purposes. After all, travelling from the demonic realm, one level below, to the mortal plane was fundamentally no different from going from the mortal realm to the Pantheon of the gods. Yes, Alycia's Barrier was in the way, but according to the lioness god, Pryshia, that barrier was cracked. Surely the work of the Angel, Purity.

The Black Guardian was going to need to know where those cracks were and how to detect them, but she already had a plan in mind for that. Thanks to this mission to the past, she now had the beginnings of how she might Ascend, and once Dreya reached the Pantheon, with all the abundant energy resources there, the sorceress couldn't begin to estimate how much power she could gain.

Ultimately, if she was going to destroy Purity, she knew she would have to go much further than the Pantheon. All the way up to the shadow realm. To do that efficiently, she would need Kullos' dimensional control device. Otherwise, Ascending one layer at a time could take decades. Perhaps even centuries. Thanks to this trip, she had one more fragment in her possession. Added to the two stored safely in Daelen's Tomb, that was three out of six: halfway there.

All of a sudden, she decided as she stepped through the portal back to Calin's Tower just a few minutes after she left, things seemed to be coming together rather nicely.

*****

Catriona burst out of her portal and, seeing Dreya, she rushed to embrace her. Unlike Mandalee, she was not covered in demon blood, so the sorceress didn't object. She was, however, slightly damp.

"Oh, fell in a river. It's all good," Cat explained dismissively when her wife queried.

"Shame you didn't take Mandalee with you. She could have used a bath!" Dreya remarked.

"Well, mine did me a world of good, that's for sure," she agreed, "and not just physically."

Dreya couldn't help noticing the woman she loved was much happier about things than she had been when she left. "I take it your little side-trip was productive?"

Cat nodded. "Yeah, but that's not the best part!"

She placed Dreya's hand on her belly, and for a moment, the sorceress wasn't sure what she was supposed to be feeling, but then the baby kicked.

"Wow!" Dreya gasped, her face lighting up in a broad smile. "That's amazing!"

Just then, Mandalee ran over with Shyleen. The White Guardian was certainly looking a lot cleaner. She was wearing her combat suit, having decided to ditch her white leather entirely, accepting that it was ruined.

"Is this a private party, or can I join in, too?" she asked.

Without a word, Cat grabbed her hand and placed it next to Dreya's. Her reaction was much the same, and Cat quickly found herself in a three-way cuddle with the two most important people in her life. Plus one leopard, of course, who promptly offered her congratulations.

When Mandalee broke the hug, however, she was wearing a puzzled look.

"Wait! I thought we'd established you were at most sixteen weeks along, on a typical half-Faery pregnancy scale."

Cat nodded. "I was. I definitely was," she agreed, "but now I seem to be at least two or three weeks further along."

"How?" Dreya wondered. "Did you go off on holiday for a fortnight without telling us?"

Cat laughed. "Of course not. I've been in the Timestream for no more than one full day, maximum."

"So, like Dreya says, 'how'?" asked Mandalee.

Cat did her best to explain that this development only confirmed a theory she'd had in her mind for a while. It didn't seem to matter whether she was in the present, the past, on another world where Time flowed differently, or even Timeless. It was as if her baby had a relationship with Time that was unique. Beyond such considerations.

"Remember, my baby is half Shadowkin, and we barely know anything about what that means," Cat told them.

"Sounds scary when you put it like that," Mandalee worried, but Catriona refuted that with an emphatic shake of the head.

"Absolutely not. My baby's going to be amazing. Perfect."

Dreya thought that was all the more reason she should find a way to reach the shadow realm, to find out more about them. By dissection, if necessary. Mentioning none of this to the others, she simply asked, "So, what now?"

"Well," Cat replied. "I suggest you pop your fragment in our Meadow, so it's safe, and then we do what Mandalee said: go and join a party."

"That's not quite what I said," Mandalee objected with a crooked smile. "Not that it's anything less than a stellar idea," she clarified quickly. "Where did you have in mind?"

"I know the perfect place," Cat replied. "Right here."

Dreya looked around sceptically. "Doesn't seem like the ideal party place to me," she pointed out. "We already got told off once for having fun out here."

Mandalee backed her up, telling Cat about the incident with the White Custodian.

Cat nodded. "That'll be Kadessa."

She knew her in her own time, fifty years in the future. She was the longest-serving Custodian in history and had a rather large chip on her shoulder about it. Kadessa was a stickler for rules and protocol who considered Catriona a 'disruptive influence'. By contrast, in Catriona's opinion, Kadessa enjoyed rules and her own authority way too much.

"But she won't be in a position to complain, this time. No, this is absolutely the right place; we're just a bit late, that's all."

"How late?" Mandalee asked, catching on.

"Oh, not much. Only about a hundred and twenty years."

"That's practically now, to a Guardian," Dreya considered. "Do you have the co-ordinates?"

Cat assured her that she did. She had been working at Calin's Tower a lot, where she had studied more about the conflict that had blighted the island in years gone by. The druidess had even helped to design the new information plaques that were going up around the Tower and along Red Street. She had got the idea from similar things she had seen on famous buildings on Earth during her honeymoon with Dreya. Calin loved the idea of having small nuggets of information about the history of the troubles on Esca Isle that people could wander up to and read. Cat had helped to construct a basic timeline of events, culminating in the ceasefire, peace talks and Armistice celebrations.

Those celebrations, about a hundred and twenty years ago from their current time zone, included the destruction of some terrible magical weapons that had been constructed during the war. Effectively turning them into a harmless fireworks display. Some people started singing. Musicians started playing. There was dancing, drinking, laughing, and the whole event turned into an impromptu party.

Catriona knew the precise co-ordinates, not just from the history books but, better still, from Calin's memories, because at the tender age of twenty-two, she'd been there.

"Wouldn't that be something?" Cat remarked. "To see the Armistice happen? To be there at that celebration of peace? Even to meet Calin herself. We've still got our perception filters, so she won't recognise us. Besides, it'll be more than a hundred and fifty years before she meets us again, and by her own admission, she got very drunk that day."

"Sounds like my kind of party!" Mandalee agreed.

*****

The Guardians portalled a discreet distance from the action, on the outskirts of Ellinsford town. They didn't want to upset the peace process by scaring people with a big blue door in midair. They began walking and soon joined up with others who were heading toward the ceremony in the centre. Before long, they found themselves in a large crowd.

When they reached the centre, Cat couldn't fail to notice that the table on which the official Armistice Treaty was to be signed was as close to her Mystery carving as her magic would allow. At that table sat four individuals.

General Gaspar from the Eastern side was human, while Vitius was of the Escanian Faery, although the conflict was not divided on racial grounds but rather religious ones. They were sitting next to each other in the middle, while their eldest child flanked them.

Upon the table lay the peace treaty as ratified by both sides, which each of the four would sign. Though there was no concept of right of succession on either side, it was a symbolic gesture: a promise that the peace brokered here today would be honoured by future generations.

The thirty-year-old son of the Eastern faction's general was called Tayne, a Black robe cleric. His Western counterpart, the eldest daughter of Vitius, was Aerith, known to be a fierce warrior.

In the sight of the crowd, in the flickering flaming torchlight, as the town hall clock struck midnight, the document received its first signature: Gaspar of the Eastern faction. He passed it across to Vitius, who added his name alongside him as the leader of the Western side. Drying sand was sprinkled on the two signatures so the ink would not smudge. Next was Tayne, representing the next generation of Eastern Esca. With much reverence, he accepted the document and carefully dipped the quill into the inkpot. Removing it, he tapped it a couple of times to dislodge any excess droplets and then slowly, carefully inscribed his signature beneath that of his father. As he did so, Aerith sprang out of her seat, flicking a concealed dagger into her hand and leapt across the table at Tayne.

The Guardians didn't even think; they just acted out of instinct. They were together, so their powers were at their peak. They Froze Time.

It took them a moment to fully realise what they'd done, but when they did, they were left with a rather important question: what now? They couldn't keep Time Frozen forever.

The Black and White Guardians left the task of answering the question to Catriona, knowing that she was more familiar with how these events played out in history.

Catriona wasn't sure.

"I know I've read something about this, but I can't remember the details."

"That's useful!" Mandalee snarked. "Sorry, but I came here for a party, not to mess around with Time some more!"

"There has to be a way to find out what really happened here," Dreya insisted.

"I think there is," Cat replied with a gleam in her eye that her companions knew well. "I have a ridiculous radical plan."

"Of course you do," her best friend remarked.

"What is it?" Dreya wondered.

"I'll ask Calin."

Cat reminded her fellow Guardians that she had been working on making all the books in Calin's Tower Timeless. That meant she could simply look up the historical record of this day, secure in the knowledge that it would be the version of history that related to the established Timeline.

"But that means travelling back to our own time, and if you leave here, we can't hold back Time with just two Guardians," Dreya objected.

"I think you can, for this small area for a short time, and a short time is all I need." She had been collating information on this very event for the new plaques, and one of the principal references Catriona had used was Calin's personal memoirs. "We know she's here in the crowd, somewhere. She's a part of these events. Do you really imagine she didn't bother to mention this moment in her writing?"

"OK, but how does that help us with holding back Time?" Mandalee wanted to know.

"It doesn't," Cat accepted, "but I know something that might."

The others weren't seeing it, so she gave them another hint.

"While two Guardians may not be enough to Freeze Time in the first place, sustaining a Frozen Timefield that's already been created is another matter." She reminded them that during the Fall of Kullos, the Catriona of that universe had helped them save their Tempestria, but the Mandalee and Dreya of that world were unable to spare the energy to even speak because they were busy holding back an onrush of true destruction, the power of *IT*. "The only way they could do that was to keep Time Frozen, and if they could do it, so can you."

"But Cat," Dreya objected, "our other selves were using some of the higher planar energy from a Heaven's Surrender blast to power their magic. Even I don't have that kind of power. You'd need a shadow warrior for that."

"Or at least some of their technology," Mandalee suggested.

"Ten points to Mandalee!" Cat exclaimed with a snap of her fingers.

"No!" both Guardians gasped at once, realising what she was suggesting.

"Yep!" Cat affirmed, nodding. "We have some shadow warrior technology or, at least, a fragment."

Chapter 18

"You can't be serious!" Dreya objected.

"I'm always serious about what I do," Cat protested. "Just not necessarily the way I do it. The fragment's waiting for us in our Timeless Meadow, where I'll have to go anyway to get back to our Time."

"To be fair, Dreya," Mandalee put in, "even Ulvarius managed to use a fragment pretty successfully for weeks. Surely you can do better for a short time?"

"But the power is unstable!" Dreya objected.

Cat shrugged. "So is blood magic, and you know what you always say about that: it just needs control."

"You are the Mistress of control," Mandalee insisted helpfully.

"No-one's suggesting you do this long-term," Cat assured her, "but I'm confident you can control it enough for what we need now."

Dreya wasn't so sure. "I can't decide whether you're being supportive or ganging up on me," she grumbled.

The Black Guardian knew her control was not what it once was, thanks to that presence in her mind. The entity that had resisted all attempts to put it back in its cage. Stabilising a fragment for transport was one thing. To attempt to use that power was another matter entirely. The presence in her mind was willing to help her control this power for what she needed, but predictably, it was demanding that more of itself be released in exchange. It knew how she felt about paying debts and was using that to manipulate her. She knew she should refuse, but then Catriona, the woman Dreya had vowed she loved even more than magic, spoke those six fateful words.

"Will you do this for me?"

"Of course I will, Cat," was Dreya's only possible answer.

"We both will," Mandalee concurred. "Although I have no idea how to incorporate higher planar energy into my magic. I guess I'll have to learn quickly."

Dreya promised to help her with that. During their time fighting Ulvarius, the sorceress had learned to feed her power to others. She'd done it again to help Mandalee after Nalani almost killed her. It was the same principle, and she could filter out the more unstable parts of the energy to make it easier for the White Guardian to work with.

Before that, while the Black Guardian prepared herself, Cat asked her friend to open a portal back to their Timeless Meadow so she could retrieve the fragment. Having done that, Cat opened her own portal to Calin's Tower in their own Time zone and quickly ran inside to find both Calin herself and her memoirs.

*****

Pushing her way through the other library users, Catriona hurried along the corridors and passageways, firing off apologies as she went. She had come to know this place as well as the Black Tower in her time working there. It was a home from home. Calling upon that knowledge, the druidess tried to stick to the less well-travelled routes and quieter sections as much as possible. As the Red Guardian sprinted through the centre of the tower, she allowed herself a small smile at the sight of the three carved symbols that translated as 'Dig Hole Here'. Symbols she had carved a few minutes ago – or more than nine centuries, depending on one's perspective.

Wasting not a moment, Cat headed for the spiral staircase that led up to her office, where she worked when she wasn't otherwise occupied saving the world. At the foot of those stairs, Cat skidded to a halt and paused to take a breath before beginning her climb. It was at times like this that she missed shapeshifting. Time was, she would have chosen to shift to owl form and fly up in favour of walking. However, her baby chose that moment to give Catriona's insides a kick as if to remind her that that was no longer an option.

As if she might somehow forget she was pregnant!

There being no other option, she resigned herself to it and climbed the steps to the fifth floor, which was reserved for staff only. It only took a minute or two more to get to her office and grab the book she needed. It was on top of the pile, still open at the page she had been studying when she was last here.

No sooner had she left her office than she was off and running again, nose in the book as she headed for Calin's private quarters. Since it was currently outside office hours, that was where she would be. Cat vaguely heard a few other staff members call out in greeting, but she ignored them. She didn't mean to be rude, but time was of the essence. She didn't want Dreya and Mandalee to have to tap into the unstable power of that fragment any longer than absolutely necessary. However, after narrowly avoiding colliding with a pair of young acolytes, a voice rang out that she could not so easily ignore.

It was the voice of an elderly woman wearing White robes and the official sash of the Custodians.

"Catriona Redfletching, stop right there this instant!" she ordered. Age had not dimmed the power of her voice, even if it was an octave lower than it had been in her youth. Cat jogged to a halt and turned to face her.

"Kadessa!" she greeted her with false enthusiasm, a fake smile plastered on her face. "I was just talking about you earlier today." Or about five decades ago. Once again, it was a question of perspective.

"It's *Mistress* Kadessa to you, young lady!" she insisted.

"We've had this debate before," Cat replied wearily, "and I don't have time to repeat it just now."

According to protocol, the Custodians were ranked behind no-one save Calin herself and ultimately the Triumvirate. However, the Guardians had carved out a niche position for themselves that existed somewhat at a tangent to the established chain of authority. That was something Kadessa found quite irksome. She maintained that there had been no change to the role of the Custodians, and she was the senior Custodian. Therefore, she was still Mistress Kadessa to anyone except those four people.

Catriona didn't actually care about the title either way, but the more Kadessa insisted, the less inclined she was to use it. That was simply her nature.

"Now, if you'll excuse me, Kadessa, I need to see Calin."

She made to walk away, but the dour, white-haired sorceress stopped her.

"When Mistress Calin is off duty, the correct procedure is to request an audience through one of her Custodians. Not to go tearing through her tower like a dragon with its tail on fire. I will not have you treating this sacred place as a playground for your amusement. The rules apply to everyone, even Guardians. If there are any more incidents like this, I shall eject you from the premises!" Being privy to the precise details of the tower's security, the Custodians were quite capable of teleporting any individual outside. "Don't test me, Catriona! Just because I'm retiring doesn't mean I will allow standards to slip. Now, if you would care to make an appointment for an audience with Mistress Calin, I will check her availability."

"Great, thanks!" Cat spat in reply. "Of course, while you do that, at a critical moment in the past, the events that led to the creation of this tower are in jeopardy and could collapse at any moment. But never mind that, *Mistress* Kadessa. You just keep on making sure your precious rules are being obeyed."

Kadessa glowered at her. "You'd say anything!"

Catriona fought to control her temper. That crossed a line for her. It wasn't so much the implication that she was lying. She wasn't as firmly against that as Dreya – Cat would lie if she believed the situation warranted it. But the idea that she would make up an imaginary catastrophe in Time just to get her own way was offensive.

"Whether you want to believe me or not, Kadessa," Cat growled through tight lips, "the fact is, if events don't unfold the way they're supposed to, it could mean the end of everything relating to this tower. You got that? Everything! Even your pension!" She paused as she was suddenly struck by something Kadessa had said. "Wait – you're retiring?"

Kadessa nodded. "I was the youngest ever Custodian," she told Cat, for about the millionth time since they'd met, "and after working here for over fifty years, I shall forever be officially known as the longest-serving Custodian. So, I've decided it's time to retire."

Cat elected not to point out that while fifty years' service was impressive for a human, a Faery could easily match that three times over. Calin herself, approaching two hundred years old, was proof of that.

Instead, she offered, "Oh, congratulations! You must let me give you something to mark the occasion."

With an impressive display of false modesty, Kadessa protested that it wasn't necessary, but Cat insisted. Opening her pocket dimension, she pulled out a bouquet of flowers. She had picked them up from Earth on her honeymoon, intending to leave them next to Daelen's body that was held in stasis in his Tomb. She thought the gesture would be appropriate since it was Daelen who had taken her to that world in the first place. Unfortunately, with everything that had happened since her return, she hadn't got around to it. Still, they were perfectly fresh – pocket dimensions seemed to have a kind of preservation effect. Now, with perhaps the fate of this world being held in the balance, she was sure her shadow warrior friend would have supported her decision to use them for another purpose. Handing them to Kadessa, the old woman's face momentarily softened as she accepted them and thanked her.

Rather than the customary, 'You're welcome,' however, Cat replied with, "I'm sorry."

"Sorry?" Kadessa echoed with a confused look. "What—?" but she didn't get any further as the flowers grew rapidly. The stems neatly wrapped around her body, and the leaves covered her mouth. The flowers wouldn't hurt her, but they did immobilise and gag her quite effectively while Cat sprinted away.

"For that!" she called back.

*****

Calin was remarkably calm and unsurprised as the Red Guardian burst into her chambers. "Come in, why don't you?" she remarked drily.

Without preamble, Cat asked, "The Armistice. What do you remember about the signing?"

"Why don't you just look in there?" Calin asked, indicating the book in Catriona's hand.

The druidess shook her head. She'd already seen what she needed to see in the book, but she wanted to hear it from Calin, too. "Picture the scene," Cat coached. "The clock strikes midnight, and the two generals, Gaspar and Vitius, have just signed the Treaty. Gaspar's son, Tayne, adds his signature. What happens next?"

When Calin told her, Cat was much relieved.

"Congratulations," the druidess smiled. "Your account matches what's written in the book."

"Well, I should think so, considering I wrote it!"

Cat quickly explained that the books in Calin's Tower were Timeless, thanks to her, but Calin herself wasn't. Therefore, any discrepancy between Calin's account and that of her book could have indicated a change in the Timeline.

"Or a problem with my memory," Calin pointed out.

"Agreed," Cat nodded, "but since they match, I'm saved from having to pick that apart, and I know that what we're doing is fulfilling history, not changing it.

"Speaking of your memory, I need to know what you looked like back then, when you were young."

There was no photography back then, but thanks to Catriona's sympathic link, Calin could project an image of herself at that age. The image was a bit hazy, but it was clear enough for her purposes.

"Got it," the druidess confirmed and thanked her. "Now I've got to get back. My fellow Guardians are doing something incredibly reckless and dangerous right now."

"Why?"

"Because I asked them to."

"Ah, I see," Calin smiled knowingly. "One of your ridiculous radical plans?"

"You know me too well!" Cat grinned and dashed out of the room.

She ran back to where she'd left Kadessa tied up and asked the flowers to release her.

"How dare you!" she demanded, her face an ever-deepening shade of red. "An assault on a Custodian! Why, I've never known such a thing in all my years!"

"Sorry, but I was in a hurry, and you were in the way."

"Impudent child!" Kadessa gasped indignantly. "This time, you've gone too far, and by the authority vested in me as White Custodian, you are hereby officially banished from Calin's Tower!" With that, she inscribed the spell in midair, and an instant later, Catriona found herself back outside.

"Thanks, Mistress Kadessa," Cat thought aloud. "Teleportation certainly beats running, and I was not looking forward to all those stairs."

Wasting no time, Cat opened a Prismatic Sphere to her Timeless Meadow. Closing it behind her, she grabbed something she needed and leapt through the portal Mandalee was keeping open, taking her back to her fellow Guardians.

*****

Taking in the scene before her, Cat couldn't help noticing things weren't quite the same as when she left.

"Is it just me, or is Aerith a few inches closer to Tayne, now?"

"It's not easy maintaining a Frozen Timefield without you here," Dreya objected, "so yes, events may have advanced slightly. Plus, as Ulvarius discovered, the power of these fragments flares up and splutters out without warning."

"Yeah, and I've never used higher planar energy at all before," Mandalee objected. "It's all very well for you, Cat. You just get one of your ridiculous radical ideas in your head and then swan off to Calin's Tower for a chat!"

"You've only got yourselves to blame," Catriona pointed out facetiously. "You two broke Kullos' control device in the first place!"

"Because you told us to!" Mandalee shot back.

Cat rolled her eyes. "I didn't tell you to lose the fragments in time and space! Anyway," she rushed on before the others could protest further, "you only need to hold back Time a moment longer. I know what to do. Just be ready to drop the Frozen Timefield the instant I say."

'*Shyleen, I need your help,*' Cat projected telepathically in the language of leopards. '*The instant time resumes, leap up, knock Aerith off-balance and get out of there quick because there's going to be magic flying your way.*'

While Shyleen got herself into position, Cat scanned the crowd, looking for someone, focussing on where she ought to be. She found her: a young dark-haired Faery woman in Red robes, holding a staff topped with her family crest. The symbol that represented the House of Vitius. Her name was Calin. As the second-born daughter, she had no official role in the day's proceedings, but she believed in the peace process wholeheartedly. She had plans for this place, which did not include continued fighting.

She had been watching the signing intently and was alert to her sister's body language even before she sprang out of her seat. Calin's face was currently frozen in an expression of horror at what Aerith was doing with that dagger in her hand. The next thing Calin knew, she, too, was suddenly holding a dagger. One with a strange, jagged blade, like a stylised lightning bolt, emitting a most peculiar magical signature. She didn't have time to worry about that, but it did provide the spark of inspiration as Calin brought forth her own magic to conjure a real lightning bolt at her sister. She didn't hold back – sister or not, Aerith's actions could escalate the conflict and cost hundreds, if not thousands, of lives. Calin had to stop her, but even as she wrote in the air, she was convinced she would be too late.

When she was mid-spell, a leopard appeared out of the darkness. Time returned to normal, and the leopard sprang at Aerith before disappearing into the night once more. It was only a glancing blow; anything more and Calin might have missed her target, but as it was, it bought her the time she needed as Aerith fought to regain her balance and the momentum to strike at Gaspar. The electrical bolt slammed into her, throwing her clear of the signing table, to land smouldering on the ground.

Calin ran forward, taking care to drop her knife to avoid anyone misunderstanding her intentions. She never even noticed someone dressed all in white streaking past to retrieve it.

She did notice that Aerith was beginning to stir; her magic hadn't killed her. Guards surrounded Aerith in a heartbeat and dragged her to her feet. Even as they looked to Vitius for guidance, Calin checked that Tayne was unharmed – he was thanks to her – and then took the pen from him so she could sign her own name in Aerith's place.

Aerith struggled futilely in the guards' grasp, screaming, "Traitor!" at her sister. "How can you side with these monsters?"

"I'm not siding with anyone," Calin replied evenly, "because there are no sides any longer. The war is over, and the only monster I see here is you."

"They're evil, don't you see that?" Aerith cried. "They desecrated our dead! How can you – any of you – even think of appeasing them after all they've done? You're all traitors!"

"We desecrated theirs, too," Calin pointed out, "out of ignorance."

The people from the Eastern side of Esca believed in placing the body of the deceased face up, allowing the soul to fly out into the cosmos to explore for eternity. Those on the Western side believed in placing the body face down so that their soul could rejoin the soul of the world, from where it had originally come. During the conflict, each side had been treating the enemy fallen according to their own beliefs, which only fanned the flames of war even hotter. Only recently had the truth come to light. Hence the Treaty.

"That's different!" Aerith insisted. "Our beliefs are right!"

Chapter 19

Calin magically projected her voice to the assembled crowd, saying, "My sister's prejudice and intolerance is something our world can ill afford. The truth is our Western neighbours believe differently from those of us on the Eastern side. Our failure to understand that cost thousands of people their lives over many generations. We accused them of desecrating our dead, and they, in turn, accused us of desecrating theirs. Then, at last, we started talking *to* each other instead of *at* each other. More importantly, we began to listen. We exchanged information, shared our knowledge, and we learned a vital truth: we're all guilty, and our crime is ignorance. We cannot change the past, but we can choose what happens in the future."

"Well said," her father approved. Turning to the leader of his former enemies, he addressed him formally, "Lord Gaspar, I humbly apologise for the unforgivable attack on your son. Aerith acted on her own in wilful ignorance, against the wishes and best interests of both our peoples. I will not shield or protect her from the consequences of her actions. Her life is yours to take if that is your wish. All I ask, I beg, is that you recognise the signature of my second daughter as the fulfilment of the Treaty."

In the end, Aerith was imprisoned but spared execution in the interests of peace, and the Treaty was upheld, thanks to Calin.

Seizing the moment, Calin once again projected her voice to make what would prove to be a historic announcement.

"With this Armistice, I propose a new struggle against the true enemy: ignorance. To combat this requires knowledge.

"To that end, I shall build, here on this very spot, a great tower. A beacon. A library. The most magnificent library in the world. At its centre shall be the Mystery of Esca Isle." She pointed to the smooth rock on which the three unknown symbols were carved. "This has lain here for centuries. It saw our conflict begin, and now it has witnessed its end. We may never know what it says or whether it means anything at all, but now that this land is safe, people on both sides of the ocean will flock to see it and puzzle over it. Then, when they come here, they will have free access to my library and the knowledge it contains. People will learn, they will understand, and then they will leave, taking some of that knowledge and understanding with them wherever they go, and we will all be richer for it. Who will support me in this endeavour?"

Tayne was the first to stand and declare, "I will! You saved my life, you saved the whole of Esca, and I am sure that one day Calin's Tower will help to save the world!"

Their two fathers each added their own endorsement, and soon the whole crowd were chanting, "Calin's Tower! Calin's Tower! Calin's Tower!"

They were still chanting even as the music started playing. The chanting changed to singing and laughing. Local brewers brought beer, ale and wine from their stores, and the party was soon in full swing.

The two leaders gave the order to begin the destruction of their most terrible magical weapons, creating a fireworks display in the night sky. Calin herself quickly grabbed a beer and downed it in one. With the events of the last few minutes, she needed it. A couple more drinks and a whole lot of dancing later, as the lightshow in the air continued to sparkle among the void storms, Calin thought she saw something. Or perhaps someone. A glowing figure. The entity appeared to have a wooden staff in their hand, at the top of which was a blue crystal. That crystal began to emit a new light of its own, high in the sky, to join the fireworks. A few moments later, the entity was gone, and that was the end of it…except, if she didn't know better, she would say that a handful of stars weren't in quite the same positions anymore.

Nobody else seemed to have noticed anything out of the ordinary, and when she brought it up, the only response was from Tayne.

"Wow, Calin, how much have you had to drink?"

Considering the question carefully, she decided, "Not enough!" and grabbed another beer as she resumed dancing and forgot all about it. Nor did she notice a trio of young women off to one side, standing in the dark with a great golden leopard.

"I knew it!" Cat cried triumphantly.

While researching the conflict on Esca Island, she had come across a few sketches of the night the Treaty was signed. It wasn't entirely clear, but the starry sky looked slightly different before and after the event. Intrigued, she had vowed to visit. Now the opportunity had presented itself, and she could see she was right. Her Angel had appeared, and once again, the stars shifted.

"Wait, this is why you brought us here?" Mandalee wondered. "I thought we came to party."

"I often have multiple reasons for doing things," Cat replied. "You know that."

This appearance of her Angel also proved something else to Catriona's mind. All the previous confirmed instances were during terrible events such as the mass murder of the village of Quernhow by Ulvarius, the start of the Demon Apocalypse, and the day the Monster destroyed Catriona's home and family. But today, there was no such disaster. On the contrary, the war was over, crisis averted. Unlike Renjaf, Cat had never believed her Angel was the cause of those catastrophes, but she couldn't rule out that they might be a herald of disaster. Today did not fit that hypothesis. So, if the link wasn't disaster, what was it? Looking up at the fireworks, Cat thought she had the answer because it wasn't really a fireworks display; it was the destruction of powerful magical weapons. It was a turning point. That, Catriona now believed, was the common thread. It even fitted with the day the stars had moved for her when she unlocked Time magic and formed the Guardianship. A major event in magical history.

Satisfied that all was now as it should be, the Three Guardians finally got down to some serious partying.

*****

Returning to the present, via Catriona's Meadow, Dreya made sure to use specific Temporal co-ordinates this time. She didn't want to accidentally skip two years again. A quick check of the date confirmed that they had returned the day after they left.

That done, they needed to verify that the Timeline was restored correctly. Dreya confirmed *Shifting Stars* was back on her shelf, and the other books that were supposed to reference it did so once more. Cat popped them all safely in her pocket dimension. She was going to need them.

Catriona checked her personal records and cross-referenced them with the Council. Both agreed that she had once been summoned to a Conclave to answer charges brought by Renjaf. Exactly as she remembered.

Meanwhile, Mandalee took a trip to Compton and had a chat with both people and animals in the local area. All confirmed that the White wizard was indeed a grumpy old recluse who rarely left his home. It seemed history had not been kind to him. They couldn't be certain of the details, but it wasn't hard to work out.

He had told people about the Angel he had seen, convinced they were some terrible threat. Nobody believed him. He did research and discovered a connection to the shifting pattern of stars. The trouble was, the further back in time he looked, the less clear the star charts became. That made it difficult to prove. Even if people accepted the idea of the stars moving, the idea that it was the work of an invisible Angel sounded ludicrous. His work was scorned and ridiculed. Opportunities that might otherwise have come his way were given to other, more stable individuals instead. When Cat had first met him, he had told her that he was refusing to help her because nobody in his life had ever done anything for him. Now she knew why.

She had worked to fix up his garden and bought him things, naively thinking that might make him more inclined to help her in return. As if a spot of gardening and a few pastries could make up for a lifetime of rejection. Cat couldn't help feeling partly responsible for that. Restoring the Timeline in the past had been her duty. It had been the right thing to do – she had to believe that – but maybe there was something she could do now.

To that end, Catriona asked her fellow Guardians to hold off on bringing their fragment before the Council as proof of a job well done. She wanted to talk to Calin first.

To appease Kadessa, Catriona went through official channels to request an audience. She even referred to the retiring White Custodian as 'Mistress Kadessa.'

Greeting Calin, Catriona asked her to confirm her memory of the signing of the Armistice Treaty. Catriona was much relieved to find it unchanged and entirely in line with history. However, the Red Guardian could fill in more details of what happened that night.

"The leopard that leapt at my sister and knocked her off balance – that was Shyleen?" Calin marvelled when Catriona explained. "Mandalee's other half, as it were?"

Cat nodded. "It was the first time she'd been able to travel through Time with us, and in doing so, she fulfilled history. You always said that even with that distraction, you didn't know how you had time to stop Aerith from killing Tayne and shattering the peace process," Cat reminded her. "Well, the truth is, you didn't, or you wouldn't have if not for us. While I was here, talking to you about this, the others were busy keeping Time frozen, which isn't easy with just two. When I rejoined them, I had to make sure things played out as they did before. There's only one way, as far as I know, to break a non-Guardian out of a frozen Timefield – the Timeless dagger."

"The jagged blade!" Calin gasped. "It just appeared in my hand. I never understood where it came from or where it went, but it was you. It was always you!"

Cat nodded.

"And the Council accused you all of selfishness and incompetence when Mandalee took that dagger from Nalani instead of the fragment," Calin remarked, her furrowed brow and pursed lips making her views on the matter clear.

Again, Cat nodded. "If she hadn't, with no dagger and no Shyleen, we couldn't have kept history on track. In theory, the Timeless dagger can only protect one individual. In practice, Shyleen is part Guardian, so there was some wiggle room, especially while we were using the power of a fragment. It was risky and probably violated half a dozen rules that I haven't even written yet, but it was the only way."

"This is why you Guardians have to maintain your autonomy, in my opinion," Calin insisted. "None of us can hope to understand the decisions you have to make, so how can the Council lay down just laws?"

Cat conceded the point, but qualified it, saying, "In the future, I'm sure the Council will have to set down laws, but hopefully, they can do so with our guidance. Even then, though, maybe a future Guardian will one day face a choice between the letter of the law and doing the right thing. A time when someone like Kadessa is in the way. Someone who is just a little too fond of the rules."

"Then I hope they realise that there are times when you just have to tie them up to get them out of the way while you save the world."

"Speaking of Kadessa," Cat segued, changing tack, "have the Council appointed a successor yet?"

Calin confirmed that they hadn't.

"Good, because I'm hoping you can help me pull some strings."

"Why? Who do you have in mind?" Calin wondered, at a loss as to why a Guardian would be concerned about the appointment of a Custodian.

"Before I can tell you that," she replied, pulling some books out of her pocket dimension, "I need to talk to you about *Shifting Stars*."

*****

Calin listened as Catriona made her case, detailing the times in known history when the entity she referred to as her Angel appeared with the Crystal Mage Staff that she now owned. The critical times in magical history when the stars shifted out of place. Calin realised she had seen such an incident herself.

"I just put it down to a combination of alcohol and stress from everything that had just happened. In the decades since, I can't say I've ever thought any more about it. But that was real? It actually happened?"

Cat confirmed it, showing her the slight change in the star pattern before and after the Armistice celebration.

"You're not alone in dismissing the incident," Cat assured her. "Throughout history, most people have."

"But not you," Calin put in.

"True," she allowed, "but I couldn't possibly know as much as I do without *Shifting Stars*. This reference has been the key to so much for me – for the world – and nobody even knows. I've kept it at home in the Black Tower these past few years, but I think it deserves better. It should be here. It should be read by others. It should be recognised…and so should the author."

"But the author is anonymous," Calin pointed out.

Cat shook her head. "The author made himself anonymous with magic. Unfortunately, he did the job too well and ended up all but completely forgotten."

To explain further, Cat pulled out Renjaf's books on mental magic. The author's name was now anonymous, having been exposed to Renjaf's magic in this Timeline. The druidess walked Calin through how it all fitted together in the same general terms as how Renjaf had explained it to her. Calin may have renounced all but the barest use of magic for herself, but she still had a keen mind for how it worked, so she quickly grasped what Cat was showing her.

"This is astonishing work!" Calin gasped.

"Even Dreya was impressed," Cat agreed.

Calin raised her eyebrows. "With such high praise from Dreya the Dark, I can see 'astonishing' is too small a word. I should have said unequalled, unparalleled. If I knew the author, I would promote this work without hesitation."

"Then it's time to tell you who it is: Renjaf."

"Of course," Calin groaned regretfully, putting it together. "Unable to bear the ridicule he must have suffered due to his work on *Shifting Stars*, he made his work anonymous, but as you say, it worked too well, and he practically made himself anonymous. In another reality, I'm sure the Melrose Academy and I would have been fighting over him."

"In another reality, you both won for a time," Cat told her, explaining about the altered Timeline.

At the end of Catriona's story, Calin reached out in compassion and pulled her close.

"This is what I was saying about the impossible decisions you have to make as Guardians," she sympathised, "but you can't blame yourself. Not for how others treated Renjaf, not for his life choices and not for doing your duty and restoring Time. It's not your fault."

Pulling away, Cat clarified, "Intellectually, I know that's true, but emotionally..." she trailed off for a moment before concluding, "...A wise woman once said, 'We cannot change the past, but we can choose what happens in the future'."

Calin smiled, recognising her own words.

"Mistress Calin, would you please help me bring all this to the Council?" Cat requested formally.

"It would be my honour," she agreed.

Cat also told her that Dreya was planning to adapt her air lensing magic to function as sight correction.

"When I was on Earth," she explained, "people wore what they call glasses. Literally, a pair of small glass panes in a frame that fits on the face, focussing the light into sharper images. We're hoping to recreate something like that with magic."

"An intriguing idea, but have you not considered healing?"

Cat shook her head. "Mandalee and I may be healers, but we're hardly experts. Healing eyes would need a delicate touch."

"There is someone who could probably do it if you could persuade Renjaf to leave his tower and get a travel permit for a human to enter Sylfrania."

Calin described a healing centre in Ainderbury, not far from Gaggleswick and the Black Tower, run by a young Faery woman who was, by all accounts, exceptionally gifted in magical healing.

"No-one quite knows how she does it, but from what I've heard, she's dealt with cases like Renjaf's before."

Fascinated to hear of such a thing practically on the Black Tower's doorstep, the druidess asked the Faery woman's name.

"Princess Zarinda," Calin replied.

Cat laughed. "We know her!"

"You do?"

Cat nodded enthusiastically. "We even invited her to the wedding. Well, she sort of invited herself, but we didn't mind."

She told Calin how Zarinda had a penchant for spying on them using far-seeing lensing magic from just inside the Ainderbury border. It was, in fact, where Dreya had got the idea for her own lensing magic.

"Looks like we need her. Or at least Renjaf does if we can persuade him."

Calin asked her Custodians to cancel all her engagements for the rest of the day, so she could accompany Catriona and the other Guardians in bringing this issue to the Council. Before that, however, Cat wanted to make another stop along the way.

Chapter 20

"Astonishing magic," Calin breathed as she stepped out of Catriona's Prismatic Sphere portal in Tedstone Warf.

Keen to approach the Council with the backing of allies, Dreya had contacted Dagamir at Melrose Academy. Suitably intrigued, he was happy to examine the particulars for himself.

"It is, isn't it?" Dagamir concurred as he stepped forward to greet his guests just outside his college. "In my research centre, I've tried to get something similar working, but I just can't get the damn things to stabilise." He offered his hand and bowed his head in respect as he shook the Faery woman's hand and introduced himself. "Dagamir!" he boomed. "Dagamir the Tenth. It's an honour to meet you, Mistress Calin. I've wanted to for a long time…" he paused and frowned before qualifying, "…at least in this version of the Timeline."

"This version?" Calin wondered.

Dagamir nodded. "I didn't exist in the old one."

Calin looked questioningly at Cat, who blushed as she admitted it was true.

"Long story. First day on the job," she confessed with a sheepish look. "Accidentally tweaked a couple of things. That's why I made your library Timeless."

Dagamir invited them into his office, where Dreya was waiting.

She didn't immediately appear to notice when they walked in until Cat startled her with a kiss on the cheek.

"You OK?" Cat asked her wife.

"Hmmm? Oh yeah, sorry, Cat," she replied. "Miles away."

"Well, for your next trip, you might want to pay a visit to Sylfrania," Cat suggested and explained what Calin had told her about Princess Zarinda.

"Interesting as that is, I think you'd better go to her, Cat. Given my history with her father, it's probably best if I don't ruffle feathers by going back home."

Of course, Cat knew that Dreya, originally named Andreyanka by her parents, was born into Sylfranian Faery nobility. Her wife had never shared any further details, insisting her childhood was entirely irrelevant. Merely a period she'd had to get through to become the young woman who took the Black Tower. The history she mentioned was that Zarinda's father, Prince Travarin, along with Squire Johanssen of Gaggleswick, had sent a team to attack Dreya a few days after she first took Ulvarius' former home. The members of that team became her elite undead guards, but rather than retaliate any further, Dreya had invited Travarin and Johanssen into her home to dictate the terms of their surrender. She hadn't set foot in Travarin's lands since, and she had no intention of doing so now unless it was absolutely necessary.

Sylfrania was compulsorily White aligned, which on the surface, might make Mandalee the best choice of Guardian to approach Zarinda. However, Sylfrania generally, and Ainderbury in particular, was also fearful and xenophobic towards humans. Therefore, of the Three Guardians, as half-Faery, Catriona, though Red aligned, would probably receive the friendliest welcome.

Still, there was much to be done before there was any point to such a trip. First, Catriona presented her case to Dagamir, who was as generous with his praise for Renjaf's work as Calin had been.

"This is the kind of work that would qualify for the Darla Award for Excellence," Dagamir told them.

Even as the words left his mouth, he remembered Dreya was present. She, of course, was the Faery woman from whom the award historically got its name.

The sorceress offered a small smile and simply said, "Darla would agree."

"Then I will gladly support you in your efforts with the Council."

Speaking to Catriona, Calin offered, "The only thing I can think of that would make your case even more watertight is if you could find another witness to your Angel's activities.

Cat nodded. "That's in hand."

All they needed now was a Council session to present their case, and between them, they had the authority and influence to make that happen.

*****

The time arrived, and the quartet stepped from a portal outside the Council building. A moment later, a second one appeared, from which stepped Mandalee with Shyleen and Ossian Miach Kaidool. The Champion of the Gods had been in Quarthonia on the Day of the Monster. He could testify to those events, including the actions of Catriona's Angel. Cat knew even more about that day, of course, but some moments were too private to be shared.

Together, the mismatched group came before the Council, where the Triumvirate opened what they were calling an Extraordinary Meeting. They had no idea how apt that epithet was.

The Guardians shared the pertinent details of their adventures in the past, correcting an aberrant Timeline, preventing interference in the events of the Demon Apocalypse and, centuries before, reinforcing the Esca Armistice. They also presented the fragment that they had successfully retrieved. As soon as these proceedings were over, it would be stored safely away in stasis in Daelen's Tomb.

Dreya may have managed to use the fragment for a short time without it blowing up in her face, but she knew better than to make a habit of it. She had no intention of touching its power again until the device could be made whole once more.

Cat moved on to discuss *Shifting Stars* and its implications. Many of the Council were sceptical at first, but with the backing of Calin and Dagamir, plus the testimony of Michael, the truth won out. The Council accepted that there was indeed some kind of entity that appeared at critical moments in magical history and, either by side-effect or by design, caused the stars – or at least people's perception of them – to shift.

Dreya took over to explain the workings of mental magic that had allowed the author to erase himself in far more technical terms than Cat could offer.

Finally, when the Council was sufficiently on the edge of their seats, clamouring to know who had managed to achieve all this, the Black Guardian offered, "We can do better than tell you."

"In fact, it would do no good to tell you," Cat added further. "The magic the author used made his name memory-proof in relation to any published work."

"You'd forget in minutes," Mandalee translated succinctly.

Indeed, Calin and Dagamir had already forgotten. They knew Catriona had told them and understood in general terms why they were present, but the name itself eluded them. In time, even the rest would fade.

"If the Council agrees it is appropriate – and I believe it is," Dreya added with a pointed look at Laethyn that told him he'd better back her on this or else, "I can unpick the magic and restore the author's name."

"Then it's up to all of us to spread the word," Mandalee spoke up, "so that this remarkable individual receives the recognition he deserves."

The Council ruled in favour of the motion, so Dreya the Dark unravelled Renjaf's decades-old magic. When she had finished, the name on all the books Catriona had presented no longer read Anonymous, but Renjaf. With the memory-proofing magic dispelled, everyone could now retain it. Calin and Dagamir's complete memory of their earlier discussion quickly returned.

Calin recommended Renjaf for the position of White Custodian when Kadessa retired, and the Council quickly carried the motion. Of course, the Council of Mages had no jurisdiction over Dagamir's decision to grant Renjaf the Darla Award for Excellence, but he brought it up anyway as a demonstration of support.

The Council quickly drew up official documents and handed them to the Guardians. The rest was up to Renjaf himself.

*****

Cat sent Calin back to her tower through a portal, while Dagamir and Michael simply teleported themselves home. That left the Guardians to visit Renjaf alone – Shyleen chose to remain outside the gate to his grounds.

The elderly man who answered the door was much more the Renjaf that Catriona remembered from her college days than the version she had met only yesterday.

"What do you want?" he demanded.

"We're the Guardians," Cat offered.

"Know who you are. I said, what do you want?"

“Well,” Mandalee chimed in, “for a start, we want to present you with these.” She handed him the official documents, awarding him the Darla Award for Excellence from Melrose and the invitation to take up the position of Custodian at Calin’s Tower.”

Renjaf squinted at them, clearly unable to make out what they were.

“Allow me,” Dreya volunteered, casting her air lensing magic. “Let me know when you can read them easily.”

“Stop!” he snapped after a moment. “You can stop your witchery now!” So, Dreya maintained the lensing magic while he read the award. “What’s this for?” he asked.

“For a start, it’s for your work on mental magic,” Cat replied, showing him the books she had acquired from Calin’s Tower in the alternative Timeline. She realised that bringing books from a defunct Timeline into this one was probably violating half a dozen regulations that the Guardians hadn’t written yet, but that wasn't going to stop her.

“Where did you get these?” he demanded, still making no move to invite them in. “They’re my work, but I never published.”

Cat did her best to briefly explain without saying too much about what his other life was like.

“The techniques you develop in these books are truly excellent,” Dreya admitted. “In fact, I would welcome the opportunity to discuss them further.”

“But that’s not the main reason we’re here,” Mandalee put in before they got too sidetracked.

Cat shook her head. “No, the main reason both for our being here and for the award is because of this…” She held up *Shifting Stars*.

Renjaf glared. “What is this, some kind of joke?”

“Your work isn’t a joke, Renjaf,” Cat assured him. “I know that’s what everybody else thought, because they never saw what you saw. I understand the trouble that caused you and what that drove you to do. But that’s all changed now.”

“What are you talking about? You’re mocking me!” he protested.

“No, I promise you, we’re not,” Cat assured him and invited him to look inside the cover, where several prominent mages had written endorsements, including the Guardians, the Triumvirate, Dagamir and Calin.

"You were right," Catriona stated flatly.

Renjaf's eyes grew wide. "I was right?"

"Yes, you were," she confirmed.

"Have you any idea how many years I've desperately wished I could hear those words, just once?"

From the emotions that flashed across his face, it was as if a great weight that he had been carrying around for half a century had been lifted at last.

"I think I have some idea, yes," Cat replied, "and I'm sorry I never thought to tell you when I was researching it a few years ago."

She may not have known he was the author, but with hindsight, she believed she could have put it together if she'd thought about it. Renjaf hadn't exactly been the most approachable individual, but now Cat felt she had a better appreciation for why that was.

"But let me try and make up for that by saying it again now. You were right…mostly," she amended. "Although if you were going to re-publish it – and you should – then you might want to consider a slight revision to your conclusion in the light of further evidence."

At that, Renjaf finally stepped aside and invited his guests into his home, and although there was no tea and biscuits on offer, he at least listened while Cat shared her research. Renjaf could hardly contain his excitement at having his work vindicated. He even accepted the Red Guardian's point that the Angel destroying the world didn't fit with the new evidence.

"Who knows," he speculated, "maybe they're trying to save it? Although," he considered, "you seem to be doing an admirable job of that yourselves."

Feeling somewhat uncomfortable in the face of that compliment, considering what she'd done to rewrite his life, Cat was keen to move on.

When she reminded him about the offer of the Custodian position, Renjaf hedged, "Oh, I don't know if that's really me. Especially at my age."

"Well, at least think about it," Mandalee encouraged him. "In the meantime, there's one other thing we can do for you if you're willing."

Dreya explained to Renjaf her technique for forming lenses in the air that enabled him to see more clearly so that he could cast it himself.

"But there's a chance that we might even be able to go one better than that," Cat went on and told him about Calin's suggestion of Princess Zarinda's healing and what it would entail. "I know how you hate leaving your tower, but—"

Renjaf cut her off. "—I only hated going out because everywhere I looked – even with my weak eyes – I could see people pointing and laughing at the crazy old man who believed in Angels that move stars in the heavens and start wars. Even though nobody knew that anymore because of my magic, I could still hear them and see them in my mind's eye, and though it was my imagination, the pain was real. You've changed that. Thanks to you, people will finally see the value in my work and in my life. While I suspect I'll never be a social butterfly, I no longer need to hide myself away in a cocoon. If you can get me into Sylfrania for an audience with this healer princess, I have no objection. Far from it. Either way," he continued, focussing on Dreya, "the lensing magic you have shown me is life-changing by itself. I'm in your debt."

"Careful," Mandalee warned with a grin, "she collects those."

"Yes, I do," Dreya confirmed. She did not smile.

"Alright then, I think we're done here," Cat concluded. "I'll make arrangements with Zarinda, and I'll be in touch."

With that, the Three Guardians left Renjaf's tower and went their separate ways.

*****

Renjaf returned to his sitting room, still reeling from how his life had changed so suddenly. Wrapped up in his own thoughts as he was, it took him a moment to realise he wasn't alone. There, standing in the shadows, was a figure in robes of deepest black velvet.

"I appreciate what you just did for me, Black Guardian, but I don't appreciate you barging into my home like this!" Renjaf objected indignantly.

"My apologies for returning unannounced," Dreya replied in an icy cool voice, devoid of any emotion, "but my business requires a certain discretion, and we have something to discuss that has nothing to do with my fellow Guardians."

"And what might that be?" he asked, wary of how different she seemed from when she was here only a moment ago. This was much more the Dreya the Dark he would expect.

"Well," she answered, "the White Guardian mentioned it as a joke, but I consider it to be a serious matter: debts. I have a thing about them, you see, Mr Renjaf. I always pay them, and I always collect. You said yourself that you are in my debt since I gave you the magic by which you now see. Even if the Red Guardian is successful in procuring a long-term solution, that changes nothing. You still owe me, and I intend to collect."

"So, how exactly do I repay my debt?"

"By doing what I alluded to earlier: tell me more about your mental magic. I have studied what you wrote. Now I want to know what you didn't write. All the extra details of cutting-edge research that don't make it into print."

Dreya drifted slowly over to him. There was nothing overtly threatening in her body language, but Renjaf felt his pulse race all the same. He knew Dreya the Dark's reputation, and only a fool would be unafraid when she turned her penetrating gaze towards them.

Still, he had been quite formidable himself in his youth, especially when it came to mental magic. He had fought in the four-year war that was now called the Demon Apocalypse. He had faced down armies of demons. So had many others. But where other mages fought them with physical magic, Renjaf would reach inside their minds and turn them on each other. Caught in the outbreak of the war, he had even used his magic to hold a demon king at bay while that cleric assassin despatched it. It wasn't just any wizard who could do that.

'*Is this to do with the other presence in your mind, Dreya the Dark?*'

Dreya heard the words quite clearly despite him not saying a thing, except that should be impossible. No-one had ever penetrated her mind when her shields were up.

'*That's because they didn't know what they were doing,*' Renjaf returned in answer to her unspoken words.

Besides her own mental discipline, given that Pyrah was apparently still alive somewhere, she had an indirect sympathic link with an Ysirian through Catriona. The idea that he could penetrate such defences was astonishing.

'*Yes, interesting company you keep up here,*' he conceded, '*but nothing that can't be countered with the right techniques*.'

Renjaf felt a stab of pain and suddenly found himself sitting down, no longer trusting his legs as he was forcibly ejected from Dreya's mind. Now the tables were turned as she barged into his brain as she had his home.

'*I had intended to simply talk about this in a civilised manner, but since you saw fit to invade my mind, I'll do the same to you and simply take what I want.*'

"But if you can do this already, what do you even need from me?" Renjaf gasped.

His defences were all shattered now, and he could feel the sorceress sifting through his thoughts to find what she wanted.

"I can break down your defences with power, but as my wife likes to say, 'power isn't everything'. You've proved that you can enter someone's mind even if they're more powerful. That's what I need. Subtlety, guile and technique will often succeed where power alone would fail. Also, there's your work on Substitution magic. The idea of creating not just illusions, but whole mindscapes that would appear entirely real. I believe that could have useful applications."

"You should be careful of magic like that, Dreya," Renjaf warned. "It could be dangerous for you."

Being alone, as he was, Renjaf's life often lacked entertainment, and for a while, he had played with those mindscapes in his own head. Entirely believable make-believe worlds that didn't even need conscious direction once a few parameters were established. More than once, he had almost lost himself in his own mind, as living there became more attractive than the world outside.

"Thank you for your warning," Dreya acknowledged, "but I believe that is my concern and not yours." After a few moments, she declared herself done. "Now, let's see what I've learned."

Renjaf could tell she'd learned quickly. The way she was moving around in his mind now was done with precision, not brute force. If he didn't already know she was in there, he probably wouldn't even notice.

"You now know things about me that I cannot allow you to share, so I'm putting a block on your mind, so you forget this meeting entirely."

Finishing up, she exited his mind and unfolded a power word.

"SLEEP."

Chapter 21

The golden-haired Sylfranian princess was sitting on a silver chair in the middle of what was not so much a building as a wooden platform with a roof held up by pillars. Her name was Zarindalauryndanorvana, but most people called her Zarinda, as long as her father wasn't around.

According to tradition, the length of a Faery's name indicated status.

Keeping track of where all of her relatives and their offspring sat in the order of things was a task too demanding and pointless for her to bother with. The last time she counted, Zarinda estimated she was thirty-sixth in line to the throne, but she was pretty sure two or three cousins had had a baby or two since then, which probably put her closer to fortieth. As such, the length of her name was somewhat exaggerated according to that tradition. However, the practice was dying out these days, so it didn't cause too much of a stir. Still, it was indicative of her parents' attitude that they clung to that tradition on the one hand while, on the other, giving her a name that, if that tradition were still enforced, would never have been permitted.

Her father's court in the province of Ainderbury was governed very much along those lines. Claiming to cling to tradition while, at the same time, applying those customs as if the town were far more significant than it really was.

Zarinda had little interest in court intrigue. She was more concerned with helping people. That was why last year when she turned sixteen, she had set up her treatment centre. Having discovered, as a child, an innate healing magic, she felt a calling to use it now that she was old enough – according to tradition.

One year on, and her centre was packed with Faery from across Sylfrania and Quarthonia, with which her father was trying to cultivate closer ties. Faery from other settlements came, too, and even – very occasionally – a few humans were granted a short visa to visit her. Zarinda was happy to heal anyone – Faery, humans, animals, even aliens from Rhynapolis, in principle. In practice, she hadn't met any yet.

By and large, Zarinda's day was going as usual. Patients came in with various illnesses and injuries; she sang, accompanying herself on her lute, and used her magic to cure them. It was satisfying work, if a little repetitive. However, after breaking for some lunch around midday, when she resumed in the afternoon, she couldn't fail to notice the Red robe mage sitting in the corner. Balance-aligned mages were rare in Sylfrania, where everyone was aligned with the Light, so the princess was naturally curious about who this individual could be. Female, the princess assumed, based on the fact that she was several months pregnant. Zarinda usually saw her patients on a first-come-first-serve basis, barring some emergency, but this Red robe seemed content to sit there and let others who arrived later move ahead of her in the queue.

The afternoon wore on, and Zarinda was done for the day, except for this one Red robe mage who still made no effort to approach her. That left the princess with little choice but to take the initiative and approach the mage herself, stepping lightly over to where the stranger was sitting.

"Excuse me, but I'm done for the day. Is there something I can help you with?"

The mage removed the hood of her robes, allowing Zarinda to see her face for the first time. Half-Faery, she observed, which was unusual. Zarinda didn't recognise her, but that was hardly surprising. There were no half-Faery in Sylfrania.

"How does your healing work?" asked the woman without preamble, a look of concentration on her face.

"I'm sorry?" Zarinda had been expecting a medical question, not a magical one.

"I've been sitting here all afternoon, and I can't make heads nor tails of it. That's rare because, if you'll forgive the conceit, I'm usually pretty good at figuring out how magic works. At first, I thought your lute might be enchanted, but it's not, is it? It's like my staff." From Zarinda's perspective, a large gap opened up in reality, from which emerged a three-foot-long wooden staff with a large blue crystal on top. It was highly distinctive and instantly recognisable as it obediently nestled in the mage's grip. "I wouldn't touch it if I were you," the mage warned her as the gap in reality closed. "Sometimes, bad things happen when other people do that.

But like this staff, your lute just channels magic and aids focus. You could probably heal just as well without it."

"Where did you get that staff?" Zarinda demanded. "Did you steal it?"

The mage blinked in surprise. "No, of course not. It was a gift. I can only assume it was theirs to give. Not the first thing you think to ask when an Angel offers you a gift, is it? 'No offence, but you didn't nick this, did you?' You just, sort of, assume it's OK to accept it. Wait – don't you recognise me?"

Zarinda shook her head. "Should I?"

The mage snapped her fingers as if suddenly remembering something. "Sorry," she apologised. Then she seemed to scratch the back of her neck for a moment, and the next thing Zarinda knew, it was the Red Guardian sitting there.

Now the staff and everything the mage had said made sense. Well, most of it, anyway.

"Of course, I'd heard you can shapeshift!" Zarinda cried. Then she immediately stood and curtseyed. "I'm honoured to meet you, Mistress Catriona."

"Blimey, you can cut that out for a start!" the Guardian remarked, belatedly remembering how formal things could be in Sylfrania, especially here in Ainderbury. "It's just Catriona. Cat to my friends. And no, Zarinda, that wasn't shapeshifting. Had to give that up because of this." She patted her swollen belly. "What you saw was something called a perception filter. I didn't want to cause a fuss by being here and then forgot about it when you came over. Sorry, I'm a bit tired. Been up for about a day and a half, I think. It's hard to keep track." She paused and considered, "Actually, if we're being formal, shouldn't I be the one curtseying to you, Princess Zarinda?"

The princess smiled. She still felt a little shy talking to the famous Catriona Redfletching, but she couldn't help but warm to her. "If my father were around, yes, but since he's not, no."

Cat returned the smile. "Ah, it's like that, is it?" Her look of concentration returned as she repeated her earlier question. "So, how does your healing work? I mean, for a start, are you a cleric or a druid? Obviously, you can't be a wizard – they don't have healing powers. Although," she considered, "Dreya once gave her power to Mandalee to help her heal. That was indirect healing, I suppose."

“Dreya the Dark gave away power?” Zarinda gasped incredulously.

Cat laughed. “I know. I was as shocked as you are, the first time. Mandalee said she needed a drink. Mind you, she often says that!”

“Dreya the Dark is not at all what people say,” the princess stated firmly.

“Dreya the Dark could and can be everything people say,” Catriona countered. “She’s just a lot more besides. Anyway, sorry, that’s the second time I’ve asked you that question and not let you answer. Although I’m not even sure I want you to answer. I love a puzzle, you see, and you, Zarinda, are the first one I’ve come across for years that didn’t involve saving the world. It makes for a welcome change.”

“Well, if it helps,” Zarinda offered, “the answer to your question is I don’t know. I don’t even have any other magic, as far as I’m aware. Except distance seeing. But I’ve been healing people and animals since I was a little girl.”

Cat’s face lit up. “And the puzzle deepens to a mystery!” she remarked. “Did I miss my own birthday again?”

Zarinda grinned, finding it impossible not to like her. “I haven’t even had any formal training or anything.”

Cat nodded knowingly. “Self-taught. I’m just the same.”

“Is that what brought you here to my little corner of Sylfrania?” Zarinda asked. “To find out how my healing works?”

Catriona shook her head as if to clear it of distractions. “Oh, no, sorry. I’ve sidetracked myself. As I said, I’m tired. The other two are hungover from a party about a hundred and seventy years ago – don’t tell the Council! Although it was at least partly Guardian business. I just limited myself to one drink for obvious reasons.”

Zarinda shook her head in wonder. “Going to a party so far in the past. I can’t imagine what that’s like!”

“It’s a lot like going to a party in the present,” Cat shrugged, “except nobody knows you, so it doesn’t matter how badly you dance.”

Zarinda laughed.

Catriona yawned.

“No offence,” Zarinda told her, “but you look exhausted. That’s one thing I can’t heal. Only sleep can do that.”

Cat nodded. “I know. Believe me, sleep is next on the agenda for all three of us. Before that, though, there’s a reason I came here: I need you.”

The princess was glad she was sitting down when Catriona said those three little words. She’d had the dream again only last night. The one that had been recurring for years. Those words were like a trigger for her, only it was the wrong Guardian saying them. It was supposed to be Dreya.

Zarinda pushed those thoughts aside. What was she doing? Catriona had come to see her, and here she was fantasising about her wife riding in to sweep her off her feet on her wedding day! She would never want to come between them. What kind of horrible person would? It was time she let go of that stupid, childish fantasy.

Swallowing all that, she asked, “How can I help?” Then, guessing, she added, “Oh, is it about…?” she gestured to indicate Catriona’s pregnancy.

Cat shook her head. “No, no, nothing like that. It’s not even about me. It’s about an old White wizard I know. Human, seventyish, extremely poor eyesight. I wonder if there might be any way for you to help with that. His eyes, that is, not his age,” she clarified. Even the Guardians couldn’t do anything about that. “Sorry, I’m tired – did I mention? And I’m aware I might not be making the greatest amount of sense right now.”

“No, it’s fine,” Zarinda assured her with a smile. “I can’t promise anything, but I’d be happy to try. He’ll need a visa, of course, but I’m sure I can pull some strings. Being fortieth in line to the throne has to have some perks. Besides, it’s a request from the office of the Guardians. Who’s going to refuse that?”

“Well, we don’t really have an office. More of a garden,” Cat mused distractedly, her eyelids drooping, “but your point still stands.”

“Who is this wizard to you? A friend? Family?”

“I lost my family a long time ago,” Cat told her, catching herself before she dozed off, “and I wouldn’t go so far as to call Renjaf a friend. I just feel I owe him. It’s a long story. More than fifty years long, actually!”

"You're not at all what I expected," Zarinda told her. "If anyone around here had your job, I'm sure they'd be all-important and serious. But not you."

The princess had seen Catriona in the grounds of the Black Tower many times, but that was when she was with Dreya and their friends. In Ainderbury, it was quite a different matter when one was on official business.

"I'm always serious about what I do," Cat promised. "Just not necessarily the way I do it. Anyway," she segued, helping herself up with her staff. Zarinda thought she looked ready to drop. "I've taken up enough of your time. Thank you, Zarinda."

Laying a gentle restraining hand on her arm, the princess asked her to wait a moment.

"I know it's not why you came, but why don't you let me examine your pregnancy while you're here?"

"Well, I don't want to keep you."

"Nonsense!" she insisted. "Look, I'm sure everything's fine, but it can't do any harm to check, can it?"

"Alright then," Cat agreed. "Why not?"

Zarinda led Catriona over to one corner of her healing centre that was equipped with privacy blinds, which she pulled closed around them both.

The princess then asked Catriona to lay on the bed while she sat beside her.

"You were right about my lute, by the way. In fact, for more intimate examinations, I've found I get a better reading if I touch the patient while I sing. Is that OK?" she asked.

Cat nodded and kept her staff safely out of the way while Zarinda placed her hand gently on her swollen belly. Closing her eyes, the Faery princess began to sing, but Cat interrupted her.

"Sorry, one last question: does it matter what you sing?"

Zarinda shook her head. "Doesn't seem to."

"Do you know Angels Among Us? It's kind of special to me. For a lot of reasons."

"Human language or Traditional Faery?"

Catriona was surprised she would know the human version and told her so.

Zarinda explained that Catriona was the reason she knew it, reminding her about the book of traditional Faery children's rhymes and lullabies that she wrote for Dreya's old tutor, Xarnas. Apparently, he had passed it on to his daughter and her Faery husband; from there, it seemed it had been copied and distributed. Cat had no objections. As per Faery custom, it was given freely.

"It's a small world!" Cat declared. "I mean, Tempestria is huge, and Time is probably infinite, but still, it's a small world." She yawned again. "OK, no more questions, I promise. Let's do this before I fall asleep right here."

So, Zarinda sang: [1]

Angels among us, stars in the night,
Watch o'er your sleep, shining so bright,
Safe in their light, as you close your eyes,
Love will surround you, 'til morning you rise.

Angels among us, shed you no tears,
Bright Angels guard you, quiet your fears,
Nature's embrace, is gentle and strong,
Love will surround you, all your life long.

Interwoven with Zarinda's song was her magic. The druidess could feel it, even if she couldn't identify it. For once, though, she chose not to analyse it. Just accept.

After a few moments, Zarinda stopped singing and told Cat, "Your baby is healthy and surrounded by magic like I've never felt before."

That came as no surprise to Catriona, considering who the father was. She wouldn't expect Zarinda to know higher planar energy when she encountered it.

"Do you want to know the sex?"

"You can tell that?" Cat asked, amazed.

Zarinda nodded.

"Alright, then."

"You're having a girl. Congratulations!"

Cat nodded. "I had a feeling, but I wasn't sure." She got up and thanked the princess.

---

[1] Fits to the tune of Rockabye Baby.

Zarinda reopened the privacy blinds. “As for the other matter, where should I have the visa documents sent?”

“Probably best to let me have them first.”

“So, the Black Tower, then?”

Cat nodded.

“That’ll ruffle a few feathers, but I’ll make sure it gets done.”

“Thanks, Zarinda. It was nice to meet you properly, at last. I still have no idea how your healing magic works, but I can see this community is in safe hands.”

With an exchange of farewells, they went their separate ways.

Chapter 22

Upon leaving Renjaf's tower, Dreya immediately returned to her own.

Time travel played havoc with one's sense of time. She'd hidden it well while facing Renjaf's mental assault, but she definitely felt as if time had caught up with her. The sorceress felt physically, mentally, magically and in all other ways, drained. She needed sleep. Right now, though, she was still too tightly wound.

She sat down with a glass of wine and allowed her mind to wander – literally. She wanted to practice Renjaf's techniques for astral projection. At some point, however, her mind returned to her body, and she just caught herself before she dozed off.

While preparing for bed, Dreya realised she'd forgotten something: she still had the fragment in her pocket. Groaning, she sat down on the bed and thought about it. Wrapped in its own Timeless field, it was reasonably safe. Nevertheless, she would feel happier if it were in Daelen's Tomb with the others. Her twin thoughts were at war with one another: she wanted to take the fragment away, yet she didn't want to move.

Both options were promptly denied her with a persistent banging on her door.

With a sigh, she called for her death knight guards to find out who it was. It was Ossian Miach Kaidool – Michael. Dreya frowned in puzzlement. He'd never done anything like this before. In fact, the only time he'd even been in her grounds was on her wedding day. Her defences didn't consider him a threat as such, but they were alert to his presence and power. Her undead gardeners had ceased their toil for the moment and were watching him intently.

The sorceress forced her brain to work. The only reason Michael would do this was in an emergency. It had better not be anything to do with Jessica or Sara, she thought. She already felt bad enough about their world being Cleansed by Purity – a double genocide on top of all the others that Angel had committed. She'd be damned if anything was going to harm the last remaining Chetsuans.

On balance, expending magical power seemed preferable to physical energy, so she levitated herself downstairs.

"This had better be important, Mickey," she warned him when she opened the door. "I'm not in the mood for a cup of tea and a chat."

"It is important," he assured her. "Potentially disastrous. And don't call me Mickey."

"This 'potentially disastrous' situation," Dreya ventured. "Does it involve Time travel?"

"Not that I'm aware of."

"If I stop it, will I gain power?"

"I shouldn't think so," he admitted.

"Then I'm not interested," she declared and tried to magically flick the door closed.

Michael's foot was faster, stopping it from shutting completely. "I think we both know you better than that, Dreya."

Dreya groaned and opened the door again, this time stepping outside to join him. "Oh, alright!" she reluctantly agreed. "But if anybody asks, I am not doing this to save the world. I'm doing it…" she trailed off.

"Yes?" Michael prompted.

She waved a hand vaguely as she said, "…I'm doing it for some other, self-serving reason that I'll think of later." Then, in response to his amused look, she raised a finger and warned him, "Look, Mickey, I'm low on energy and even lower on patience, so don't imagine I won't do a Kullos and rip your power away if you piss me off. There's plenty of room in that Tomb for you and Daelen!"

"I'm saying nothing," Michael promised.

"Smart boy."

*****

When Catriona returned home, she was looking forward to an early night and some much-needed sleep. She reached the steps leading to the front door, where the black, red and white roses remained in bloom all year round, thanks to her magic. The druidess had reshaped them after their wedding, however. The heart shape was beautiful on her special day, but long term, she felt it would have got a little saccharine. When she stopped for a moment to smell the black ones, she almost immediately heard Dreya's voice, as if the act had summoned her, communicating via their Timeless Meadow.

"I'm at Michael's place," she told her. "You'd better get over here. There's trouble."

Cat pulled a face and groaned, "But I'm knackered!"

"We all are," Dreya agreed, "but I think we need to deal with this."

"Ugh!" Cat replied, which her wife took to mean she was on her way.

*****

Mandalee and Shyleen arrived only a moment before Catriona. Michael greeted them warmly and led them inside his home.

"Love what you've done with the place," Mandalee offered.

The ancient temple had come a long way from the ruined state it had been in when they first saw it on the way to fight Kullos' army. There was still work to be done, but it was clearly a labour of love for the Champion of the Gods.

'*I, for one, would appreciate it even more if I were actually awake,*' Shyleen offered.

Mandalee could only agree.

Michael led them to an ornate lounge room, and sitting there, waiting for them, alongside Dreya, were two people they knew and one they didn't: the two Chetsuans, Sara and Jessica, and someone who looked a bit like a male Chetsuan, except with a golden skin tone rather than a shade of purple.

"Heya loves!" Jessica called out, immediately jumping up to hug her friends and stroke Shyleen, who purred in appreciation.

Sara was fiddling with some kind of technology that Mandalee didn't understand but looked delicate. Still, the Chetsuan carefully put it down to step behind her sister and offer her own hugs.

"Sorry to drag you out here," she offered. "Dreya's told us you've all been on your feet for about a day and a half."

"A day and a half?" Mandalee cried. "Try a hundred and seventy years!"

She knew it didn't work like that, but it was how she felt, and her friends did not contradict her.

With an apologetic look, Jessica introduced the newcomers to their guest while Sara got back to fiddling with whatever she was working on.

"This is Laoghaire, our friend from Lavos."

He stood and offered his hand, which a somewhat bleary-eyed Mandalee and Catriona shook in turn.

"Call me Lao."

"It's nice to meet you, Lao," Mandalee offered politely.

"Yeah," Cat agreed, "but what are you doing here?" Realising that was rude, she apologised. "I'm afraid you're not catching us at our best, right now."

Lao waved that aside. "When I've been up for more than a century and a half, maybe I'll be in a position to judge. Sadly, I'm afraid to say your beds will have to wait because I came here to warn you."

"About what?" Cat asked.

"I have reason to believe that somewhere on your world, some people from mine have built an enormous bomb, and it could go off at any time."

When Dreya had got to Michael's home, and Lao delivered his warning, she had decided the other Guardians needed to hear it, too.

"That's why I called you," the sorceress concluded.

"Oh, great. Thanks, Dreya," Mandalee grumbled. "I'm so glad you chose to share this with us. I mean, come on," she scoffed, clearly not believing it, "how could anyone from Lavos get over here in the first place, let alone plant a bomb?"

"That's a good question," Cat agreed. "How *did* you get here, Lao?"

Mandalee swore, realising that if Lao had managed to get to Tempestria, then the idea of others doing likewise wasn't so ridiculous, after all. She was sure she would have thought of that if her mind were not half asleep.

"Cat, love, is that really the most important thing, right now?" Jessica asked.

"Probably not, but it's where I'm starting," the druidess insisted, choosing to sit down before she fell down. What she ended up doing was a blend of the two, as she missed the sofa and sat down on the floor in front of it instead, claiming, "Meant to do that!"

Laoghaire, more impressively in Catriona's opinion, actually found the seat he was aiming for and explained that on his world, in the aftermath of preventing dragon genocide with Sara, Jessica and Michael, he had used video surveillance technology to analyse the Prismatic Sphere portals. It had taken a lot of time and research, but he and his technical team had finally found a way to replicate the process with technology.

At the same time, however, there were growing concerns that not all of the extremist anti-dragon elements had been weeded out of their society. At least one faction was still out there, plotting something; Pro Dragon Intelligence was sure of it. Finally, intelligence operatives uncovered some alarming evidence – more video surveillance capturing the image of what appeared to be a Black robe wizard, of all things. Of course, it could have just been somebody dressed up, but the video clearly showed him levitating things, juggling with fireballs and frying computer technology with electrical bolts from his fingertips.

PDI analysed the video using every technique they knew and found no evidence of camera trickery. The magic was real.

"We didn't want to jump to conclusions and assume he was from Tempestria – there could be other worlds of magic for all we know."

"There are," Dreya confirmed.

Sara nodded. "There's Phitonia for a start."

Dreya shifted uncomfortably at that. She still hadn't told them. She could never tell them.

Lao nodded. "Obviously, we knew that from what Jessica could do."

With a twinkle in her eye, Jessica made a potted plant next to Lao's seat grow a little.

He smiled as he continued, "But it didn't seem like the kind of magic you do. More like what you told me Dreya here can do…" his eyes widened, "…no offence."

The sorceress shrugged. "None taken. It sounds like the very least of what I can do. It also sounds like the renegade Black wizard that's been causing us a few headaches in recent years. Tell me, on your video surveillance, did he ever have a dagger on him with a jagged lightning-shaped blade?"

Lao wasn't sure.

To help, Mandalee opened a portal to Catriona's Meadow, retrieved the Timeless dagger and showed it to him. The Lavosian dug out his Portacom, which he unfolded and activated.

"Is it OK if I take a photo of this?" he asked.

There were no objections, so he tapped his device a few times, and a tiny light flashed. An image of the dagger materialised in midair, and Lao tapped his Portacom a few more times. "I've asked it to search for anything in the database that matches that image," he explained.

A moment later, the projection of the dagger was replaced by a kind of three-dimensional photograph of a wizard in Black robes. Something was hanging from his belt. At first, it was too small to make out properly, but as the image zoomed in, it became clear: according to the computer, it was a '99.7% probability match'.

"That's obviously before Mandalee took it from Nalani," Cat mused as her friend returned it through the portal.

"Who?" Lao asked.

"Think of her as an agent of the Black robe wizard," Sara spoke up.

PDI had set up some technology to scan for the energy signature of a Prismatic Sphere portal, and eventually, they got a hit. PDI agents, including Lao, were on their way within seconds of the alert. Even so, by the time they got there, the wizard was gone, and the portal had closed. But Lao's team had built another device to try and analyse the origin of the portal based on the residual traces.

"That's what you learned to do," Cat remarked to Dreya.

Her wife nodded. "Is that how you got the co-ordinates for our world?" she asked Lao.

The Lavosian opened his mouth, but Michael got in first. "Actually, that was me."

At the end of their time on Lavos, having foiled the plot and retrieved the fragment of Kullos' dimensional control device, the new pro-dragon government was keen to establish relations with Tempestria. "I gave them co-ordinates for my place, here," Michael explained. "In case they ever found a way."

Lao nodded, "The reading I got from the portal wasn't that precise, but according to the analysis, it was a '73.3% probability match', which was enough to convince me that the wizard was from Tempestria. Just probably a different part of Tempestria."

'*Such as Elvaria,*' Shyleen suggested to Mandalee.

"Like another continent," Mandalee translated for Lao's benefit.

"Question: what was that wizard doing on Lavos?" Sara wondered.

"Working with anti-dragon extremists, from what we could tell."

Dreya shook her head. "There must be more to it. We know he's got two of the fragments. That, in concert with everything else he's done, proves he's a typical Black robe: he wants to gain power. How does meddling in your world help him do that?"

"Dragons?" Jessica suggested. "It's why you conquered Phitonia," she pointed out.

"You conquered their world?" Lao gasped, eyeing the sorceress warily.

Dreya shrugged. "I had a spare afternoon. Don't worry, Lao," she assured him, "I have no plans to conquer Lavos." He started to look relieved until she added, "Funny thing about being a Guardian of Time – these days, I just don't have time."

"Relax, Lao, she's winding you up," Mandalee assured him.

"Mostly," Cat put in. If her wife ever felt it was necessary or advantageous, she wouldn't shy away from such a conquest. It was just staggeringly unlikely that there was anything that would interest her on a world of technology, so Lavos was safe from her schemes. Probably.

"Anyway," the Red Guardian continued, "whatever this wizard wants with your world, with the greatest of respect, I'm currently more concerned about this bomb."

Lao nodded. "I understand, but the two things are related."

He explained that things went quiet for a few years, Lavosian time, but then certain items of technology began to go missing in seemingly unrelated thefts across Weslend. Worryingly, many of the components were similar to what was used to construct the terrible weapon that Michael and the Chetsuans destroyed. According to the plans they uncovered, this device was much more straightforward – a simple bomb – but it was clearly intended to be powered by higher planar energy.

"Long story short," Lao summarised, "despite our best efforts, a bomb exploded in the capital. Thankfully, with the help of the dragons, we managed to evacuate everyone in time, and there were no fatalities, but I wouldn't rely on that miracle happening a second time."

Lao told them there were easily enough stolen components to make a second device, and according to the intelligence reports, it was destined to be used on Tempestria. Also, an analysis of the wreckage confirmed higher planar energy, but the fragment had mostly disintegrated in the blast.

Dreya and Michael shared a wide-eyed glance. They were more aware of the true power of higher planar energy than any of the others.

"How bad was it?" asked the demigod, dreading the answer.

"A whole city block, pretty much," Lao replied.

Dreya's frown deepened as she shook her head. "No way was that a fragment. If it were, you wouldn't have a city or anything else for miles around."

Michael backed her up. "That's a conservative estimate. A blast powerful enough to blow up the fragment itself would probably take out most of Weslend."

Chapter 23

In response, Lao took out a small sample bag containing what he told them was the only significant piece of the fragment they could find. It was a splinter of metal, barely half an inch long.

He passed it to Dreya, saying, "I was hoping that analysing it with magic might yield more information."

Dreya took the metal splinter carefully in her hand and was walking over to Michael to get his view when Mandalee spoke up.

"Dear gods, it's my fault!"

"I bet it isn't," Cat replied. Her friend often blamed herself.

"No, this time it really is!"

She reminded her friends of what happened during the Fall of Kullos. She and Dreya used all their power to shatter Kullos' control device, but that wasn't the only thing that broke that day. In the process, her treasured Pureblade, too, smashed into innumerable metal splinters.

"But we swapped our StormClaw Island for the one on the original Tempestria," Dreya pointed out. "Any splinters of your Pureblade should have ended up on the other world that was unmade."

"I don't care. This is from my Pureblade," she insisted.

"We're wasting time here, guys," Cat interrupted, banging the table irritably, "and I'm too tired to do that. Bottom line is there's a higher planar bomb. No matter how big or small the power source, we need to find it and stop it. Any suggestions?"

"Isn't this the part where you're supposed to come up with one of your ridiculous radical plans, love?" Jessica asked with a grin.

Cat's withering look shot her down in flames. "What part of 'too tired' aren't you getting?"

"Actually, I have a solution," Sara spoke up, having apparently finished tinkering with her tech. "Or the beginnings of one." She reminded the others that they had located the fragment on Lavos with a tracking device. Frustratingly, it had stopped working soon after they arrived back. Now, having had a chance to consult Lao, she'd finally figured out what was wrong with it.

"Astound us," Cat prompted her.

"Nothing," she replied.

"Huh?"

"It works fine," Lao insisted, "or it would do if someone weren't jamming the signal."

"With Lao's help, and thanks to some advances in Lavosian tech, I've modified it to cut through that jamming signal," Sara explained. "Plus, I've extended the range about a hundredfold, and now I've built a second one."

"Put one here and one in Elvaria," Lao concluded, "and something's bound to turn up."

"I have an alternative suggestion," Michael volunteered. "I think we can narrow things down with some common sense." To Lao, he pointed out, "This bomb would need Lavosian expertise to build and install, yes?"

Lao nodded.

"So how could aliens operate on Tempestria without anybody noticing?"

"Perception filters?" Mandalee suggested.

Lao shook his head, convinced they didn't have the technology for such things.

"Maybe they don't need them," Sara suggested with a thoughtful look. "Maybe they're at a sci-fi convention."

"This is no time to be thinking about snogging elves, sis!" her sister quipped. Then she caught on. "No, wait, I see what you're getting at. If you want to hide a book, you put it in a library. If you want to hide aliens, you put them with other aliens."

Sara nodded. "In Rhynapolis."

Rhynapolis had been established from the remains of Kullos' army camp. The aliens who surrendered were granted amnesty on the grounds of having been lied to, abandoned and stranded in this world. Most of them decided that if they were going to build a new life, they might as well do it where they already were. The Allorian authorities agreed that since they had done the work to construct the city, that gave them a rightful claim to it. It was situated at the southern edge of the Rhynas Desert, more-or-less where Qiapolis had been before it was destroyed in the Demon Apocalypse. After some debate, the name was approved, and Rhynapolis was born.

That also fitted with something Cat had discovered but not yet shared. She was just about to correct that when a White robe wizard burst into the room, eyes wide with a mix of terror and desperation.

"Oh, thank the gods you're here! When you weren't at the Black Tower, this was the only other place I could think of to look!"

"Come on in and join the party," Michael remarked with a sardonic smile. "As you can see, it's open house!"

"Sorry," the wizard apologised, "but it's an emergency: there's a small army attacking the Council."

"And you can't deal with it yourselves?" Mandalee shot back.

'*How did they cope before there were Guardians?*' Shyleen wondered. A point her friend was happy to relay.

The wizard told them that the attacking magic was laced with higher planar energy, and they weren't confident that their shields would hold.

"It's Keir, isn't it?" Dreya offered. The wizard nodded. "White Secondmage," the sorceress explained as an aside to the others.

"Please, I need to get back!" Keir pleaded. "The White order is looking to me to lead them."

"Why? Where's Maia?" Cat asked.

"Not serving today," Keir answered, explaining that she had taken her son to the Open Day at Melrose Academy.

Catriona was instantly alert – or at least as alert as fatigue would allow.

"Is Melrose under attack, too?"

Keir frowned. "Not that I know of – they'd surely send word if they were."

"Go and find out."

Keir could obviously teleport, so it was a simple enough request. He stammered an objection, but Cat was not in the mood.

"Just do it!" she groaned, exasperated.

Suitably scolded, Keir teleported away.

Seconds later, he returned, even more terrified than before. "You're right, Red Guardian," he confirmed. "They are under attack, but they can't get a message out because there's an anti-magic field!"

"Thank you," Cat replied. "Now, please go away. We're busy."

"But you'll come and help, right?"

The druidess didn't say a word. She just rubbed her tired eyes and glanced at Dreya who, knowing what her wife wanted, used her magic to forcibly teleport Keir back to the Council building.

"The Council and Melrose," Cat remarked, "and I'll bet my staff we're next."

"What!" the others demanded.

Catriona ignored them as she concluded, "Plus, at least one higher planar bomb, ready to explode."

"At least?" Mandalee wondered, then she realised. "Of course – there are two missing fragments."

Sara turned to Lao and asked, "You said the enemy forces had stolen enough components for two explosive devices – one for your world and one for ours. Could they have enough for a third?"

Lao looked pale. "Possibly," he admitted.

"So," Dreya mused, "we're looking at a major, multipronged attack."

Lao nodded. "I'm afraid so."

"We have to do something, quick!" Mandalee declared, even as she swayed on her feet.

"No!" Cat refuted, using her staff to help her up and look confident. At the very least, she looked annoyed.

"What do you mean, 'no'?" Mandalee wondered.

"I mean no," she insisted. "Come on, don't you find the timing of this just a little too convenient?"

Michael caught on. "Someone knows how exhausted you must be right now and is trying to take advantage.

Dreya glowered. "They're trying to force us into rash action, so we'll make a mistake."

Cat nodded. "Someone's playing games with us, so it's time to change the rules."

"You have a ridiculous radical plan after all, don't you, Cat?" Mandalee surmised.

Catriona returned a grim smile. "I'm way past ridiculous and radical, and heading straight into desperate and dangerous. Who's with me?"

The other Guardians, the Chetsuans and Michael all raised their hands.

Lao hesitated. "I thought I was coming here to stop a bomb, not a conspiracy."

Michael spoke up to remind him, "When we travelled to your world, we thought we were going to collect a fragment, not prevent genocide."

"Funny how things work out, isn't it?" Sara observed archly.

"Fair point," Lao conceded. At last, he raised his hand. "Oh, what the hell?"

Cat acknowledged that with a smile and a nod before immediately issuing instructions.

"First, defences." She asked Jessica to use the plants surrounding Michael's home and water from the pond to create thick barriers of greenery and ice walls. Plus, since they were close to the Rhynas Desert, plenty of sand blew down from the North. "Can you fuse sand into glass yet?" she asked.

Jessica was hesitant. "Well, I've never actually—"

Interrupting her with an annoyed glare, Cat insisted, "The correct answer is, 'Yes, Cat, of course I can, because I believe in myself'."

The last time Jessica had doubted herself and her magic, Cat had gone with the hand-holding approach. This time, on the verge of falling asleep where she stood, she had neither the time nor the patience, so she was using the 'throwing her in the deep end' approach, as Jessica herself would probably put it.

Understanding what Cat was doing, the Chetsuan put on a determined smile as she replied, "Yes, Cat, of course I can, because I believe in myself."

"Then do it."

Jessica rushed outside to comply. Michael offered to help with some magic of his own, but Cat stopped him.

"Not yet. I think I'm going to need you first, depending on Sara."

"Me? What can I do?"

Before getting to that, she asked Mandalee and Shyleen to go with Jessica instead. Both for protection and to talk to the animals thereabouts to hopefully get advance warning of an attack.

As they left the room, the druidess reminded Sara what had happened when they tried to return from dealing with Ulvarius. They had skipped two and a half years when they were pulled into the future by Sara's device.

"Do you still have that device?"

Sara confirmed it was in her room, gathering dust on a shelf.

"Well, bring it here and clear off the dust."

Sara agreed and got up to fetch it – Lao by her side – but reminded Catriona, "it needs a fragment to work."

The control device fragment they had found on Lavos had somehow called the one the Guardians had taken from Ulvarius and pulled them into the future from Catriona's Meadow. Once again, the Guardians would need two fragments, and currently, they had only one in their possession.

Cat nodded. "That's why I need you, Michael," she told the demigod. "Go and fetch one, would you?"

"It's not safe to keep using these fragments," he objected. "With or without a bomb, one of these days, one of them is going to explode!"

"I know it's not safe, Mickey. Desperate and dangerous, remember? Don't worry. It won't be for long."

"Alright, Cat," he acquiesced, "but if it blows your legs off, don't come running to me."

A brief smile was all she could spare.

With that, he left the room to collect the containment box they had used to safely bring back the fragment through a portal from Lavos. Once he had that, he would open a portal from his new home to his only previous one.

Cat turned to her wife – the only other person still in the room, but Dreya could already see where her plan was going.

"We're going to Earth for a bit, aren't we?" the sorceress surmised.

"Yes, we are," Cat concurred, "and don't give me any crap about us not going off-world."

Dreya shook her head. "I still maintain that as a rule, we shouldn't, but under the circumstances, well, it's worked before."

After they had defeated Kullos, the Guardians were in no fit state to return to the battle against his army, so they had spent a few days recovering on Earth. This time, there were no significant injuries to worry about. They just needed rest.

"But why use Sara's device?" Dreya wondered.

"Insurance," Cat answered. "There's more to this situation than meets the eye. Too many unknowns. Maybe we could travel to Earth and return at the right time. Even if we arrived back too late, we could probably go back in time and fix it. But do you want to risk everything on maybe and probably?"

Dreya shook her head, accepting Catriona's point. This way, Sara's device would give her a beacon to lock onto with her portal from Catriona's Meadow. Catriona was right; this was the best insurance they could get. Pulling power from the fragment again was a risk, but since it would be only a few seconds, she agreed it was one worth taking under the circumstances.

The others all returned at once. Michael had chosen to bring the fragment they had retrieved from Lavos. He didn't believe it would make any difference, but since that one had worked before, why take a chance on the other?

Sara, too, was taking no chances. Putting the device down on the table, she steadied it with both hands while Lao used a small brush to clear away the dust.

"How long do you need?" Cat asked her.

"Five minutes?" she considered. "Ten at most."

"Then activate it ten minutes after we leave," Cat told her.

"People are approaching," Mandalee warned her friends, "and the animals don't think they're friendly."

"Defences are up," Jessica reported.

"Good," Cat acknowledged.

"Now, I know you can all take care of yourselves," Dreya spoke up, "but just in case, I'll get you some reinforcements."

Guessing her meaning, Cat asked, "Are you sure that's a good idea? What if they attack the Black Tower, too?"

Rather than answer directly, her wife opened a portal home and called for her elite guards. She ordered them to activate all of the Black Tower's dormant defences, including a barrier of higher planar energy that should prevent entry by any means other than a portal. Having complied, four death knights and three sinister ghouls appeared in their midst before Dreya closed the portal.

"The Black Tower stood against all comers for three hundred years before I came along," Dreya declared with total conviction. "It's not going to fall again while I'm in charge of the place."

With that, she instructed her elite guards to defend their friends with lethal force against anything that might attack.

Then she pointed to Michael. "Until I return, he's in charge."

Her guards acknowledged her order, and the Guardians opened a portal to Daelen's base on Earth.

"See you in ten minutes!" Mandalee called out as she and Shyleen joined her friends and stepped through.

All those that remained watched the blue Prismatic Sphere close, and Sara started a timer, counting down the seconds.

That's when the attack began.

Chapter 24

The defenders quickly went to patrol the perimeter of their defences. All except Sara, who was keeping an eye on the timer while working on her technology, and Lao, who stood in the doorway, gun in one hand, Portacom in the other. His device already had an open connection to Jessica's mobile phone. He had no idea how either device could function when this world had no satellites, but then he had no idea how any of this world's magic was possible, and he knew better than to ask.

The attacking force numbered close to a hundred. Frankly, between them, it was nothing the defenders couldn't handle, but that wasn't the point. Michael had set up wards to prevent teleportation, but it wouldn't stop portals. Therefore, Lao was vigilant for the merest hint of a blue shimmer in the air in case anyone, anticipating their plan, tried to steal the fragment. Besides the risk of losing the fragment itself, the Guardians were relying on Sara's technology to guide them back in ten minutes.

After those ten minutes, if all went to plan, the Guardians would return at the peak of their powers, and Michael could take the two fragments safely away. Therefore, they focussed exclusively on defence.

Despite Jessica's best efforts, it took less than ninety seconds for the attackers to put their first hole in her glass dome. Behind the glass was a wall of ice, but wizards set about melting it. Fortunately, it happened near her position, and she simply used her magic, plus a bit more sand and water, to repair the damage to both.

When another gap appeared near Michael, penetrating all the way through, the demigod used it as an opportunity to send a swarm of biting insects out to harass their enemies. One particularly bold wizard, ignoring the flies, cast fire at Michael through the gap. Obviously, he had no idea who he was dealing with. Ossian Miach Kaidool had fought shadow warriors with their focussed beam cannons. Compared to that, this wizard's fire, even laced with a bit of higher planar energy, was about as threatening as a candle. Michael sent out two tendrils of his own power that twisted and writhed like snakes. They latched on to the wizard and pumped venom into his body. He began screaming for help, and the clerics in his group displayed the level of their solidarity by ignoring him as he died in agony.

Michael called out for Jessica, who dashed around the perimeter to restore the defences.

Dreya's death knights used such holes to thrust a sword into whatever body might be on the other side, while the ghouls, who were not constrained by a constant physical size, could squeeze through any gap, however small, and freeze the soul of whoever was closest.

Whenever Shyleen saw a breach in the barrier as she patrolled, she quickly found Jessica by her scent and growled to get her attention. Words were not necessary.

At ten minutes, it promised to be the shortest siege in history, but it certainly kept Jessica busy, as she had to run around, plugging the gaps wherever she found them. She quickly gave up using the plants against the attacking force. Warriors just sliced through them with their weapons, and she couldn't spare the effort to actively bind wizards' hands. Catriona might be able to handle all that – and more – at once, but Jessica wasn't at her level. That wasn't a lack of confidence, just self-awareness.

Six minutes in, there were two simultaneous breaches at opposite sides of Michael's grounds. At one end, the invaders were greeted by ravens of death, instilling fear and panic. At the other, death knights met them with steel, which, while more conventional, was no less effective.

It was unclear whether those breaches had been genuine attempts, or mere distractions, as a portal began to open inside Michael's sitting room. Knowing it was too soon to be the Guardians since the beacon was not yet active, Lao and Sara hesitated not a moment as they blanketed the opening with their weapons fire. The portal promptly closed before it fully opened, and Sara breathed a sigh of relief.

The Guardians had been fully confident in their friends' abilities to maintain their defence for even longer than ten minutes, if necessary. However, there was one threat they knew they couldn't counter: Nalani. With her speed, even one minute would be an eternity in which she could grab the fragment and go, almost before anyone else knew what was happening. There was no evidence she was involved with this, but they knew she was linked with their unidentified Black robe wizard adversary. Therefore, if a portal opened before time, Sara knew she couldn't afford to allow it to stabilise for even a second.

The next four minutes seemed like forever, but they held their nerve. The breaches were contained, the damage repaired, and no further portals opened.

Finally, it was time.

At the demigod's order, Jessica, Michael and Dreya's guards retreated into his home, so they were all together. All were ready with their different weapons, just in case anyone other than their friends portalled in. It no longer mattered if the rest of the ancient temple fell to the invaders as long as that one room was secure. Sara activated her device, as she had only once before, and prayed.

Seconds ticked by – Sara estimated each one lasted at least an hour and a half – until a blue Prismatic Sphere opened, out of which stepped the Guardians. Mandalee was first, deciding to trust in her magically resistant bodysuit in case of any mistakes.

"Don't shoot!" she cried. "It's just us!"

*****

The Three Guardians looked much better than they had just ten minutes earlier because it had been somewhat longer than that for them.

They had slept well, and then Dreya and Mandalee had gone to get them some food. Mandalee still had several bags of new clothes from their shopping trip with Daelen the first time they visited Earth. The White Guardian realised that, with the time difference, that was more than a decade ago, so they were probably considered old-fashioned styles by now, but that couldn't be helped. Dreya's black velvet dress was perhaps a little formal for what was mid-afternoon there, but it would do. Catriona still had nothing to wear.

"How did you guys manage on your honeymoon here?" Mandalee asked just before they left. "Or did you two spend all your time here… 'kissing'?"

"We used our perception filters," Dreya answered.

Unfortunately, they needed to be charged from time-to-time, and it made sense to do them all while they were here. So, Cat found herself staying behind to launder their clothes and clean up.

Thanks to their friendship with the Chetsuans, Cat had become better-versed in Earth culture, so she now understood their reference to 'Cinderella'.

When they returned, Mandalee made a show of inspecting her best friend's cleaning and remarked, "I think this is the part where I say, 'you missed a spot'."

Cat nodded. "Yeah, and then I ram my staff up a part of your anatomy that you only have thanks to me," she replied sweetly.

"I suggest we skip both of those," Dreya offered.

After waiting a few hours to allow their food to digest and discuss their plans, they were ready to get back to business. In theory, thanks to Sara's beacon, they could have stayed longer and still returned on time, but that would have been selfish and unprofessional.

They opened a portal to Catriona's Meadow and immediately felt what they could only describe as the pull of Time. They had felt the same thing when they returned from fighting Ulvarius, but being new to such things, they hadn't recognised it. They could override the pull by using Temporal co-ordinates, but they didn't want to. Instead, Dreya used spatial co-ordinates only and allowed the pull to drag them to where – or rather when – they needed to be.

As soon as the portal was fully stabilised, they could see they'd got it right.

*****

Now that they were back in Michael's home, they immediately set to work.

Cat asked for a situation report, and Michael gave her a succinct summary.

Not for the first time, Ossian Miach Kaidool wondered how he found himself taking orders from Catriona. Was it that he was so used to being Daelen's second, or 'sidekick' as his Chetsuan friends liked to call it? Or was it something about Catriona herself? She'd changed since he'd first met her. She seemed…not stronger as such, but more aware of her strength. She didn't give orders in the unthinking way Daelen had, at times. In fact, she was much better at accepting valuable input from those around her, but she still acted like she was in charge. He didn't know if she necessarily thought about it in those terms, but it was true. He wondered what Daelen would make of her now if he were still alive.

As if responding to his thoughts, Catriona advised him to return both fragments safely to Daelen's Tomb.

"Jessica and Sara should join you," she advised, "and take one of the trackers. Go wherever the strongest reading takes you."

The Guardians needed Lao with them so they would have someone with experience of Lavosian technology. The two teams could stay in contact through their respective communications devices, should they need to.

Dreya opened her own portal to Walminster and sent her elite guards through to deal with matters there. The Guardians had discussed this while on Earth and were convinced that there was no way Lavosians could have planted a bomb in the Council building without anybody noticing. That wasn't to say the mages there were safe – with portals, the bomb did not need to be at the detonation site. On Lavos, the two sites had been on opposite sides of the world.

The undead revenants of the people that had attacked Dreya in her own grounds had proved extremely useful over the years. They had helped her to harness and control far more higher planar energy than she could have alone, and so they were perfectly capable of handling whatever rabble were attacking the Council with that same power now.

"Do only what is necessary to remove the attackers' source of power," the sorceress commanded. If it was a fragment of Kullos' control device – which she very much doubted – they would have to take it away to the Black Tower for safety. If, on the other hand, it was just a crude imitation, made from the splintered remains of Mandalee's Pureblade – though Dreya still couldn't understand how that was possible – they could simply contain the power and destroy it.

"No indiscriminate slaughter," she cautioned them with a raised finger.

With a twinkle in his eyes, Michael, who was about to leave with the Chetsuans, remarked, "An act of mercy from Dreya the Dark?"

Shooting him a cautionary scowl, she replied, "I've warned you about comments like that, Mickey. No, I just think the Council should fight their own battles for a change instead of bleating to us!"

Michael acknowledged that with a nod – it was actually a fair point – then left. Jessica's defences were down by now, without her to maintain them, but he wasn't worried about the attacking force. His home wasn't the target. They were after the Guardians, more fool them.

The attacking force entered the ancient temple unopposed until the Guardians met them in the entrance hall. It was a large area with black and white patterned floor tiles, columns at either side holding up the high ceiling, and standing plants in the alcoves between them.

The Guardians knew they couldn't afford to waste too much time and energy on this mob. Not with one or possibly two bombs ready to explode. They wanted to give these people a chance, but they needed the area surrounding Michael's home to be secure again, and not just for Michael's sake. The Guardians intended to evacuate Rhynapolis for safety while they dealt with the situation there, but they didn't want to leave the aliens stranded too far from home. This was the closest settlement, and they obviously had precise co-ordinates, but the Guardians couldn't very well save the aliens from an explosion by dumping them in the middle of a hostile force.

Dreya drove the attackers back with her magic. She could kill them all in a moment if she wished, but she would prefer not to expend unnecessary power.

Mandalee, her dragonclaw daggers a muscle-twitch away from her hands, quipped, "Sorry, there was an open house party here earlier, but I'm afraid you've missed it."

Ignoring her remark, one of the attackers – a man whose sword was entirely the wrong balance for him, in Mandalee's expert judgement – demanded, "Where is he? Where is Oss...assee…ian Mia…rrach Kai…eeaaa…dool?"

The Guardians winced at his terrible pronunciation.

"Not here," Dreya answered, "and be grateful for that, after mangling his name like that! What do you want with him?"

"We want his head!" a Red robe cleric answered.

Cat gave a facial shrug. "I can see why you would – he's quite handsome." The others regarded her strangely. "In his own way," she qualified.

"He means we're going to kill him," a Dark sorceress clarified, apparently not realising Cat's misunderstanding had been sarcasm, "and you're not going to stop us!"

"We actually are," Dreya contradicted, "and since I outrank you on the Council, I'm ordering you to stop."

"You can't give orders, Dreya," she returned. "You're not Black Secondmage anymore, and I don't recognise your authority as Black Guardian."

"Oh, really? Do you think you'll recognise my magic when it kills you?"

Trying to stop things from escalating unnecessarily, Cat asked, "Why are you after Michael anyway?"

"Because he destroyed all our homes!"

Cat frowned. "Recently?"

"Don't be stupid!" the first man retorted. "We're talking about all his battles with Daelen and Kullos, all the destruction he caused!"

"He didn't cause it," Mandalee shot back, "he was trying to help Daelen stop Kullos or the dark clone! I know their battles were terrible and the damage costly, but without Michael and Daelen, things would have been a lot worse."

"We lost friends and family thanks to Michael and the others," the sorceress growled. "The shadow warriors may be gone, but he's still here, and we deserve vengeance!"

That got the mob cheering.

"It's alright for you privileged Guardians!" the first man sneered.

'*Privileged?*' Shyleen remarked. Growling to demonstrate exactly what she thought about that word.

"You don't know what it's like, any of you!" the man continued his rant. "What have you ever suffered? What have you ever lost?"

Dreya and Mandalee both gasped at once, mouths gaping wide at the remark. No words were necessary, just a shared glance. They knew what was coming.

The mob grew louder, backing up the man's words, and Catriona snapped, unleashing her magic. The standing plants proliferated, snaking out to snare the intruders. Wrapping around their limbs, they began to pull taut.

Staff in her hand, blue crystal glowing, her voice was quiet, but it cut through the noise all the same.

"What have I ever suffered? What have I ever lost? When I was a child, I watched my father disintegrate before my eyes. I saw my mother fighting valiantly but futilely against the Monster that attacked our village. My home was destroyed. I lost friends. OK, yes, maybe I was lucky that my Angel came to chase the Monster away and rebuild my home, but the people, my friends, my parents…they were still gone.

"You say I'm privileged to be a Guardian of Time and Magic, and I am, but not the way you mean. Do you think it's never occurred to me to go back in time to try and save my parents? It would be futile because even with all we can do, we still would have no way to fight whatever that Monster was, but it's still a temptation."

Calming down, she told the plants to relax their grip as she made one last entreaty for the mob to understand, surrender their source of higher planar energy and leave.

"For a while, I believed all shadow warriors were as bad as each other, but then I got to know Daelen and realised I was wrong. He never wanted to fight here, but he had to stop Kullos, or Kullos would destroy us all. But even when I blamed Daelen, I never blamed Michael. He was there on the Day of the Monster, and he tried to stop it. The Monster was too powerful even for him. He knew it could destroy him, but he fought it anyway. He did the same for all of you. He fought in the Demon Apocalypse, too, probably saving your parents and grandparents, and ensuring that you all got to be born.

"Now, last chance: will you please stand down and go home? We have reason to believe someone is trying to blow up the alien community, so we need to be in Rhynapolis, not wasting our time here."

There was a stunned silence for a moment, and Catriona dared to hope she was getting through to them, but then the first man spoke up again.

"Let 'em burn!" he scoffed, stirring up the mob's hate once more.

"We don't want those alien freaks here!" a female cleric spat.

"Yeah!" another called out. "Let them all burn!"

More voices were raised in unthinking anger and hate, chanting, "Burn them! Burn them! Burn them!"

Lao had unfortunately chosen that moment to enter the hallway from Michael's sitting room. He had been monitoring Sara's tracking device and was growing ever more concerned about the power build-up it was reading. From the bearing and distance, having seen a map of the area, he was convinced it was in this alien city, Rhynapolis, and they needed to get there fast.

"Freaks like him!" one of the others shouted, pointing.

"Burn the aliens!" cried another.

"Burn them! Burn them! Burn them!"

Chapter 25

Dreya had heard enough. The world was never going to move forward as long as there were people like these in it. She took a pace forward, visibly allowing her power to build, crackling in her hand.

The Black robe sorceress at the head of the mob stepped forward, accepting the challenge.

"You don't scare me, Dreya. You've gone soft since you hooked up with these two. You think you're so powerful with higher planar energy fuelling your magic, but thanks to this," she brandished a metal splinter, "we have the same power!"

Even without the signature of higher planar energy, Mandalee would always have identified it as a splinter of her old Pureblade.

Dreya snorted. "You're deluded if you think that's enough to make your powers anywhere near mine, but thanks for showing it to us. Makes things much easier."

Together with the other Guardians, she Froze Time. Stepping forward, Dreya simply plucked the splinter from the sorceress' unmoving fingers and walked away again.

Rather than cancel the Frozen Timefield, they retracted it to encompass the splinter only.

The enemy sorceress gasped when she saw what had happened, and as the mob watched on, Dreya turned her sharp gaze on the splinter and unfolded her power word, "DISINTEGRATE."

It was the safest disposal method. Despite the name, Dreya's power word didn't just turn the object into dust. It also transported the remains and the energy into the void between planes where it could do no harm.

"We need to go!" Lao warned the Guardians. "Now!"

He didn't care about the mob's hate-fuelled words. After the initial revelation of Sara, Jessica and Michael on his world, similar groups had sprung up. Such bigotry was, ironically, a trait that transcended species.

"Be right with you," Mandalee assured him. "Just after we dispose of this lot."

The plants were still restraining them, but the Guardians couldn't just leave them like that. Nor did they want to waste their energy fighting them, but Dreya had the perfect solution. She opened a portal to just outside the Council building in Walminster.

Dreya's elite guards were still handling the situation there, so she called to them, "You can deal with this lot, too!"

With perfect timing, Cat made the plants let go, so Dreya could push them through with her magic. As soon as they were gone, Dreya closed her portal, and Mandalee opened another one to Rhynapolis. She spent quite a bit of time over in Alloria, these days, when she wasn't doing Guardian business, and so was more familiar with the co-ordinates.

As they stepped through with Lao, the White Assassin caught the Black Guardian's arm and remarked, "Dreya, you never warned your guards not to kill that lot."

The sorceress nodded. "You're right. I didn't."

"Good."

*****

Laoghaire stared at the tracking device in puzzlement. He even shook it a couple of times as if in doubt as to whether it was working.

"It doesn't make sense," he remarked, chiefly to himself.

"What's wrong?" Mandalee asked him.

"The reading – it's gone down," he explained, still not taking his eyes off the display. "The power was building up, but suddenly, it's gone down to—"

"—To where it was half an hour ago?" Cat suggested.

Lao finally looked up in amazement. "About twenty-nine and a half minutes, actually."

Mandalee winced and snapped her fingers. "Forgot about Temporal lensing, didn't I?"

Cat nodded.

'*Still, thirty seconds out isn't bad,*' Shyleen told her.

"No, it's not," Dreya agreed.

The White Guardian spun to face her. "You heard her?"

"I've been experimenting with some of Renjaf's mental magic," she offered, by way of answer, "and I found a way to tune into Shyleen's frequency."

'*But how do you know my language?*' asked the leopard.

"I don't," Dreya admitted. "Translation magic. It's cheating, I know, but I keep feeling I'm missing part of the conversation."

'*We'll have to be careful what we say about her, in future,*' Shyleen remarked to Mandalee.

Cat and Mandalee both laughed.

Dreya, acting indignant, demanded, "What have you been saying about me when I can't understand you?"

Cat kissed Dreya's cheek and replied, "Nothing you need to worry your pretty little head about, dear."

"What is wrong with you people?" Lao demanded. "Have you forgotten a bomb's due to go off at any moment?"

Cat checked the timepiece on her wrist. "Not for at least half an hour," she disputed, an amused look on her face.

"You do know we've got Time magic, right?" Dreya checked.

Lao blinked, stunned as he realised the implication. "You mean, the reason the power reading has gone down is that—"

"—I opened a Temporal portal to half an hour ago," Mandalee finished for him. "Well, more-or-less," she conceded. "Forgot about Temporal lensing – portals make past events seem closer than they are."

"That's why we were half a minute out," Dreya explained. "No big deal."

Lao was visibly relieved. "Sorry," he breathed. "New to all this. I thought you weren't taking the threat seriously."

"We're always serious about what we do," Cat insisted. "Just not necessarily—"

"—the way we do it!" the other two chorused.

"Relax," Cat told him. "We're going to save the world, same as always."

"But why half an hour? Why not a day or a week?"

"Because non-specific co-ordinates can be dangerous," Cat explained, "except for short hops like this."

"Plus," Dreya put in, "we have to factor in the distance between Rhynapolis and Michael's place."

Mandalee addressed his blank look. "We don't have your communications technology, Lao, or your travel machines, and as far as we can tell, none of the aliens has teleportation magic. That means if someone in Rhynapolis knew or suspected something was wrong and decided to go for help, they would have to head for Michael's place. They know him, and Sara and Jessica have helped out here a lot. Travelling there takes about an hour."

Catriona took up the explanation. "If we went back in time, say, two hours, and warned these people, somebody could set out to try and get help from Michael…"

Laoghaire finally caught on. "…Then they could be there before we left, which could change the events that led us to come here."

Dreya nodded. "Planned paradoxes can be useful tools. Accidental ones are best avoided."

"Besides which, any aliens coming for help would be in the middle of that alien-hating mob," Mandalee pointed out.

Lao's eyes widened. "I can't see that ending well!"

Cat nodded. "Now do you see why I was keen for us to get some rest before diving into our next adventure? Someone was trying to force us into rash action, hoping we'd make mistakes like that."

She also explained that she had quite deliberately sent Allorian-based Michael, Sara and Jessica to deal with matters in Elvaria, while they came to Rhynapolis themselves.

"I'm betting whoever planned this would have expected it to be the other way around because it's more logical. This way, hopefully, I've completely screwed up their plans."

Lao smiled grimly. "Whoever that someone is, they're obviously going to have to do a lot better if they want to outsmart you."

Cat patted him on the shoulder encouragingly. "Now, let's see about evacuating these people, shall we?"

Rather than collapse the portal, Mandalee reduced the size to a discreet micro-portal and tethered it to her: a technique Catriona had invented on Earth to help her maintain a connection to Tempestria. When they found a suitable spot, she would widen it and anchor it in place so that the people of Rhynapolis could escape to safety.

*****

Rhynapolis had certainly come a long way since the Guardians were first in that area. Back then, of course, the place had been surrounded by a shield of higher planar energy keeping everyone inside. That was long since gone, taken down by Dreya's elite guards. Kullos' fortress still remained in the middle of the settlement, but even that had changed. There were many more windows where walls used to be, making the place open and inviting instead of dark and foreboding.

Even before the battle against Kullos' forces, there had been the beginnings of permanent construction, as if some already suspected they might never see their homeworlds again. There were many more now. This was now their home. The Guardians would do everything in their considerable powers to prevent it from being destroyed by the bomb that was ticking away somewhere nearby. But in the end, they were more concerned with saving the people first and ending the threat of the explosive device and its power source second. If necessary, buildings could be rebuilt. People couldn't. Catriona knew that from bitter experience. Still, if there were to be any collateral damage, she hoped the people of Rhynapolis wouldn't blame them the way that mob had blamed Michael.

From what they knew of Rhynapolis, the people had established their own administration inside the former fortress. Since none of the aliens appeared to have any significant magical abilities, the Council of Mages felt they had no jurisdiction. As for the regular Allorian authorities, frankly, even fifty years since the Accords at the end of the Demon Apocalypse, they still had enough to do without dealing with this alien city as well.

Depending on one's point of view, the aliens had either been granted the freedom to live their own lives or abandoned to fend for themselves.

Either way, they were certainly making a good go of it. In fact, the way members of a dozen or more species were interacting with each other as the Guardians walked through the city with Lao, Cat thought it quite inspirational.

The tracker led them to the fortress, although when they entered, they found it had been turned into an enormous indoor marketplace called the Rhynapolis Arcade.

Laoghaire remarked that it was not unlike the marketplaces in some of the less technologically advanced parts of Lavos. Cat and Mandalee's frame of reference was different, of course. There were similar centres of commerce on Elvaria, and while it wasn't as lavish as the shopping mall they had visited on Earth, it was impressive, nonetheless.

As for Dreya, she found she was having uncomfortable flashbacks to her time in Axford Market on Phitonia. Before Purity came to wipe out all intelligent life for failing to live up to her twisted standards of perfection. It was worse that she couldn't share the memory. If she told any of the people beside her, her Chetsuan friends might also learn the awful truth. Having seen their world before she ended the threat of the dragons, Dreya had gained a unique insight into their lives before Daelen, and the truth was she admired them. It had been a harsh world, a hard life, even before the dragons took them away to be experimented on. They'd learned to fight at an early age, so they were both formidable in their different ways, but they'd been through enough. Dreya was resolute that they deserved to live their lives on Tempestria unburdened by the knowledge of the destruction of a world they could never see again anyway. And so, she buried her feelings and remained silent.

According to the signs, the reception was the first room on the left, and they hurriedly entered. The blue-skinned man working in reception betrayed recognition of the Guardians with his widening eyes.

Without preamble, Catriona told him, "We need to talk to whoever's in charge of this place immediately."

"And anything you have in the way of security needs to hear it, too," Mandalee added.

The man's apologetic expression suggested he was going to politely refuse or perhaps ask them to make an appointment.

Dreya cut him off. "We wouldn't be here if it wasn't an emergency."

She allowed her power to crackle in her hand to emphasise the point. It usually helped to motivate people, and it didn't let her down now.

The man didn't even speak. He just nodded and led them to an adjoining room where a dozen people were assembled in a rough semicircle, discussing whatever matters were on the agenda that day. That agenda was about to change.

"Excuse me, Administrators," the blue man apologised, "but you have some important visitors."

Seeing who was in their midst, they all rose to their feet to greet them and introduce themselves.

Cat forestalled that, saying, "I'm sorry, but we don't have time for that. We need to evacuate this building, possibly the entire city, because we have reason to believe there's a bomb primed to explode in the heart of Rhynapolis."

Everyone began talking at once until Dreya launched a small fireball at the ceiling. It was low power, so it did little more than singe the paint but was enough to engender a stunned silence.

"Sorry," she apologised, "but if we don't stop this bomb, you won't have a ceiling anymore, or anything else for that matter."

"We understand you have questions, but we don't have time to waste," Mandalee insisted.

One of the administrators, a burly man of a reptilian species with dark green scales, raised his hand, and Cat nodded, granting him permission to speak.

Introducing himself as Brakkis, Head of Security, he asked, "How long have we got?"

"At least twenty minutes," Lao volunteered.

"We can stretch that out," Cat added, "but we have to find the bomb first."

Brakkis took charge, ordering his eleven colleagues and the secretary to spread the fire alarm. With a remarkable lack of debate, they each ran to a cupboard in which there sat a dozen large handheld bells. As soon as they had one each, they left the room and scattered into the corridors, ringing them loudly.

The security chief still looked troubled. "We can evacuate the Arcade," he said, "we have contingencies for that, but not the entire city."

"You can with time," Cat assured him. "That's why we're here, to give you that time – in case we can't disarm it before it explodes."

Offering no argument, which the Guardians appreciated. Brakkis simply asked, "What do you need?"

'*If only the Council were this co-operative!*' Mandalee sent to Shyleen. She broadcast the telepathic message, and from the hidden smiles, she knew the others had heard, too.

The White Guardian asked Brakkis to take her to the assembly point, so she could anchor the portal for the Rhynapolis citizens to evacuate. Shyleen remained with the others. Their unique bond would help Mandalee find them again.

Lao remained in charge of the tracker since he understood the technology, and the others followed him where it led. Winding through the maze of passageways, they reached a long, narrow corridor that led straight to a dead end. Ahead of them was a blank stone wall, and to the left was an access door with an adjacent keypad. It wasn't something one would expect to see on Tempestria, but then, this was a city of aliens. As such, it was full of strange things. That made it the perfect place to hide alien technology – nobody would pay it much attention. What would attract attention was the sign on the door:

KEEP OUT – UNDER CONSTRUCTION

DANGER OF DEATH

Chapter 26

"I'm betting the 'Danger of Death' part is accurate," Lao suggested. "Trying to go through that door without the correct keypad sequence would be bad for your health."

Strangely, according to the tracker, the source of higher planar energy was directly ahead, behind the wall, not the door, but there didn't appear to be any other way in.

Presumably, Lao suggested, the door led to a corridor on the left-hand side, allowing access to an adjacent room through another door a little further on.

The Lavosian put his tracker away in favour of his Portacom.

"Don't worry," he assured them. "I deal with things like this all the time on my world. I'll soon have the right code." With that, he began to furiously tap the screen.

While he was working, Mandalee came rushing back. "People are being evacuated," she reported. "I quickly popped through the portal myself to make sure it was safe."

A quick consultation with the animals suggested there was nothing unusual in the vicinity. That didn't preclude the possibility of people portalling or teleporting there, but she couldn't stand guard over them. Brakkis had sent some of his security team through for that.

Looking around, Mandalee remarked, "This place brings back memories!"

At almost the same instant, Lao announced, "Got it!"

He was about to punch in the entry code when Cat screamed, "Stop!" and slapped his hand away.

"Why? What's wrong?" he asked.

"You deal with things like this on your world all the time," she replied, repeating his own words back to him. "So, it made sense for you to take the lead. If Jessica and Sara were here, they probably would have deferred to your knowledge of Lavosian technology. But this is our world. A world of magic. If we wanted to hide something, we wouldn't do it like this. As Mandalee says, this place brings back memories; we've been here before."

The White Guardian had seen past the superficial changes and realised this narrow passageway had once been the access to

Kullos' throne room. Their Chetsuan friends had held his guards at bay in the very spot in which they were now standing. The stone wall in front of them, blocking off the corridor, was new.

"You think that door's a trap," Mandalee realised.

Cat nodded. "It's the kind of thing I do – set a trap with an easy escape, then if they take the bait, they fall into the real trap."

Dreya spoke up then. "Whoever built the bomb here must have exact co-ordinates, so they don't even need a door. Just a permanent portal."

"So, how do we get in?" Lao asked.

"I take the wall away," Cat replied. She'd mastered stoneshaper magic many years ago. It was easy, and they didn't have to worry about the ceiling crashing down because it had got along perfectly well before the wall was built.

"Be ready," she warned.

Lao took his gun off safety, Mandalee's dragonclaw daggers flicked into her hands, Shyleen's claws came out, too, and Dreya pricked her finger on her own knife to access blood magic.

Cat reached out with her druid senses. The stone was moving all the time. Tiny, imperceptible vibrations. All she had to do was encourage them, coax them, magnify them. The friction generated heat, and that, too, she multiplied until the rock began to soften and melt, making it easier and easier to move. Working in concert with nature, it required minimal effort, and soon the stone parted with a groan to open up into a makeshift doorway.

Kullos' throne room itself looked much like it had before as they stepped through, except now there were cables everywhere, spilling out from the throne itself and connecting with technology that was unknown to the Guardians but all too familiar to Laoghaire.

"Dear gods!" he breathed. "They really are doing it again."

At the heart of all that technology, there lay a glass box containing several small metal splinters – the splintered remains of Mandalee's Pureblade. Above that, there was a large digital display, counting down the time to detonation. They had twenty-nine minutes left. Doing a quick calculation, Lao realised that it had taken about twenty minutes to get here from when they arrived. Maybe a touch over. Therefore, the countdown must have been at about forty-nine to fifty minutes when they portalled in. Had they not travelled back in time by half an hour, they would have had only nineteen or twenty minutes when they arrived in the city. In that case, they would have found the bomb just in time for it to blow up in their faces. He wasn't sure even the Guardians could have reacted in time to do anything in that situation. If Sara and Jessica had come here instead of the Guardians, they would have been killed for sure.

He also realised that at the same time as he was here with the Guardians, he was also at Michael's temple home, watching those same Guardians return from Earth.

Time travel made his head hurt. He didn't know how the three beside him kept track of it all.

He didn't have much time to reflect on that, however. Behind the throne there was, as Dreya had predicted, a glowing blue portal, through which came twenty armed Lavosians, ready to fight to protect what they had built.

*****

Elsewhere, the Chetsuan twins had accompanied Michael through the portal to Daelen's Tomb. This was their first visit there since saying their goodbyes to their friend, the fallen shadow warrior. The one who had taken them from their world to save them, or more accurately, to save their world from them, because as biologically engineered plague carriers, they would kill every other Chetsuan they met.

It was hard to see his body, unmoving and lifeless, surrounded by shadow warrior technology that was beyond even Sara. But they had to steel themselves to it. Daelen StormTiger was dead. His troubles were over. It was the living who needed them.

Sara programmed her detector to ignore the power of the fragments of Kullos' control device that were inside the Tower of Dreams, and scan beyond the walls of the Tomb. It gave them a bearing and distance. That the direction was South was a given, since the rocky outcrop of the Tomb was the northernmost point of Elvaria. From the distance reading, however, they knew the source of higher planar energy it was detecting was about as far south as they could go without getting wet. The south coast. Tedstone Warf. Melrose Academy.

Sara rolled her eyes. "I don't know why I bothered building this thing!" she grumbled, brandishing her tracker. "Cat knew the other bomb would be there without any gadgets."

It would, however, help them narrow down its exact location within the school, and in situations like these, every minute, every second they saved could be precious.

Another portal took them outside the main school complex, from where they could get a more accurate reading. Unfortunately, they seemed to have portalled into the middle of a warzone as a force of wizards, clerics and warriors were attacking the building, trying to break through the shields that the Melrose staff were desperately working to hold together.

Inevitably, the big blue door in space had attracted attention, and half the warriors rushed towards the companions as the mages threw their magic at them. Michael shielded while he and the Chetsuans fought, but none of that was getting them any closer to where they needed to be. A fact Jessica highlighted to Michael.

"I know," he replied, "but I can't shield us and open a portal at the same time!"

Sara and Jessica shared a glance, both thinking the same thing. No words were needed.

"Drop the shield," Jessica told Michael.

"What? I can't—"

"Trust us!" Sara insisted, taking her sister's hand.

Michael did as they asked. Opening a portal inside the school would only take a few seconds, but a lot could happen in a few seconds. Still, all he could do was trust them.

Sheathing all weapons, Sara and Jessica, standing completely still, took a deep breath and focussed their will. When they were together, they were unstoppable…well, except that one time against Dreya, but they couldn't let that give them any doubts. That was a unique situation. Here and now, they knew they could do it. Together.

Their eyes flashed with a golden light as they chanted, "You don't want to harm us. You don't want to harm us. You don't want to harm us."

All at once, the magical attack ended, and the warriors ceased their charge, coming to a natural halt. They all looked confused, as if they knew they had been doing something but couldn't remember what.

It wasn't easy for the Chetsuan twins to use their telepathy against about sixty minds at once, but they didn't need to hold it for long.

Marvelling at the power of these two young Chetsuan women, the Champion of the Gods opened his portal while they kept the attackers at bay.

Prismatic Sphere now ready, he could restore his shields, allowing the Chetsuans to cease their mental attack and run. The force resumed their assault as soon as the mental hold was gone, and the girls jumped through the portal like their tails were on fire.

"Go and find the bomb!" he called after them. "I'll handle the evacuation."

Just before Michael could join them, however, a golden lioness, moving impossibly fast, knocked him off his feet.

He managed to throw the three-hundred-pound furball off him but standing between him and the portal, was a young woman with dark brown hair in a single braid down her back, which she was stroking with one hand while she played with a vicious-looking knife in the other.

"I hear you're a creature of the gods," she remarked, "so you might recognise my companion."

Looking again at the lioness, Michael's eyes widened.

"Pryshia!" he gasped.

He did indeed recognise her. Long ago, the gods created Ossian Miach Kaidool to help Daelen stop Kullos. Motives were many, but they reached an agreement all the same. Each gave a portion of their own life essence to combine into a single entity. A demigod. Of all the gods there present, there was but one who failed to participate: the lioness god, Pryshia. She wasn't going to give away anything of herself for any reason, but she didn't say that outright. She stood in a ring with all the other gods and began the magic, but at the last possible moment, she stopped and withdrew from the circle, forcing all the others to expel a little more of themselves to make up the shortfall. That weakened them, allowing Pryshia, always the bully of the Pantheon, to rule over them all as their queen.

She was not a kind ruler, delighting in tormenting, even torturing the other gods for her amusement.

Thus she had continued until the day an Angel Descended, abandoning her war with the shadow warriors to Cleanse the mortal plane of evil. Especially those who had dared commit the ultimate blasphemy in Creating a facsimile of that which the Creator had made perfect in the Beginning.

In doing so, Purity had fractured Alicia's Barrier. Seizing the opportunity, the other gods banded together and did to Pryshia what she had done to the leopard goddess, Shyleen – Banished her down to the mortal realm. She found herself on a world called Phitonia and, from there, made her way to Tempestria, thanks to reaching an accord with a mortal wizard.

Pryshia appeared to an angry young girl, Nalani. She was already a zealous fighter who held a grudge against the mortal with whom Shyleen had bonded. With a little manipulation, Pryshia moulded Nalani into a weapon. Nalani would murder Mandalee, and Pryshia would exact vengeance against Shyleen. With luck, Pryshia thought, she would be able to extract enough power from Shyleen's dying essence to re-Ascend and retake her rightful place as Queen of the Pantheon.

It had already taken longer than she had expected, thanks to two failed attempts, and she wasn't any closer now. That wizard had promised her that Mandalee and Shyleen would be here, separated from the other Guardians, so they wouldn't be able to use their Temporal magic effectively. This time they were supposed to die, and she and Nalani were here to make sure of it.

Except the Guardians weren't here. Only their friends were. Pryshia didn't really care about the aliens one way or the other, but this demigod could be useful. He was a creature of the gods; therefore, as far as Pryshia was concerned, she was his Queen. That made him hers to use as she saw fit, and his death would serve her needs very well indeed.

"And you must be Nalani," Michael realised.

The girl nodded. "Right, and now that we've been introduced, close this," she pointed to the portal behind her.

"I can't," he insisted. "My friends, all those people, they'd be trapped."

Nalani shrugged. “If you don’t, I’ll just go through and kill them all myself. Maybe they’ll stop the bomb, maybe not, but they won’t stop me.”

Inside the building, a man had spotted the portal and, thinking it represented escape, ran through it.

Nalani stopped fidgeting and, with a blur of action, slit the man’s throat and shoved him back through the portal to die in a river of his own blood.

“And I’ll do that to anyone who comes out,” she told Michael. She fixed him with a threatening glare. “Close it. Now.”

She was right, Michael accepted. His Chetsuan friends were formidable fighters, but there was no way they could stop Nalani. They’d never even see her coming, she was so fast. None of the people trapped in Melrose would stand a chance. So, as much as he hated it, with a whispered apology, he closed his portal, trapping his friends and everyone else inside.

*****

Over in Rhynapolis, Lao fired his gun at the attackers, but his aim was slightly off, and the laser hit the wall, mere inches from one of the control panels.

“For the gods’ sake, Lao, put that thing away before you kill us all!” Dreya warned him, reaching out with her magic and stopping two hearts. Even their attackers were armed with knives and swords rather than guns, and Dreya herself planned to avoid any physical magic.

“Leave this to us – you focus on the technology,” Cat told him.

She melted the stone floor, so their attackers found themselves ankle-deep in mud, slowing them without the need for temporal magic.

Mandalee didn’t even bother with her super-speed, preferring to conserve energy for the greater challenges that were sure to come.

Trusting in their protection, Lao swapped his gun for his Portacom, scanning the technology. There was a redundancy in the readings that he couldn’t understand. It was as if the system were measuring everything twice. Why? It wasn't just there in case one broke down; he was sure of that much.

Within five minutes, all the attackers were dead, and Mandalee stood guard by the portal while her friends joined Lao next to the Pureblade splinter housing.

Had they been dealing with a fragment of Kullos' control device, Dreya would have had to extract it and return it to Daelen's Tomb with the others. These cheap imitations, however, were of no use to her whatsoever. Yes, they contained power, but only a fraction of that contained within a fragment. Enough to take out most of this city, but insignificant compared to what Dreya wanted: the power to destroy an Angel. She doubted this was enough power to trim Purity's toenails. It wasn't worth the effort to stabilise the power. Better to simply destroy the splinters and vent the power harmlessly away.

Dreya didn't see the point of all this technology, just to blow up one city. She could do that with a sneeze if she wanted to, but it would be a waste of power. It would gain her nothing.

Fixing her gaze on the splinters, then, using the casing as the perimeter of her containment field, she mentally checked the preparation of her power word and focussed on the splinters, as she had with the one that stupid sorceress had laughingly used to threaten her inside Michael's home.

"DISIN—"

With a cry of "Stop!" Lao suddenly knocked into her, interrupting the magic.

Dreya's eyes widened, and Cat immediately knew why. Power words were like folded magic. Rather than inscribe the language of magic during the casting, it was all prepared beforehand, ready to let fly in the time it took to say one word, which would unfold and unleash the magic. But it was vital that the magic was folded and unfolded correctly. That was something Ulvarius, the first wizard to experiment with power words, had never understood. That was why he could never get the magic to stabilise.

The sorceress was visibly struggling with the effort, her body trembling, her face flushed red. Beads of sweat began to appear on her brow.

“Dreya!” Catriona cried out. She desperately wanted to help her wife, but she knew there was nothing she could do. There was a battle for control going on inside Dreya’s mind. The magic was stuck half-unfolded, but it couldn’t stay that way. It had to go to completion, but now it was many orders of magnitude harder to control.

Eyes flashing, Cat lashed out and threw her water bottle at Lao’s feet, where the spilt water grew into an ice prison, rising up his legs to his waist.

“The spell has to finish. Disintegrate something. It could obliterate this entire room!” Or, if she couldn’t send it out, it would disintegrate Dreya’s brain, instead. “Give me one good reason why she shouldn’t disintegrate you!”

Chapter 27

As soon as they got inside Melrose, the two sisters made their way to the main entrance, where most of the senior staff were trying to maintain the shields against the assault. Dagamir was easy to identify thanks to his swashbuckling outfit and the sword at his side, so they approached him and warned him about the bomb.

"Dear gods!" he breathed. "We've been so focussed on the trouble outside, we didn't even think there might be something worse inside!"

"We're going to try and deal with it," Sara told him, "but in the meantime, you need to evacuate."

"Don't you think we've tried that?" he shot back. "We can't teleport through the magical shields, and if we drop them, there won't be time to do anything!"

"That's OK, dearie," Jessica assured him. "We've got Michael with us. He can get you all to safety."

"Hang on, where is he?" Sara wondered, realising he wasn't with them.

Dagamir accompanied them back to the corridor where they'd portalled in, just in time to see a man get dumped through it. There was blood everywhere. Then the portal closed.

They ran over to the man, but they were too late. He was dead.

Dagamir cried out in shock, recognising him. "Yanis!"

"I'm sorry," Sara sympathised, "but if we don't act fast, we'll be joining him."

Dagamir ran his fingers through his hair, at a loss as to what they could do.

"Think, Dagamir!" Jessica urged him. "If Michael's got trouble, we need another way out of here. There's got to be something!"

"I don't know," he faltered. "Maybe we'd be better off taking the fight out there."

Sara shook her head. "Judging by the power readings on here," she held up her device, "if that bomb explodes, it won't make any difference whether we're in here or out there. We need to get away – far away."

"Or, better still," Jessica offered, "stop the bomb from going off at all."

Looking at the device in Sara's hand, Dagamir reasoned, "I take it that's telling you where this bomb is?"

She nodded.

Making a decision, he told them, "Right, I'm coming with you. Maybe there's something I can do to help with that."

They dashed through the school corridors, stumbling every time another blast of magic shook the building. Along the way, he literally bumped into a White robe sorceress hurrying the other way with a young boy in tow.

Dagamir apologised, but the White Triumvirate representative waved it aside as she recognised the two purple catlike aliens that accompanied him.

"You two!" she cried. "Does this mean the Guardians are here, somewhere?" The light of hope that grew in her eyes dimmed just as quickly when they shook their heads.

"They've got other troubles," Sara explained briefly, desperate to get to the bomb, quickly.

"As have we," Jessica added. She was about to explain further, but Dagamir shook his head slightly and subtly drew her attention to Maia's son.

The two sisters shared a glance. This was something they'd seen a lot in this world. On Earth, too, if only in the movies. Perhaps it happened in real life there, too, Jessica pondered – shielding children from the reality of their situation. No-one had ever done that on Phitonia. When she and Sara were children, the dragons were everywhere, and they knew they could be snatched or killed at any time. Their parents had never shielded them from that. Nor did they hide the fact that there were evil Chetsuans out there, too, that might do the same or worse.

This school was under attack from the outside – this boy must surely realise that, given how the building shook with every blast. Jessica really didn't see the point of trying to hide the existence of the bomb from him. Surely, he had a right to know. However, this was clearly neither the time nor the place for such a debate.

Dagamir suggested a telepathic conference with Maia, and she agreed. It was easy to tell from Maia's expression the moment he mentioned the word 'bomb', but it was equally evident from Dagamir's face that she'd also said something significant to him.

"A portal!" he gasped. "I've been trying for years, but I can't make them stabilise."

The last time Melrose was under attack, the White Guardian had created a portal in the basement to get everyone away. Once the danger had passed, he'd tried to analyse it from the outside. Using that experience, he'd adjusted his magic, but it hadn't helped much.

"You two came through a portal," he realised. "Maybe if I could gain an impression of one from the inside, that might help me stabilise mine."

He'd travelled through portals himself, of course, but he hadn't tried to analyse the magic for fear of offending the Guardians to whom he quite literally owed his life. However, with the new mental magic techniques he had learned recently from Renjaf's lost research, Dagamir believed what he could gain from within the minds of these two alien girls would be every bit as clear as if he were inside a portal himself.

"Alright, but we need to get to the, erm—" Sara looked pointedly at her tracker.

Without further comment, they ran in the direction it showed them until they reached a staircase.

"What's up here?" Jessica asked.

Dagamir shrugged. "Just old storerooms. Junk, mostly. I keep meaning to have a clearout."

Maia crouched down to talk to her son.

"Rivius, can you do something really important for me?"

He nodded.

She sat him down on the bottom step and continued, "Stay right here while I go with Mr Dagamir and his friends. If anybody comes looking for us, tell them where we are. Can you do that?"

When Rivius nodded once more, his mum hugged him and praised him. "Good boy."

Wasting no time, the four climbed the steps quickly and charged through the door at the top.

Inside, the room was filled with technology, rigged up to a box containing pieces of metal that were emitting the telltale signature of magic and higher planar energy. Not the fragment they had expected, but more splinters of Mandalee's Pureblade. That was just as well, Sara pointed out, because Michael had the containment box.

"Looks like someone's done the clearing out for you, Dagamir," Jessica remarked.

"Without my authorisation, too," he nodded pensively. "I don't remember signing the paperwork to purchase all this technology, either."

According to the countdown that was clearly on display above the splinter housing, there were less than twenty-five minutes left.

Sara shrugged, trying to look on the bright side. "We've had worse countdowns."

Remembering the time they saved Lavos, her sister smiled and nodded.

That was when they were attacked.

A dozen renegade wizards came at them, and the four were forced to defend themselves. Maia lashed out with a lightning bolt that narrowly missed one of the control panels.

"Don't do that in here!" Sara cried. "If you hit the tech, you could kill us all!"

"Just shield us," Jessica advised. She and her sister were wearing their magic-resistant bodysuits, but there was no sense in taking chances.

Dagamir's sword rang out as he drew it, moving to attack. The blade flashed, glowing red and crackling with magic, but it remained firmly under control, posing no risk of unintentional damage.

Likewise, the Chetsuans went for their dragonclaw knives rather than risk their guns around all that technology.

They killed the wizards in short order, but it had delayed them. The timer was now down to under twenty minutes, and they were no closer to stopping the bomb or evacuation.

Sara volunteered to check out the technology while Dagamir took a stroll in Jessica's mind.

After a moment, he offered, "I have what I need to stabilise my portals now; I'm sure of it. But I need time."

"Then get to it," Sara told him. "We can take care of things here."

So, with barely a nod, Dagamir left the room to see to the evacuation. He didn't pause to wish them luck. He trusted these friends of the Guardians to deal with the latest crisis without relying on such an ephemeral concept.

Maia felt like a spare wheel. She tried to remain on guard, but she wasn't sure what she could do in the event of more trouble if she couldn't use direct magic to defend herself and the others. Maybe Dagamir had the right idea, she considered. The sorceress had previously thought his sword merely a part of his flamboyant style, matching his outfit that was more adventurer than wizard. Now she knew otherwise. He knew well how to use his sword. Combining that with his sharp mind and potent magic, he could deal with any situation in the most expedient way.

Clerics were allowed to use whatever weapons they chose. The White Guardian even wore body armour like the two aliens before her. Maia had always resisted changes like that for wizards, but now she was beginning to see it might be wise to re-evaluate some of her opinions; change some of the rules.

A loud noise broke her out of her introspection. For a moment, she was worried the bomb had gone off. An irrational idea, since if it had, she wouldn't be alive to worry about it. On reflection, she realised it hadn't sounded like an explosion so much as something getting smashed. As she looked around, though, there was no damage that she could see.

The four companions picked their way around the technology in the centre of the attic room, following the direction of the noise. There they found a previously hidden portal.

Peering through to the other side, they were astonished to see the Guardians and their Lavosian friend, Laoghaire, who was currently half encased in ice that slowly grew upward, threatening to engulf him.

*****

"Have you any idea how dangerous it is to interrupt a power word?" Catriona hissed.

"No," Lao returned, "but I know we'd all be dead if I hadn't!"

"What are you talking about?" Cat demanded. The woman she loved was in pain, struggling for control, fighting for her mind and her life, and the druidess couldn't see past the fact that Lao had caused it. Meanwhile, the ice prison continued to grow, reaching up to his chest, making it hard to breathe, and the cold was beginning to take its toll on his body.

Mandalee rushed over and placed a gentle hand on her shoulder.

"Cat," she implored her softly, "let him speak."

The White Guardian understood her friend's reaction. When Shyleen was hurt, all she wanted was the blood of whoever had caused it. But this was different. She didn't believe Lao would have done what he did without a good reason.

Her best friend's touch was a lifeline to Catriona's reasoning, and she slowed the progress of the ice.

"Alright, Lao," she accepted in a warning tone, "I'm listening, but this had better be good."

"You were right about there being more than one bomb," he told her, shivering with cold. "It's on the other side of that portal, and the two sites are linked. Just like they were on my world. If you suddenly remove the power source here, the power will rush in from the other side, and—"

"Blow us all to bits!" Mandalee realised. Turning to her friend, she cried, "Cat! It's not his fault! He had to stop her. Now you have to stop before you kill him."

Cat shook her head. His explanation made sense, and she knew she should stop, but she was too scared and, as irrational as it was, her anger was still there. But now it had no focus, and the ice slowly resumed its progress up Laoghaire's body against her wishes. She tried to make it stop, but it wouldn't obey.

"Cat, listen to me," Mandalee implored her. "Your magic is tied to your emotions. Your magic is out of control because your emotions are. You have to tell your magic to stop, and it has to know you mean it." As long as her emotions were all over the place, her druid powers didn't know what she wanted. That made them unpredictable.

"But Dreya could die!" Cat wailed desperately. Tears in her eyes.

The ice was nearly up to Lao's neck. Mandalee opened her mouth, but it was Dreya who, with heroic effort, gasped, "Oh…ye…of…little…faith!"

It was as if she was trying to squeeze each word through a tiny gap. Then, something suddenly gave way. Looking up at the ceiling, she cried out, "DISINTEGRATE!" Her power launched upwards and removed the ceiling with a concussive blast, leaving a gaping hole in the roof. Loose debris fell all around them – fortunately, none of it was big or heavy enough to harm them. The whole structure groaned, but thankfully it was strong enough to hold.

"It'll take more than that to finish me off."

The entity in her head had seized the opportunity to free more of itself, but that was a worry for another day.

All at once, Catriona realised she was about to murder an innocent person, regained control and shattered the ice prison, melting it, evaporating the water and gently warming Lao's body.

After an enormous hug of relief for Dreya, she tentatively approached Laoghaire.

"Lao," she began, deeply ashamed of her reaction. "I am so sorry. I should have listened. Let you explain. I'm so, so sorry."

The Lavosian offered her a grim smile. "If I believed someone had put my wife in danger, I'd lash out, too."

Cat's face lit up. "You're married?"

He nodded. "Ten years," he replied.

Mandalee frowned, "How—?" then she remembered. "Of course, time moves faster there."

"Maybe we should stop the bomb now, socialise later?" Dreya suggested, though she did join them and offer Lao her hand. "You acted fast and saved us all from my rash action. Thank you."

"Now that that's all sorted out," Mandalee put in, "I'd say it's about time we Froze Time so that the people here can evacuate before they run out of time." She pulled a face and remarked, "Only three. That's rubbish!"

"Three?" Lao wondered.

"From time to time, we like to see how many times we can get the word 'time' into one sentence," Cat explained, "and I guess this is one of those times." With a grin, she declared, "Five – a new record!"

Laoghaire shook his head in disbelief. “You people are ridiculous!”

“Yes, I suppose we are,” Mandalee nodded thoughtfully. “Anyway, you still have the Timeless dagger, right?”

Lao frowned for a moment and then remembered he’d wedged it in his belt. “Sorry. Completely forgot I had it,” he replied. Reaching around to where it was hidden under his shirt, he made to hand it back, but the White Guardian stopped him.

“We didn’t forget, and you’re going to need it.”

Cat nodded. “It will let you operate within a Timeless field. Otherwise, you won’t be much use to us when we Freeze Time.”

“I really wouldn’t do that!” came a familiar voice.

Turning around, they noticed Jessica and Sara on the other side of the shimmering blue portal.

Sara had accessed the technology on that side, and like Lao, she had recognised the redundancy in the systems, but without the distractions their friends had had to deal with, she’d had time to figure out what it was for.

“It’s monitoring the flow of time on each side of the portal,” she explained. “It’s a Guardian trap!”

Chapter 28

The bombs were building power, preparing for detonation in less than twenty minutes, but if the system detected any discrepancy in time flow rate on either side of the portal, both sides would explode prematurely. A blast on either side would travel through the portal to the other side and set off the bomb over there. It would also travel through any other portal within range of the blast.

"If we remove the splinters on one side, that will set off the bomb on the other," Sara added. "Whatever we do, everyone dies."

"The evacuation!" Mandalee gasped. "If we don't Freeze Time, there isn't enough time to get everyone away. If we do Freeze Time, the bomb will explode prematurely and kill everyone, including those who have already been evacuated!"

"That's evacuations, plural," Jessica put in and told their friends what Dagamir was doing.

"Dear gods, what can we do?" Maia fretted from her side of the portal.

"Oh, don't worry," Cat replied from the other side, "I have a—"

"—Ridiculous radical plan!" chorused her friends from both sides.

"Sorry to be so predictable, but yes, I do."

Grabbing Mandalee, Cat crossed over to the other side of the portal, leaving Dreya with Shyleen.

The Black Guardian worked hard to school her expression to reveal none of her irritation. It had happened again. Catriona was with Mandalee, not with her. Why did the fates keep doing this?

Even as she pushed that thought to one side, another fought for her attention. The Guardians had begun to see the consequences of splintering the Timeline three hundred years ago. How could they possibly know all the consequences of what they had done at the Fall of Kullos when they used Creation magic? It sometimes worried Dreya that on the original Tempestria, the one that was unmade, she and Catriona were not together. They were never in love. Was the cosmos pushing back with some unknowable force, trying to tear them apart? Well, Dreya decided, if it was, then bring it on. Demons, shadow warriors, Angels, the cosmos itself – bring it all on. If fighting reality itself was what it would take to keep her relationship with Catriona, then so be it.

"We can't Freeze Time when we're separated like this," Cat was saying, "but we can slow it down, and this technology," she spat the word, "isn't going to detect any imbalance in Time because there won't be one."

From what Sara had told them, she had quickly realised there was a flaw in the programming. It was only monitoring time at the two sites relative to each other, not using any external frame of reference. Plus, whoever thought up the idea forgot one crucial detail: the Three Guardians were actually Two and Two Halves. Uniquely, the White Guardian could be in two places at once, since Mandalee and Shyleen had their own special bond. A bond so strong that even when her friend was on another world separated by the vastness of space, she intuitively knew that Shyleen was in danger on StormClaw Island on Tempestria. Now they were merely on different continents, separated only by an ocean. By contrast, that was nothing more than a puddle.

Dreya had demonstrated that she could tap into that link, thanks to the techniques she had picked up from Renjaf's books, and Cat had shared a bond with Mandalee for years, even before she met Dreya. Together with their enhanced sympathic connection through the Guardianship, they couldn't possibly be any more 'as one'.

Even so, balancing the Timefield on each side would require nothing less than total concentration, especially with the other facet of Catriona's plan. If there should be any more attacks, they would be utterly incapable of defending themselves.

Sara and Lao were going to be busy, too, handling the tech side of things, and Dagamir had left them to evacuate Melrose. Jessica, naturally, was guarding her sister, but that left no-one to guard Shyleen and Dreya. Cat supposed she could ask Maia to cross over to that side through the portal, but she wasn't sure how much she could trust the White leader, given their history. Still, there didn't seem to be any alternative, as much as Cat wished otherwise.

However, at that moment, her wish was granted in the form of Brakkis, the lizard-like head of security who arrived on the scene on the Rhynapolis side, sword in hand.

"Sorry," he barked gruffly. "Heard a noise. Thought you might be in trouble."

"Just me," Dreya replied. "I'm afraid I did a bit more damage to your building, but if you could overlook that for a moment and guard us, I'd be grateful."

Brakkis grunted his agreement. "A new roof's a small price to pay to save a city. Do what you've got to do."

Mandalee echoed Shyleen's earlier remark, saying, "Shame we don't get co-operation like that from the Council of Mages, eh, Maia?"

Dreya could see from Maia's face that the White Guardian's snipe had hit home and spared some mental magic to find out what was going on inside the White leader's head.

The Triumvirate representative once again found herself feeling rather useless. As a sorceress in the faction of Light, she believed in using magic to help people; when did aliens become better at that than her Order? Looking back on the ways in which she had obstructed the Guardians, even trying to disband them, Maia couldn't be more ashamed. She had accused them of incompetence and selfishness when those things could not be further from the truth. In fact, Maia counted herself lucky that they were not of a mind to charge her with those same failings, because she wasn't sure she could honestly plead 'not guilty'.

On the back of all of Dreya's reforms, it had been too much change too quickly for her to cope with, and she'd pushed back.

"I was wrong about you," she confessed. "Completely wrong. Get us through this, and I swear things are going to change. Justaria, Laethyn and I will sit down with you, at your convenience, and discuss how we might help you more. Not limit you. Certainly not control you. Help you."

"Well, if we didn't have reason enough to get this right before, we certainly do now," Cat acknowledged.

'Perhaps some leopards can change their spots, after all,' Shyleen remarked.

Mandalee laughed but was too busy to share the joke.

Dreya withdrew her mental magic to avoid getting distracted.

The Guardians had to focus their Timefield on the technology, slowing the countdown. If they encompassed all the space of the two rooms in their Timefield, their friends would slow down, too, and couldn't help. The Timeless dagger could make one person immune to their Temporal powers, but if they tried to split that power six ways, its magic would be too diluted to be effective.

Sara and Laoghaire were frantically exchanging technical ideas that the others didn't understand, trying to disable the time monitoring system. So far, Catriona's plan was working – the detectors were satisfied there was no difference in time flow rate on either side of the portal. The fact that both sides had slowed down was irrelevant. It only mattered that they were the same. Still, one small slip or lapse in concentration would mean the end for all of them and many more besides. When this building was Kullos' fortress, it might have contained such a blast, but now, being so much more open, the explosion was bound to escape into Rhynapolis.

On the other side, Melrose and half of Tedstone Warf would be devastated. Between Dreya's teleportation and Mandalee's super-speed, there was a chance that they might be quick enough to close the evacuation portals on each side. That would save the lives of those who thought themselves safe already, but it was a slim chance, and it would still leave many trapped in the inferno.

Keeping the Timefields stabilised, Cat reached out with her magic to connect with the power of the metal splinters on her side. Dreya was more used to this than she was, but she couldn't do it from the other side of a portal. Besides, she had her own job to do.

Fortunately, both Sara and Lao had confirmed the system was not monitoring the balance of power on each side. Given the inherent instability of the splinters, that would be impossible. That meant that the technology didn't have a problem with Catriona siphoning off the energy from her side and sending it to the splinters on the other.

Tampering with the power in the splinters was dangerous. Adding more power to those on Dreya's side was potentially catastrophic. But the sorceress was siphoning power from the splinters on her side and sending it through a micro-portal at the exact same rate. Therefore, as long as she and Cat got the timing right, there should be no net increase.

By transferring the energy in this way, they could avoid an explosion. The problem was where to send it responsibly. Dreya couldn't send it safely out into the void between the planes, as she had planned, because she couldn't be sure how the technology would react to being exposed to somewhere outside their world. It would have to remain on Tempestria, but that meant that anyone on the other side of the portal would suddenly have access to a lot of higher planar energy.

Anyone or anything.

Fortunately, Catriona already knew where to send the power and, more importantly, when.

On their last Temporal adventure, she and Mandalee had fought in the outbreak of the Demon Apocalypse. They had been there primarily to protect Renjaf, ensuring his survival so that history could get back on track. However, while they were there, a group of Greater Demons managed to summon a powerful demon king from the deeper planes of hell. There was no mention of that in the Temporally protected history books.

At first, Cat couldn't understand where the demons had been getting the power to summon such a creature. Even with blood magic from their self-sacrifice, it simply wasn't enough. Then she'd spotted it: a tiny blue shimmer. A micro-portal, through which was pouring an alarming amount of higher planar energy. Catriona had closed the portal, but the damage was done as the demons had used the power to enhance their magic. An analysis of the portal's origins told her it was a Temporal portal, but the time co-ordinates were imaginary, indicating it was from the future, relative to their own present. As for the spatial co-ordinates, they were in Northern Alloria, a little way north of Michael's restored temple home. The place they had once fought Kullos – now the alien city of Rhynapolis. What she'd been unable to figure out at the time was why there seemed to be a Lavosian element to what she was sensing. When Lao told them about a bomb using technology from their world, she had her answer.

Now the Temporal co-ordinates made sense. They were now. The micro-portal Catriona had spotted more than fifty years ago was the one that Dreya had just opened. The power she had sensed was the power they were sending now. It was going to allow the demons to summon a demon king to spread death and destruction across Alloria, but that was OK because Mandalee, White Guardian and Assassin had already slain it.

In other words, the Guardians were making a hell of a mess of Time, secure in the knowledge that they already cleaned it up half a century ago.

Their actions must have got someone's attention, though, because a new portal opened on each side. Enemies were coming through to stop them, but with Jessica on one side and Brakkis on the other, they were cut down even as they emerged.

No hesitation. No mercy. No chance.

At last, the enemy forces either gave up or ran out of people to sacrifice, and the splinters on the Melrose side were completely drained. Not only that, but Sara and Lao's latest collaborative effort also paid off, as they simultaneously hacked the system from both sides. Deleting the time monitoring subroutine from the program made it safe for the Guardians to close the portal whenever they wished. As the last of the higher planar energy drained from the systems in Melrose, the technology there went dark. Even the countdown timer was now blank.

With that, the danger to Tedstone Warf was passed, and it was only a matter of time before Rhynapolis was safe, too. To extend that as much as possible with Time magic, Catriona rejoined Dreya and Shyleen.

Mandalee stayed behind for a moment to ask her friends, "Will you guys be OK without us?"

Jessica nodded. "Yeah, we'll be fine, thanks, love. We'll make sure the evacuation's going alright and then help deal with the attacking force outside."

"We need to find Mickey as well," Sara put in.

As if on cue, Dagamir came back to tell them, "My portal is stable, and almost all the students are safe." Turning to Maia, he added, "Your young lad is still on guard duty out here, so you might want to take him and get both of you to safety."

He didn't say, 'Because you're no use to anyone here,' but Maia heard it all the same.

But she wasn't useless. She was Maia, leader of the White faction of Light. OK, maybe it was too dangerous to use her magic in this room with all this technology, but that was because her magic was dangerous. She was dangerous. A determined look grew on her face, and her magic crackled around her.

"Our troubles might be over in terms of the bomb," she allowed, "but this school is still under attack. Once my son is safely evacuated with all the other students, I'll remain behind," she insisted, "It's time to go on the offensive."

Maia of the Light was in a bad mood, and those people outside were going to make her feel better by dying so that they couldn't harm anyone ever again.

Satisfied that everything was under control, Mandalee left them with the promise, "We'll pop over and help as soon as we're done on our side."

With an exchange of farewells, as Maia watched, the portal closed, time returned to normal, and everyone took a few breaths to calm their nerves.

*****

With a grin, Jessica broke the silence, saying, "Hey Sara, love. You realise that in those Earth movies, this is the part where everything would suddenly come back on, don't you?"

Sara laughed, "Yeah, and the countdown would start again, too!"

Her sister joined in her laughter, but they both abruptly stopped as everything burst back into life and the countdown timer lit up:

Five minutes to detonation.

Chapter 29

Outside Melrose, having closed the portal, Michael asked, "What now?"

"Now you surrender yourself to Pryshia, Queen of the Gods," Nalani stated simply.

"And why would I do that?"

"Because the gods created you, and she commands it."

"Pryshia didn't create me. She refused. Therefore, I'm going to do likewise."

Nalani's eyes lit up. "I was hoping you'd say something like that because now I get to have some fun and kill you!"

The dark-haired woman sprang at him, dragonclaw daggers in her hands, relying on her speed, as always, but Michael had been discreetly working his magic as soon as he saw her, preparing for the attack he knew would come. Insects swarmed around the demigod like millions of tiny guards or a constantly moving shield. That slowed Nalani enough for Michael to block her strike with his sword. He connected with such force that Nalani flew backwards to land on her back fifty yards away.

That gave him time to deal with the force of rebels that had chosen to face him rather than continue their attempt to break into the school. Sending out his power, he threw them all back to join the others in Melrose grounds and formed a containment field around the building.

"That should keep them out of the way," he remarked to himself.

Nalani came at him again, probing for a weakness she could exploit, but once again, he was able to swat her aside.

"How?" she demanded after her third failed attempt.

"The dragonclaws or your speed?" he asked.

"Both," she answered.

"Well, here's an idea: why don't I sit down with my enemy and have a cosy little chat where I explain all the ways I have to beat you so you can work out how to counter them," he scoffed. "I think not."

The fact was that Michael had been around for a long time. He had fought alongside and against shadow warriors, and while he couldn't beat them, he was exceptionally good at slowing them down. That, even more than his power, was why he always gave Daelen the edge in his centuries-long struggle. His Sword of Maruk was shadow warrior technology – a gift from Daelen StormTiger – made from an alloy unknown on the mortal plane. Dragonclaws were all very impressive, but shadow warrior weapons did not break so easily. The Guardians knew how much force – both physical and magical – had been needed to shatter Kullos' control device. Even then, Michael was convinced that it had only been possible because it still had relatively weak points from when it broke the first time. Michael had been there that first time, and he knew that force had almost ripped Tempestria apart. Of course, the world wasn't called that then. It only became Tempestria after that act of cosmic violence. Strangely, he couldn't recall the original name.

In the same way, it would take considerably more than a mortal with super-speed and dragonclaws to even make a dent in his sword.

As for countering Nalani's speed, once again he had centuries of training with Daelen StormTiger to thank. Whenever he fought Kullos, of course, Michael had been Fated to die. Against his dark clone, that was not so. The clone often killed him anyway, out of spite, but when that didn't happen, he would take full advantage of the time, preparing for the next battle. Over the centuries, that training paid off, and he improved.

Shadow warriors were fast – not as fast as Nalani or even Mandalee, but still pretty fast – and he'd learned how to counter speed.

He didn't have temporal magic like the Guardians, but even so, he knew time was largely a matter of perception, and as a creature of the gods, he had perception beyond that of mortals. Plus, there were his insects. They had many functions. The reason insects were so hard for mortals to swat wasn't that they were too fast. It was because, to the flies, the weapon that was trying to squash them was moving incredibly slowly. Perception of time was linked to metabolism, and a fly's metabolism was much higher than that of a mortal. To his flies, Nalani wasn't all that fast. They could see her coming. Ossian Miach Kaidool was linked to them and their perception. By using them as a mobile shield, he knew the instant

Nalani touched them and could have his strike in the right place at the right time.

The fight continued for several minutes. Pryshia tried to give him two targets to hit, but still, they couldn't get at him. Satisfied with his defence, Michael decided it was time to go on the offensive so he could be done with this and help his friends.

He brought forth his Murder of Ravens in Fugue to try and instil fear in Nalani's mind, but none of their squawking did any good. Pryshia's grip on her mind was too strong. When Nalani sold her soul, she gave away all control over her emotions to her god. Now she felt only what Pryshia allowed her to feel, and fear was not permitted. With swift strikes of her blades, she sliced each one of the birds in half.

That failed attack distracted Michael enough to make him slightly late with his block. Nalani penetrated his shield of insects, and her blades sliced deep into his chest. Though the wound was serious to a demigod, it was not life-threatening.

With perfect timing, ignoring the pain, he managed to grab Nalani's left wrist in a vice-like grip. He knew there was no point in disarming her and throwing away her dagger. No matter how far he threw it, she would be able to retrieve it in mere seconds, and he would have achieved nothing. So, instead, he snapped her wrist.

She screamed for a moment before it was abruptly cut off. Apparently, pain was another feeling Nalani wasn't allowed, and Pryshia was already giving her the magic she needed to heal her injury. Healing a break like that too fast could cause long-term problems, but Pryshia obviously didn't care about that. All that mattered was that Nalani could fight.

In a way, Michael felt sorry for Nalani, but the reality was that she was trying to kill him, besides putting many others in danger by preventing him from helping his friends to either stop the bomb or evacuate innocent people. For their sake as well as his own, he couldn't let sympathy stop him from killing her if he could.

The angle of her attack with her right-hand dagger forced him to let her go and throw her out of range, or he would lose his own hand in retaliation.

Michael sent out his magic in the form of two dark tendrils, like shadowy snakes, swaying back and forth, preparing to strike. Nalani was too quick for them, for now, but he kept probing patiently. All the demigod needed was one strike, and Nalani would be immobilised long enough for him to finish her. He just hoped he could manage it this side of the bomb exploding.

Over the next several minutes, Nalani and Pryshia found a way to penetrate a few times, scoring many deep lacerations that would most likely be fatal against anyone mortal. Fortunately, Michael was a bit more than mortal.

Throughout the fight, his insects had been biting Nalani every chance they got. His enemy was often fast enough to swat them before they could, but it didn't matter how many insects Michael lost; it cost him next to nothing to conjure a thousand at a time. All that mattered was that enough flies made it through her defences and landed on her skin to serve his needs, because he'd thought of a way to modify the tiny creatures. Rather than simply making their bite carry poison, they carried it in their blood. It didn't matter if she was quick enough to kill them before they could bite. Every time she swatted them, their blood splattered on her bare skin, and the poison naturally seeped into her own body.

Nalani called herself a Cleric of Nature, and while he knew from his friendship with Mandalee that she was nothing of the sort, she still had clerical powers. As a cleric, curing poison was little trouble, but that relied on her knowing she was poisoned. Each fly contained a dose of poison that wasn't even enough to affect a mouse, but what about the effect of a hundred or a thousand? Michael was gambling that the effect of the poison would build so slowly, so gradually, that she would either fail to notice or dismiss any effects as fatigue until it was too late.

At last, she stumbled, and Michael could see the moment of realisation dawn. Pryshia sent her healing, but that didn't matter. The poison itself wasn't the weapon. It was a distraction, and it had worked perfectly. The serpentine tendrils of magic struck – one attaching itself to each arm. She struggled frantically, and in time Michael was sure she would break free, but again, that magic was only intended to put time on his side for a moment.

Pryshia leapt at Michael, but his insects gave him plenty of time to swat her away as he rapidly closed the gap between himself and Nalani, swapping his sword for his warhammer. Made of hardened, unbreakable petrified wood, it would imprison those it struck in the same material. The only time he'd seen it fail was when he fought the ‘void-creature’ or, as Cat put it rather more succinctly, the Monster. But Nalani didn’t have that kind of power.

Even as he swung his weapon, Nalani managed to get one arm free, but even she couldn’t be fast enough to prevent what was to come. She reached out as if to push him away, but she could never be strong enough to move him. His warhammer struck her full in the chest, leaving some of itself behind, which grew and spread all over her body until it fully encased her, immobilising her. He could finish her off later when he’d dealt with Pryshia.

He turned to face the lioness who styled herself Queen of the Gods, and that was the moment when Melrose Academy exploded.

“No!” he cried.

His friends, Sara and Jessica, were trapped in there. He’d trapped them when he closed his portal. All those people had been relying on him, and he’d failed.

Fire and magic fuelled by higher planar energy ripped out from the central building and travelled rapidly outwards, incinerating the attackers. When it met Michael’s containment field, it was stopped in its tracks, but already he could see his shield was buckling. He needed to reinforce it, or the explosion would spread out into the city, but he didn’t have enough power, especially after his fight with Nalani and Pryshia.

“No!” he repeated, this time with determination, not despair. There was nothing he could do for his friends, now. Everyone inside that inferno had perished, but he would be damned if anyone else in this town was going to die because of his failure. Turning back to a stunned Pryshia, the furious demigod growled, “I can’t understand you, but I know you can understand me, so listen. I can’t stop this by myself. I need your power. The power of a god. I know you like to horde power for yourself, but if you don’t let me have it now, my containment field will collapse, and you will die. And don’t imagine you can outrun the blast. Even you can’t run that fast, and you know it. Give me your power, and I swear by all the other gods in the Pantheon that I will portal us both away. You’ll live to fight another day.”

The lioness turned her head to look pointedly at the prison of petrified wood.

Michael nodded, understanding. “Very well,” he accepted. “I’ll release her and take all three of us away. Do we have a deal?”

Ossian Miach Kaidool felt his power grow in response. "Thank you," he sighed in relief as he weaved that power into the containment field, creating a reinforcing latticework to keep the blast inside. The explosion repeatedly rebounded off the shield, disintegrating all the structures within, before gradually dying down until all that remained was smouldering rubble. At last, Michael could power down the shield to a sustainable level to prevent the fire from spreading beyond its boundary.

The famous Melrose Academy was no more, and Michael prayed for the souls of anyone who had still been inside when it ceased to be. It was important that they were remembered. He would certainly never forget those two perky purple girls from Phitonia. Their lives had been too short. Far too short.

Pryshia, obviously not given to sentiment over this atrocity, pawed at him insistently.

He nodded. "Very well, I'm a being of my word."

Michael opened his portal, and then, drawing his Sword of Maruk, he struck the petrified wood with the flat of the blade. Cracks began to appear, spreading, multiplying, widening until a young woman with dark braided hair forced herself free as if hatching from an egg.

She immediately spun her daggers into her hands and advanced on him with Pryshia, but Michael dived through his portal too fast. They followed him blindly, and Michael closed his portal. In a flash, his enemies realised where he'd brought them – right in the middle of the grounds of the Black Tower, home of Dreya the Dark.

The undead gardeners had already swapped their tools for weapons, becoming warriors once more. Animated skeletons pulled themselves out of the ground, spells of fire and ice and lightning powered up, all laced with higher planar energy. Hell hounds howled, and werecats growled. The plants began to writhe and snake towards them, thorns growing to an inch long, each as hard as steel and dripping with venom. Finally, four death knights and three ghouls emerged from the Tower – Dreya's elite guards, apparently returned from dealing with the force threatening the Council.

"I'm a being of my word, Pryshia," Michael repeated, "but I know you're not. Did you really think I'd be stupid enough to trust you? I told you I'd portal us away. I never promised it would be to somewhere safe."

With everything that was happening, Dreya had powered up all of her Tower's considerable defences in case anyone was foolish enough to try and take advantage.

"To be honest, I'm not even sure if I'm safe here," he admitted, "but I'm willing to take the risk. Are you? Do you want to take on the Black Tower and me at the same time?"

Apparently not keen on the idea, Pryshia and Nalani fled.

Dreya's defences surrounded Michael, and while they weren't actually attacking him, they weren't exactly welcoming, either.

He held up his hands in surrender. "It's alright, I'm going!" he said and opened a portal home.

Chapter 30

Catriona thanked Brakkis for his help but advised that he should now leave them and evacuate just in case.

"What if you get attacked again?" he asked.

"There'll be no time," she assured him. "Literally."

Acknowledging that with a nod, Brakkis left the room.

Shyleen accompanied him. She disliked being away from Mandalee, but she understood the strategy.

Waiting a few seconds to make sure they were clear, the Guardians Froze Time.

As Lao looked on, everything stopped. Not just the countdown, but all the sounds and any sense of change were gone. The micro-portal was now a fixed blue dot rather than fading and sparkling as the light reflected its dimensions.

"Keep focussing on the technology, Lao," Cat admonished him. "We want advance warning if we're doing anything it objects to."

"There's nothing to focus on," he argued. "It's stopped, just like everything else around here. How can you do this?"

"With faith and trust and faery dust," Mandalee quipped. She answered the quizzical looks, saying, "I've been watching too many movies with Sara and Jessica!"

Dreya gave a more serious but equally unhelpful answer. "There is no 'how'. Not really. We just do."

Cat nodded. "We're the Guardians of Time and Magic. The magic is innate; if we want Time to stop, we just will it so, and it does."

It was strange. Lao's tracker confirmed that power was being transferred out of the splinters through the micro-portal, but because there was no time inside the room, it displayed the transfer rate as infinity.

"The only reason you can witness this is because you have the Timeless dagger."

It was also why she'd had to send Shyleen away. They couldn't be certain if the magic of the Timeless dagger could protect her and Lao at the same time, and this situation needed Lao.

“Does this mean you have all the time in the world to do this, then?” he asked.

Cat shook her head. “There’s probably a theoretical physical limit to how long Time can be out of balance with the rest of the world, but in practice, we’d all be exhausted long before then, anyway.”

On the back of that thought, she wondered if there might be a theoretical limit to how long Tempestrian time could be out of sync with the rest of the universe and what that might mean for the world if ever that limit should be reached.

Discarding thoughts of hypothetical future dangers, she refocused on the real and present ones before them.

After an eternity, or no time at all, or somewhere in between, the micro-portal closed. Almost all the power had been harmlessly vented away, but some still remained.

“Why stop now?” Lao wondered.

“We don’t have a choice,” Cat replied. “I closed the portal.” Realising he wasn’t getting it, she rolled her eyes and clarified, “I closed the portal fifty years ago – or a couple of days, depending on how you look at it. At the time, all I knew was that it was letting in dangerous amounts of higher planar energy. How was I supposed to know I needed to keep it open for a bit longer? I hadn’t done this yet!”

Lao could feel a headache developing and decided to stop asking questions in the hopes of warding it off.

The Guardians quickly decided that a bit of residual power was actually a good thing. They now knew that Kullos’ throne was linked to more shadow warrior technology underneath. It was too dangerous to leave it lying around. It had to be destroyed.

Rather than cancel their Timeless field, they pulled it back to form a shield around the room and left through the hole Cat had put in the wall.

Dreya focussed one of her power words on what was left inside. After the earlier events, she hadn’t reconstructed ‘DISINTEGRATE’, so she went with ‘SHATTER’ instead. Vital components broke apart, systems shorted out, the splinters exploded out of their housing, and a further blast of magic put a crater in the ground. When the dust settled, the Guardians dispelled the shield and went back in, advising Lao to stay outside for his own safety.

Mandalee sliced through any technology that was still fixed to the walls and pushed it all into the crater. Once they were satisfied, Cat used her magic to open the crater broader and deeper, burying all the smashed components. She had to be more careful than when she'd destroyed Daelen's training centre on Earth because she didn't want to bring the whole building down on top of them. Still, it only took a matter of minutes for everything to be deep enough for her to begin growing the stone once more, crushing everything into dust.

Job done, the Guardians cancelled all their Time magic. If anybody tried to come at them now, they could deal with them without fear of setting off an explosion. Moreover, since it had all happened in range of the Timeless dagger that Lao still had tucked into his belt, no Time magic could ever interfere with what they'd done. Unlike a Temporal Black Spot, it wouldn't prevent observation-only Time travel, but the Guardians could see no need for that in this case.

No enemies came, but almost immediately, Lao's Portacom bleeped insistently, and the Lavosian put his now redundant tracker away in favour of checking his messages.

It was from Sara, sent about ten minutes ago. It read:

2ND BOMB! HELP!

Even as Dreya opened a portal, Mandalee swiped the Timeless dagger from Lao's possession, saying, "Sorry. Need this back."

They could drop it safely back in Catriona's Meadow on the way. It would take literally no time at all. She jumped through, swiftly followed by Dreya.

"Use the evacuation portal," Cat advised him. "You'll be fine."

In the blink of an eye, the portal closed, and the Guardians were gone.

*****

The three looked in horror at the remains of the school. It was obliterated. The fires were gone, but there was still a reddish glow in places where the energy had not yet completely dissipated. There was no conceivable way that anyone could have survived what had happened, but Dreya snapped them out of it quickly.

"Time portal!" she declared. "We can change this."

The others nodded and stood back as she cast her Prismatic Sphere. The co-ordinates were a bit vague, but for a ten-minute hop, the risk was minimal. Except, when they tried to enter the portal, they rebounded off painfully.

Looking at each other in puzzlement, they each tentatively tried to reach into the portal, but it was like there was a shield blocking them. Closing it, Cat attempted one of hers. Same result. Mandalee tried, too, but still, the magic wouldn't work.

As an experiment, they tried travelling back further in Time, up to half an hour. This time, the portal let them through, and they could watch events unfold, but when they tried to sever their ties to Timelessness in order to interact, they couldn't do it. It was as if the co-ordinates they were trying to use didn't exist.

At a loss as to what else to do, they walked through the school like ghosts until they found the stairs they wanted and climbed them.

Walking through the door into the attic room confirmed they were in the right place. They knew being here like this was a bad idea. Guardians couldn't hide from themselves in Time, and seeing themselves could cause dangerous paradoxes. Fortunately, there was plenty of technological clutter in that attic room that they could hide behind. Staying well hidden, they heard Mandalee and Catriona's past selves come through the portal and work to stop the bomb. They syphoned off the energy and left. Then, as soon as the portal closed, everything around them whited out, and they were forcibly ejected from the area until they were standing outside Melrose once more.

"It's a Temporal White Spot," Cat realised, remembering reading about them in the *Chronicles*.

They had once encountered a Temporal Black Spot when they tried to watch events that formed the Lake of Tears, Ulvarius' last major act of tyranny before he committed suicide. Another historical appearance of Catriona's Angel. That area was off-limits to time travel, most likely because it was too dangerous to risk anyone tampering with it. A Temporal Black Spot was surrounded by wards to prevent entry.

A Temporal White Spot was worse.

In theory, they could exist in times and places where Time itself had been damaged. Temporal White spots were physically impossible to breach. All routes through all dimensions would take one away from the event horizon.

Outside, just beyond the limit of Melrose grounds, Michael was locked in combat with Nalani and Pryshia, but the Guardians could see he was more than holding his own, so there was no need to enter the Timestream to help. He was a big boy who could obviously take care of himself.

Sara and Jessica, on the other hand, were lost forever.

The Guardians saw the explosion that killed them, and the deal Michael made with Pryshia to contain it so it could harm no-one else. In deepest despair, they followed him, unseen, as he travelled through his portal to the Black Tower and then home.

*****

As soon as Michael closed his portal, the Guardians entered the Timestream, materialising in front of him and scaring him half to death.

"Dear gods, where did you come from?" he gasped, then thought better of it. "Actually, forget that; you need to get back to Melrose about ten minutes ago. It blew up and – dear gods – Sara and Jessica were in there, and—"

"—We know," Cat nodded sadly, cutting him off, "and we've tried. We've been trying for a while, we've tried everything, but we can't get there. We can't change it. It's physically impossible. Something about that explosion damaged Time."

"I don't understand!" Michael cried. Intellectually he did, but emotionally he just couldn't grasp it. "What are you saying?"

"What we're saying is," Mandalee began, then stumbled over the words, unable to go on as the tears welled up in her eyes.

"Well, we're saying…" Cat tried, but she, too, broke down and couldn't speak the words.

"We're saying they're dead," Dreya stated. Unlike the others, she wasn't crying. More like all the emotion had drained out of her. "And it's our fault."

"Your fault?" Michael wondered.

"We had no business letting them get involved, and we certainly shouldn't have left them on their own like that," Dreya asserted.

"But we did," Mandalee put in.

"Because we're selfish and incompetent," Catriona concluded before her sobs robbed her of her ability to say more.

*****

Lao and Brakkis had been the last to leave Rhynapolis through the evacuation portal to Michael's home with Shyleen. Picking out the demigod in the crowd was simple, so they made their way over to him. Once there, Michael broke the news that Sara and Jessica had been killed. The Lavosian didn't even know them that well, and he was in shock. He could only imagine how the others were feeling.

Slightly embarrassed to be there, intruding on their grief, Brakkis gruffly offered his condolences and suggested they go inside.

"My security team and I will deal with the alien crowd on your doorstep. You've done enough. More than enough. We're all in your debt. Least I can do is take things from here."

At a loss for words, Michael nodded and ushered the others inside. He couldn't begin to express how he was feeling. His two Chetsuan guests had helped him build his new home in more ways than one. They had lived with him since they returned from Lavos. At first, it had been a temporary arrangement – the girls had been understandably uncomfortable living in the Black Tower with only the undead for company. But the Guardians got lost in Time for over two years, and by the time they returned, the three of them had got used to living together and didn't want that to change. In truth, Michael had quickly begun to see them as family. Something he had never imagined he would have. The demigod had hoped to have many more years with them. He supposed everybody hoped that about their loved ones, and he knew, inevitably, things had to end. But not yet. Dear gods, not yet. Not like this.

Michael felt sorry for Lao, who didn't know what to do with himself. He would sit down, stand up, pace, and sit down again, all the time refusing to let go of Sara's tracking device as the last piece of her in this world.

Mandalee and Catriona were in floods of tears by now. The former clinging to Shyleen, the latter to her wife, who seemed to have retreated into herself.

Even as Dreya held Catriona close, she thought back to her casual wish that their adventures would bring Catriona closer to her instead of Mandalee.

This wasn't what she'd meant.

"I'm going to miss movie night," Mandalee sniffled randomly, breaking the silence.

Cat gave a brief laugh through her tears and nodded.

"We should do that," Michael asserted. "Soon. In their memory. I'm sure I can work out how Sara put the technology together."

"I'll help," Lao volunteered.

"I'm going to miss seeing Jessica working on my grounds with her druid magic," Michael offered after another long pause.

"I'll come and do it," Cat promised, sitting up a little. "Whenever I can."

"Her magic had got so good," Dreya contributed. "Every time I saw her, she could do more."

Cat nodded. "I was proud of her…" She frowned, then, realising, "…and I don't think I ever told her."

"She knew," Michael assured her.

"Still should have told her."

Chapter 31

“You can tell me now if you like, love!” came a familiar voice from the doorway.

Everyone turned to look, not believing their ears, and when they saw who was standing there, they began to doubt their eyesight, too, but it was true. It was Jessica and Sara. They both had a few injuries, and Sara was clinging onto her sister, having hurt her ankle, but they were alive.

Everyone leapt up at once, crowding around them, fighting to be the first to hug them.

The Guardians, Michael and Lao, were all talking over each other, asking what happened, how they escaped, why didn’t they let them know they were OK, and so on.

Sara raised her voice to cut through it, “We’ll be happy to tell you all about it, but can you please let us sit down?”

Jessica nodded. “Yeah, my sister weighs a ton!”

“I do not!” she protested.

Everyone made way for them and quietened down except for Catriona and Mandalee, who found themselves arguing over who should heal them. Finally, they realised they were being ridiculous and worked together to heal them both. Their injuries were minor, considering what they’d been through, and Sara’s ankle wasn’t broken, so Jessica soon declared that they were ‘right as rain’.

Michael and Lao offered to make everyone some tea. Dreya helped, boiling the water with a spell she could do in her sleep when she was in her teens.

At last, everyone settled down to listen as the two Chetsuan sisters explained what happened after the Guardians closed the portal between the two sites.

*****

Five minutes to detonation.

“Five minutes?” Sara scoffed. “That’s ages, right?”

“Yeah,” her sister agreed, trying to stay positive. “Didn’t Dreya say she took the Black Tower in that time?”

Dagamir nodded. “She’s mentioned that to me, too.”

Jessica summed things up, saying, "All we have to do is stop the bomb, or leave, or both."

"Or contact the Guardians," Maia suggested.

"Good point," Sara concurred and dug out her phone, calling Lao's Portacom. There was no answer.

"I'm no expert," Dagamir admitted, "but if they've Frozen Time where they are, I don't think that will work."

"He's right, sis," Jessica concurred. "Give me your tracker."

Sara handed it over, which freed up her other hand to send a message:

2ND BOMB! HELP!

The second bomb was under the floorboards, which Jessica tore up with woodshaper magic.

Four minutes to go.

Sara lay down and tried to access the system. One minute later, she got back to her feet, giving up.

"Every time I shut it down, it just comes back on, like there's an override."

"Actually," came a voice from the door, "that would be me!"

Out of the shadows stepped a Black robe wizard. His face was completely shrouded in his hood. Even his voice was disguised, somehow.

"Hope you don't mind me dropping by. An extremely helpful young lad on the steps told me where you were."

"Rivius!" Maia gasped. She stepped forward, her power crackling in her hands. "If you've harmed him in any way…"

The wizard laughed. "What would be the point? He's going to blow up like the rest of you in…" he peered over at the timer, "two-and-a-half minutes."

"You'll die, too," Dagamir pointed out.

The wizard shook his head. "I have a portal on the other side of this door."

Dagamir drew his sword. "Thank you. That's all I needed to know."

He stepped forward and swung, but the wizard lashed out with magic. The bolt was aimed at Dagamir's chest, but somehow the sword seemed to attract it, absorb it. Unfortunately, the force was too much for Dagamir, the weapon flew from his grasp, and he collided with Sara, knocking her to the floor. Jessica attacked him with her dragonclaw daggers while her sister, confident in Jessica's ability to take care of herself, tried to use the distraction to disarm the bomb. The wizard was wise to it, however. Knocking Jessica back, he sent out an energy beam at Sara. It was a beam of higher planar energy, which confirmed that this was the same wizard who had stolen the two fragments. Jessica recognised it almost before it began. She'd seen Dreya use such a weapon, as well as Daelen before her.

But Jessica had also seen Catriona counter this power because power wasn't everything. The Chetsuan girl had never done it herself, but that didn't matter. She could do this. She believed in herself. It was as if Time slowed down to accommodate her need as she threw out a vial of sand and fused it into polished glass. Nature's Mirror. It formed in the path of the energy beam and reflected it back. Or at least, it tried.

The mirror shattered on contact and reflected multiple smaller beams that shot off in all directions, ricocheting off the walls, but it had bought the others time.

Maia's shields flared around them, protecting them from harm. Dagamir's sword had returned to his outstretched hand, and he was ready to attack with steel and magic.

With ninety seconds to go, the wizard tried to lash out again but let out a grunt of annoyance when it didn't work. Jessica remembered her Guardian friends saying Ulvarius had experienced the same problem when trying to use one of the fragments.

The wizard knew time was running out, so he gave up on his new powers and fell back on tried-and-tested, inscribing the language of magic in the air with one hand while he yanked open the door with the other. Maia knew what he was doing: he was still worried Sara might find a way to stop the bomb, and he was determined not to let her.

"No!" she cried, preparing her own magic. "You will not harm her!" Her magic flared in her hands, and a blast of compressed air flew out towards the wizard.

At the same time, two lightning bolts fired from the wizard's fingers, one for each of the aliens. Dagamir used his sword to attract and absorb one of them, and Maia threw herself bodily in the path of the other, taking the full impact, while her own magic threw the wizard forcefully against the door. Maia's shields tried their best, but at the last moment, the Black robe wizard had managed to lace his magic with some higher planar energy, and Maia's shields collapsed. She felt a brief stab of pain and then numbness as she collapsed to the floor.

One minute to detonation.

The wizard fled, but Dagamir was hot on his heels. He felt the Black robe work his magic to close the portal from the other side, but he wasn't going to let him. He'd worked on portals for years, and while he may have only just figured out how to stabilise them, he'd already learned a lot about them on his own. His sword sent out a stream of magic that wedged the portal open.

The Black wizard briefly tried to fight it but then, worried about the time, gave up and teleported away.

Thirty seconds.

"We have to go!" Dagamir yelled.

"Get my son!" Maia shouted back desperately.

He dashed down the stairs and grabbed Rivius, running back to the portal, while Jessica got Sara to her feet. She winced in pain, having twisted her ankle when she fell, but with Jessica's help, she hopped quickly over to the portal.

They suddenly realised Maia wasn't with them.

"You have to go!" the sorceress called out. "I can't move!"

Ten seconds.

A combination of the Black robe wizard's attack and the way she landed had paralysed her. Ordinarily, she could teleport herself, but the whole place was now surrounded by a containment field. Conventional magic couldn't get through, and there wasn't time to get her to the portal. In principle, it might be possible to teleport to the portal, but she didn't know how to be that precise. There was only one thing she knew for sure she could do: save the others. Maia sent out a wave of compressed air, throwing them through the portal to safety.

Five seconds.

"Close it!" she cried desperately.

"I'm sorry," Dagamir replied softly.

The portal closed.

Two seconds.

One.
Detonation.

*****

The Black robe wizard's portal had taken them to the Council building, but in the aftermath of the attack there, nobody would have noticed one wizard coming and going.

Both Jessica and Sara had tried to call Lao in hopes that he would tell everyone they were OK, but unfortunately, both of their phones were dead.

"They don't like being struck by lightning," Sara explained, "so we gave up and asked Dagamir to portal us here."

Although naturally delighted and relieved that their friends were safe, the Guardians were still troubled.

"We never should have let you get involved," Cat said, echoing her wife's earlier remarks. "The fact that we got lucky doesn't change that."

"Woah there!" Jessica protested. "Lucky? We didn't escape because we got lucky. We escaped because we're brilliant."

"Even so, we had no right putting you in danger in the first place," Mandalee said.

"You didn't put us in danger; we put ourselves in danger," Sara insisted, "and we'd do it again because it was right. We chose to help today, and you can bet we'll be right there with you in the future, too."

Jessica nodded. "Too right! Try and stop us, and you'll have a fight on your hands, so don't waste your energy trying, OK, loves?"

"But you could be killed," Dreya put in, "and if anything happened to you…" she hesitated, her eyes flicking briefly towards Lao. She wasn't comfortable expressing such emotions, especially in front of a stranger, but she buried the feeling to conclude with, "…I would be upset."

Jessica's face softened. "That's sweet, Dreya, love, but you're not indestructible yourself for all your powers."

The sorceress knew the truth of that. If Purity were to attack tomorrow, she would undoubtedly die along with everyone else on her world.

“But we’re the Guardians,” Cat countered. “We have a responsibility.”

“As I understand it,” Lao put in, “it’s a responsibility you’ve chosen, just as I’ve chosen PDI to help protect innocent lives on my world.”

“Not just on your world,” Michael pointed out.

Lao conceded the point with a facial shrug.

“I’ve been a Protector of your world for a long time,” Michael rumbled. “Now, Tempestria has Three Guardians, and as far as I’m concerned, it couldn’t be in better hands, but that doesn’t mean you should be alone in your struggles. Getting help from others doesn’t make you selfish or incompetent; it makes you better Guardians.”

Accepting the words of Tempestria’s eldest protector, the Guardians found themselves standing a little taller as a weight was lifted from their shoulders.

Even so, their thoughts turned to Maia, the late Triumvirate representative for Light magic. The woman had been a thorn in their side at times, but her heart had been in the right place. She would be sorely missed.

“It wasn’t just her, either,” Sara put in when Mandalee expressed her feelings. “Dagamir told us all the students had been evacuated, but we know some of the staff were still holding the shields together against the attack from outside.”

“Well, we can’t go back and change it,” Mandalee sighed regretfully, standing up while Shyleen stretched out the kinks in her muscles, “so I suppose we’d best go and see the Council.”

Her friends agreed.

After shaking hands with Lao, they excused themselves and portalled away.

“It’s time I was heading home, too,” Laoghaire declared. “Could you help me out with a portal home, please?” he asked Michael.

“I thought you could do it with technology?” Sara wondered.

“Only one way,” he replied. “The tech is about the size of this room. A portable version is a few years away at least.”

After seeking Lao’s permission to enter his mind for precise co-ordinates, Michael opened a portal to Lavos.

Before leaving, he gave Sara and Jessica each a long embrace. “I’m so glad you’re both alright.”

“Don’t be a stranger,” Sara told him.

“Yeah, don’t wait ‘til there’s another crisis before you come back,” Jessica offered.

“Well, given the experimental tech, I don’t think the PDI are likely to authorise pleasure trips, but I’ll do my best.”

Michael shook his hand vigorously, thanking him for his warning. Things would have been a lot worse without it.

With that, Lao stepped through the portal and waved from the other side before Michael closed it.

*****

The area surrounding the Council building displayed all the hallmarks of recent battle. Some patches of ground were charred and blackened, while others were stained red with spilt blood. The walls were pockmarked where the shields had failed under the onslaught of powerful magic, but the structure was generally intact.

When the Guardians stepped through the enormous, ornate doors, it was clear there had been many injuries among the Council mages, the treatment for which still continued, provided by the druids and clerics among them. Particularly encouraging was the way some of the druids and clerics were working together, combining their different talents to heal some of those wizards who were more seriously injured. Perhaps these events would help to forge greater bonds of appreciation and respect between those diverse groups, Mandalee considered. Then at least something good could come of it.

Dagamir was distinctive as always, even when facing away from them. Standing with one leg on a chair, elbow resting on his knee, while his other hand absently caressed the hilt of his sword, he reminded Dreya so much of his ancestor in this very chamber, more than three centuries ago. It was also noticeable how he was locked in discussion with Justaria, glancing only occasionally in the direction of the de facto leader of the Black robes, Laethyn, who sat with his left boot off, nursing a slight injury to his leg. It was hardly serious, so the healers’ attention was naturally focused elsewhere.

Mandalee frowned when she realised that the chair on which Dagamir had his foot was the seat of the late White robe leader, Maia. She couldn't help feeling that was a bit disrespectful, which was at odds with the impression he had so far made on her. She was already feeling guilty about celebrating the safety of their Chetsuan friends when the friends of many others had been lost. By contrast, Dagamir seemed not to have a care in the world. That rankled her.

'*Giving him the benefit of the doubt,*' Shyleen suggested, '*He doesn't yet know that you couldn't go back in Time and save everyone.*'

Mandalee conceded the point, but neither that nor his gregarious greeting, when Justaria drew his attention, did anything to change her feelings.

"Guardians!" he boomed, effortlessly gaining the attention of everyone there present. "Once again, we are all in your debt, as I'm sure everyone here now realises!" he added pointedly, his raptor-like gaze sweeping across the Council chamber.

He didn't quite insist on the kind of response Dagamir the Third once sought, but nevertheless, his words elicited a general murmur of agreement and the exchange of some rather guilty looks from those who would have voted to replace or disband the Guardians.

Catriona winced as she and her group approached Dagamir and the two remaining Triumvirate members.

"The vote of confidence is appreciated," she accepted graciously, "but I'm afraid we weren't as successful as we would have wished. Unfortunately, well, I don't think this is the time to go into the technical details, but the bottom line is, we can't go back and change what happened at your school, Dagamir."

The wizard with the sword met the news with a cavalier shrug.

"Never mind," he replied dismissively. "The work to educate the next generation of mages will continue, I assure you. Schools can be rebuilt, after all. It's people that can't."

Mandalee's frown deepened. "That's what we're saying. We couldn't save any of your people."

"My people?" Dagamir wondered with a puzzled look, clearly not understanding.

Dreya could scarcely believe what she was hearing – and people called her cold and heartless!

"Sara and Jessica told us that there were still teachers and other staff holding back the defences when the second bomb went off," the sorceress explained.

A broad grin of relief spread across Dagamir's face.

"Oh, no," he shook his head, "they're quite mistaken, I assure you. For once, being short staffed worked to our advantage."

"Short staffed?" Cat wondered. Arguably the world's most prestigious magical academic institution had trouble finding staff? That didn't seem to ring true.

"Well, even that aside," the druidess went on, addressing the whole Council, "it's still our sad duty to report the loss of Maia."

Mandalee's rage was growing that nobody here seemed remotely concerned about the absent White robe leader. Yes, they'd been at odds at times, but she was still sad about the woman's death.

Dagamir exchanged a confused glance with Justaria and Laethyn. Indeed, looking around, everybody else seemed to be doing the same.

"I'm sorry," Justaria broached with a blank, uncomprehending look, "who's Maia?"

Epilogue

Right at the beginning of these writings, gentle reader, I, Arshes Megane, your humble narrator, made a promise: that everything I wrote would be true.

I stand by that statement and would argue that I have kept my word. However, whenever I have mentioned Maia, White robe Leader and Triumvirate representative for Light Magic in my mother's time, there is a problem.

She never existed.

When I gaze through Time, I can't see her. The Original Three Guardians remembered her, as did Michael, Sara and Jessica, so I suppose one could say that she at least existed in their minds.

The best explanation for that – the only commonality – was that they had each handled at least one fragment of Kullos' dimensional control device. It wasn't just about higher planar energy, though. Interrogation of the prisoners taken during the assault on the Council of Mages revealed no recognition of the name. They had used higher planar energy stored in the splinters of Mandalee's shattered Pureblade, which, while lesser, was fundamentally no different. It made more sense to believe it was to do with the control device itself and its connection to the higher planes, where Time operated differently. It was conceivable, then, that someone with even partial access to the higher planes could have some resistance to the effects of this terrible weapon.

Maia's seven-year-old son, Rivius, did not remember his mother. To him, it was as though he'd never had a mother. His father, Rowen, did not remember having a wife. Maia's clothes and personal belongings were no longer present in their home. How could they be? Maia never existed. Yet they had had family photographs taken together; in some of which there was an inexplicable person-sized gap between father and son.

Equally baffling to both was what Rivius was doing at Melrose that day, all by himself. There was no way Rowen would have allowed that.

Maia also existed in some records but making official documents Timeless was a work in progress in that age, which led to contradictions. The things she did in her life still happened.

There is just no apparent explanation for *how* they happened since Maia never existed to do them.

When the Guardians pointed out some of these contradictions, some people could vaguely grasp that there were problems that could not be explained away as errors in the records themselves. After all, the Triumvirate system, by definition, required three people, yet there was no indication that there had been a White faction leader to fulfil that role for many years. The wizard Keir was White Secondmage, that much was certain, and people clearly remembered him standing in on the Triumvirate from time to time. But standing in for whom?

Well, for nobody, it seemed, but that didn't make any sense.

Catriona's Conclave to answer grievances filed by the White wizard Renjaf were confirmed in this Timeline, but who represented him? The original stored by the Council was blank on the issue. My mother's personal Timeless copy of the transcript indicated that it was Maia.

On a practical level, the Triumvirate system was restored via Keir's promotion, but that didn't explain why that was suddenly necessary when they had apparently got along just fine without anyone in that post for twenty years or so.

Aunt Mandalee has always chosen to believe that if Maia had lived – if she had existed – she would have reversed certain amendments she had made to the legal status of the Guardians. Specifically, the clause regarding their autonomy to make their own rules. She likes to imagine that having seen them in action, coming up with original solutions to brand new problems as the minutes counted down to disaster, Maia understood that the Council must never interfere. Guardians would have to obey basic fundamental laws, like everyone else, of course, but beyond that, the rules of Time magic could only be properly devised by those who understood it. Those who were connected to it.

Aunt Mandalee is convinced that, in another reality, Maia would have torn up the disaster of those legal amendments and enshrined the status of the Guardianship into Tempestrian law for eternity. Sadly, in reality, that never happened, forcing my aunt to waste her time and energy fighting battles it should never have been necessary to fight.

But once again, gentle reader, I am getting ahead of myself.

*****

Maia was far from the only casualty of that terrible weapon, and it would be wrong to focus on her to the exclusion of all the other people who were caught in the blast when the Melrose bomb exploded, all of whom never existed.

In my age, gentle reader, we now know this was the first known instance of the unmaking effects of the weapon used by our enemy, the void-creature, a.k.a. my father, Daelen StormTiger. Or a version of it, at least. A technological version that was mercifully only possible thanks to the splinters of Aunt Mandalee's Pureblade.

What makes this weapon so dangerous is that it creates gaps in Time.

It is entirely different to the effects of Time Intervention.

Due to the actions of the Guardians, Dagamir the Third survived the battle against Ulvarius and went on to have children. Consequently, three hundred years later, his descendant, Dagamir the Tenth, was born and grew up to become Principal of the Melrose Academy – which itself only existed thanks to that same Time Intervention.

The two Timelines are different, but in either case, there is a clear progression of cause and effect. The world made sense.

In the grand scheme of things, it doesn't matter to the cosmos whether that one particular school existed or not. As long as the Timeline makes sense. When the void-creature's weapon unmakes people, that is no longer true. Our fear is that such damage, if severe enough, could allow the chaotic entity known as *IT* to gain enough influence over the cosmos to unmake everything.

How do we define 'severe enough', gentle reader? The answer is we can't. The question is impossible to answer because *IT* does not operate according to the rules of the cosmos. While *IT* remains outside the cosmos, even Time doesn't apply to *IT* in any rational way, but when operating inside the walls of reality, *IT* must conform to the rules of Time.

That makes Time the best and only defence that we know of. In short, any damage to Time must be considered potentially disastrous.

Even more worryingly, as the nature of this weapon attests, through the invasion of the void-creature, *IT* already has a foothold in the cosmos!

In my age, we have developed defences: certain types of Timefield can block the Time destroying aspects of the weapon, but the void-creature keeps adapting his weapon even as we adapt our defences, so our defences don't always work. Even when they do work, Temporal magic doesn't stop the blast itself, so people still die, but at least we remember them to mourn them. That may be small comfort to those who suffer their loss, but it's the best we can offer.

Sometimes, the Guardians and I can Intervene in Time, try to save people, but the more time and energy we spend on that, the less we spend on finding ways to stop the further attacks of the void-creature and the closer we get to the increasingly severe void storms tearing Tempestria apart.

By analogy, there's an arsonist out there who's busy setting our world ablaze while we're still trying to put out yesterday's fires. We can't win this way.

The Red and Black Guardians still insist they can find a way without rule-breaking, without risk, but in my opinion – and Aunt Mandalee and Shyleen agree with me – it is futile to continue as we are. That's why I've stopped Time the way only I can, to bring my father here from the past to help us.

The others still believe what I'm doing is too dangerous. I believe danger is relative. If I'm wrong, everything could be unmade, but if we continue as we are, that will happen anyway. Whether it happens now or later, if everything is unmade, then, either way, Tempestria will never have existed in the first place, so what's the difference?

A sneak preview of the sequel
to *Splintered Time*

Shattered Lives

The Salvation of Tempestria
Book 6

Gary Stringer

Available Spring 2023

Chapter 1

It was the aftermath of the multi-pronged attack that saw the Melrose Academy school building destroyed and Maia, White Triumvirate representative, unmade. Forever erased from Time. As one would expect, gentle reader, there was much to be done.

Out of respect, the Council organised a memorial service for Maia and all the others who were lost that day. A strange concept, that: a memorial to celebrate the lives of people whom nobody remembered because they never existed.

After that, though, the Council returned to business-as-usual with the newly promoted Keir taking Maia's seat. The Guardians had had little reason to interact with him before. Time would tell what that relationship would be like.

However, in much the same way as in the aftermath of the Fall of Kullos, the Guardians were quick to extricate themselves from the clean-up and reorganisation. They needed to stay focussed on the bigger picture.

*****

From all that had happened since the Guardians began to try and recover the fragments of Kullos' dimensional control device, it was clear that their real nemesis was from the future.

"That's the only explanation that makes sense," Cat insisted.

During the events that led to the Fall of Kullos, the would-be Guardians had benefited from help from the future. Since then, the interference had been less benevolent.

"Nevertheless, we can't do anything about future threats," Dreya pointed out. "All we can do is deal with the Black robe wizard that's been plaguing us these past few years."

"And the only link we have to him is Nalani," Mandalee added. "If only we could get her to co-operate."

'*That does not seem likely,*' Shyleen opined.

"Actually, I think she would be willing," Michael told them, "if you could convince her of the truth. When I was fighting her outside Melrose, just before she was fully trapped in my petrified prison, I think she broke through Pryshia's control. Just for a moment. Just long enough to give me this."

He showed his friends a small slip of paper, which read:

HELP ME

At the time, Michael had thought she was futilely trying to push him away with one hand. It was only later that he realised she'd been hiding that slip of paper in his pocket. With everything that had happened since, there had been more important things to deal with, so he hadn't brought it up until now, several days later.

"Well, that's one line of enquiry," Sara spoke up, "but I think Jess and I have another."

Jessica nodded. "Yeah, we reckon we should have a look around Daelen's base on StormClaw Island."

"It's a good idea," Michael concurred. "Somebody must have been there since Kullos was defeated in order to get their hands on Mandalee's shattered Pureblade."

"It *is* a good idea," Dreya affirmed, "except we already looked, though I don't know what we expected to find."

The place was still wrecked following the battle of the shadow warriors. Sifting through the mess, they had been unable to find anything to explain how it was possible for Mandalee's Pureblade to still have been in their world. No matter how many pieces it might be in, it should have been transferred to the original, doomed Tempestria through the Cosmic Rift, along with everything else that had been contaminated by the power of Heaven's Surrender. The only reason the fragments of Kullos' control device still existed was that Kullos had sent them through portals in time and space. Thus, they were not on StormClaw when the transfer took place. The same was not true of Mandalee's Pureblade. If there had been any more portals, the Guardians would surely have noticed them.

Mystery though it was, it was largely academic now. Given how many splinters of the Pureblade had been used in various attacks, Mandalee was convinced there could be none left. That danger was passed. Now they could return their focus to the control device fragments. They had three of six, while their Black robe wizard enemy had two. The sixth and final fragment had been sent into the future, so there was no way to retrieve that, yet.

"Nalani is definitely our best approach now," Cat agreed.

"I see what you're saying, love," Jessica acknowledged diplomatically, "but I still think you should let my sister and me look around StormClaw, just in case."

"If you're still feeling guilty about us nearly being killed in the Melrose explosion, don't be," Sara insisted.

Her sister nodded. "You have to let us help. We know the layout of Daelen's bases better than anyone. There might be something you guys missed."

Mandalee shook her head. "We know you're trying to help," she assured her friends, "and we appreciate that, but I don't see how there could be anything to miss: the place was obliterated."

"Including the basement?" Sara asked pointedly.

The Guardians shared a puzzled glance. "What basement?" Cat asked.

"Exactly!" Jessica cried. "You see? You don't know as much as you think you do!"

Sara reminded her friends that when they met, and for a few years before, their job had been to look after all of Daelen's facilities. He had maintained a system of permanent portals connecting seven worlds, of which there were only two from which they had been banned. The first was Phitonia because they were plague carriers who would kill anyone they came across and many more as the disease spread. The other was Tempestria, for fear of alerting Kullos to their alien presence. That left five bases with which they were intimately familiar.

Moreover, before taking up permanent residency on Tempestria, the Chetsuans had been able to spend a brief time on Daelen's Phitonian base as part of Dreya's schemes. The shadow warrior had turned the surrounding perception filter into a containment field through which their disease could not cross. From what they had seen, the Phitonian base matched the other five, so there was no reason to suppose the Tempestrian one on StormClaw was any different.

"The basement was where all of Daelen's technology was stored," Sara told them.

"Of course!" Cat realised. "We're being thick! There was shadow warrior technology underneath Kullos' throne room in his fortress. It makes sense that Daelen would have had something similar in his base on StormClaw."

Mandalee nodded. "You're right. We're just not used to thinking in terms of technology."

"There can't be anything to power it, though," Dreya pointed out.

Daelen had ripped power from all his bases to fight Kullos. Subsequently, solar energy generation had enabled them to get the lights back on, but shadow warrior technology couldn't run on that. It needed higher planar energy.

Dreya had command of such power, of course, but she was loath to use it for such a purpose.

"That probably wouldn't work anyway," Michael offered. "It would most likely require the right signature – Daelen's signature. Although I may be able to help with that."

Other than his weapons, Michael's only possession from the old days, fighting alongside Daelen, was a ring. It contained a low level of higher planar energy because it was actually a shadow warrior device. Sara had used it to test her fragment detector, but its original purpose had been to grant him access to the technology in his Tomb. That suggested it would allow him access to any similar technology on Daelen's base.

He wouldn't be able to power the technology for long, but Sara insisted that wasn't a problem. She had experience with Daelen's systems and would need only a moment to change the security to grant access to Dreya's signature. Then she could power it, should it prove worthwhile.

"It has to be worth investigating, at the very least," she concluded.

"Sounds like a family outing to me!" Cat declared.

Michael looked around at his companions: the Chetsuan twins, one human, one leopard god, one Faery, one half-Faery who was pregnant with a girl child that would be somehow half Shadowkin, and himself, a demigod.

"Strangest family I've ever seen," he remarked.

"And all the better for it, love!" Jessica insisted.

There were nods all around – even Shyleen began to purr appreciatively.

Michael grinned. “Couldn’t agree more, my dear!”

Printed in Great Britain
by Amazon

13803363R00153